12/18/24

REQUIEM FOR
A MOUSE

A Cat in the Stacks Mystery

REQUIEM FOR A MOUSE

Miranda James

Berkley Prime Crime
New York

BERKLEY PRIME CRIME
Published by Berkley
An imprint of Penguin Random House LLC
penguinrandomhouse.com

Copyright © 2024 by Dean James
Penguin Random House supports copyright. Copyright fuels creativity, encourages
diverse voices, promotes free speech, and creates a vibrant culture. Thank you for buying an
authorized edition of this book and for complying with copyright laws by not reproducing,
scanning, or distributing any part of it in any form without permission. You are
supporting writers and allowing Penguin Random House to continue to
publish books for every reader.

BERKLEY and the BERKLEY & B colophon are registered trademarks and
BERKLEY PRIME CRIME is a trademark of Penguin Random House LLC.

Library of Congress Cataloging-in-Publication Data

Names: James, Miranda, author.
Title: Requiem for a mouse / Miranda James.
Description: New York: Berkley Prime Crime, 2024. | Series:
A Cat in the Stacks mystery
Identifiers: LCCN 2023058343 (print) | LCCN 2023058344 (ebook) |
ISBN 9780593199527 (hardcover) | ISBN 9780593199534 (ebook)
Subjects: LCSH: Harris, Charlie (Fictitious character)—Fiction. |
Librarians—Fiction. | Cats—Fiction. | LCGFT: Cozy mysteries. | Novels.
Classification: LCC PS3610.A43 R47 2024 (print) | LCC PS3610.A43 (ebook) |
DDC 813/.6—dc23/eng/20240102
LC record available at https://lccn.loc.gov/2023058343
LC ebook record available at https://lccn.loc.gov/2023058344

Printed in the United States of America
1st Printing

Book design by Tiffany Estreicher

REQUIEM FOR
A MOUSE

ONE

IIIIIIIIIIIIIIIIIIIIIII

I felt the delicate touch of a tongue in my ear. At the same time a warm, furry body nestled against my head. I suppressed a groan as I detached the cat and set him aside on the bed.

"Thank you for your kiss," I said to the affectionate Ramses, the younger of my two felines. I threw off the covers and sat up. Ramses rubbed against my side and offered a plaintive meow.

A glance at the clock showed me that I had overslept. I must have forgotten to set my alarm last night. It was nearly seven o'clock, and normally on a workday I was up at six.

"Where's Diesel?" I looked at Ramses as if he could tell me the whereabouts of my Maine Coon cat. Ramses meowed again, a mournful sound. "Well, if you're that hungry, you should have gone downstairs with Diesel and found something to eat. I have to hurry."

Ramses jumped off the bed and disappeared through the slightly ajar bedroom door into the hall. I went into the bathroom, disrobed, and turned on the shower.

Twenty minutes later I entered the kitchen. Diesel, the Maine Coon, greeted me with a warble. Azalea Berry, the formidable septuagenarian who ran my household like a well-oiled machine, stood at the stove. Without turning, she said, "I guess that little scamp woke you up like I told him to."

"Yes, he did. I forgot to set my alarm last night." I took my usual place at the kitchen table. Azalea set a plate in front of me. Scrambled eggs; two sausage patties; a large spoonful of her thick, cheesy grits; and two pieces of buttered wheat toast lay before me. I picked up my fork and started eating. Azalea poured a cup of coffee. I felt completely spoiled, but Azalea resisted any attempts on my part to cut back on breakfast. She insisted it was the most important meal of the day, and I couldn't argue with her.

Besides, as I had often admitted to myself, I loved her breakfast meals. I really didn't want to miss one. I would rather have had breakfast than any other meal. The fact that she generally prepared lunch and dinner as well during the week was another matter entirely.

"How's that new girl at the library working out?" Azalea remained in place at the stove, but she had turned to regard me with approval as I ate.

"She's a good worker," I said after I swallowed a mouthful of grits. "Odd, though. I really can't get hold of her personality. She blurts out things without thinking, and they're usually not particularly tactful." I had to suppress a laugh. "The first day she worked, she told Melba she thought the green dress she had on made her look like a cucumber." Melba Gilley, my friend since childhood, was the administrative assistant to the Athena College library director.

"My goodness," Azalea said, taken aback. "I don't see that going over well."

"It didn't." Melba's expression could have curdled milk. "She told Tara that she loved cucumbers, turned on her heel, and left the room." I explained that Tara Martin was the young woman's name. "Tara didn't appear to realize she had said anything wrong. Melba's tone apparently didn't register with her."

"She said anything like that to you?" Azalea asked, her eyes narrowing.

"Several times," I replied, "but never anything really unpleasant." Her remark about my puffing a little as we reached the top of the stairs at work had nettled me a bit. I didn't feel in the least like a tired steam engine. I shared that with Azalea.

"That child needs to learn some manners." She turned back to the stove.

"She needs to learn not to blurt things out," I said after a bite of toast. "She can think what she likes, but her lack of tact puts people's backs up. The thing is, she doesn't seem to realize what she's done."

"She tries much more of that with Melba, she'll learn." Azalea dished up another breakfast plate and set it on the table across from me. She had apparently heard someone coming downstairs. I had been too intent on my eating to notice.

"Good morning, Charlie, Azalea. Boys." Stewart Delacorte, my longtime boarder, flashed his attractive smile at us as he swept into

3

the room. "Azalea, you're a marvel. I didn't think I made that much noise coming down the stairs." He indicated his plate.

"My hearing's as sharp as it ever was." Azalea fixed him with her gimlet gaze, and Stewart grinned broadly.

"Of course," he said as he dug into his grits.

Azalea poured coffee into his cup, and he added cream to it. "I'm not as old and decrepit as some people like to think."

I noticed a certain heat in her words, and I wondered who had dared imply something like that. After a moment's reflection, I decided it must have been her daughter, chief deputy of the Athena County Sheriff's Department.

Stewart, braver than I was when it came to teasing Azalea, promptly said, "Is Kanesha out of the hospital yet?"

Azalea snorted. "She's lucky she didn't end up there." She threw a towel down on the counter and marched out of the room. She came right back, however, and set a plate of bacon on the table. She had cooked that for Diesel and Ramses, mostly. Then she disappeared again.

Stewart and I exchanged amused glances. Kanesha Berry had been trying for years to get her mother to retire. Kanesha didn't like the thought of her mother still working in her seventies, but Azalea was even more strong-minded than her daughter. Azalea had taken care of my aunt Dottie in her declining years. After I inherited the house, Azalea informed me that she intended to keep taking care of the house—and me—until the day she no longer could. I didn't argue, because she intimidated me. Not so much as she used to, but I didn't dare cross her, and she knew it.

"I guess Haskell is already up and at work," I said, referring to

Stewart's partner, a sheriff's deputy, who shared the suite on the third floor of the house.

Stewart nodded and swallowed. "He had to be at work at seven. I'm hoping that nothing happens to cause him to have to work late. We don't want to miss the big shindig out at the farmhouse tonight."

"For both your sakes, I hope nothing interferes with your plans." I had been doling out bites of bacon to the cats, and in between I managed to gulp down the rest of my breakfast. I was going to be a few minutes late to the office.

I got up from the table and set my empty plate in the sink. After swallowing the last of my coffee, I told Diesel it was time for work. He accompanied me almost everywhere, and he loved going to the office. He knew Melba would be there, and he adored her. She lavished affection on him every time she saw him, even multiple times a day. We bade Stewart and Ramses goodbye and left the kitchen.

The mid-January day was chilly and overcast, so I decided that we would take the car today instead of walking the short distance to the Athena College campus as we did in more comfortable weather. Stewart kept Ramses occupied with bits of bacon while we sneaked out the back door into the garage. Diesel hopped into the backseat of the car, and soon we arrived at the old antebellum mansion that held the library's administrative offices and the archives and rare-book collection. I worked three days a week as archivist and rare-book cataloger, a job I thoroughly enjoyed.

Diesel and I entered the building through the back door, and he ambled ahead of me to Melba's office. I caught up with him, and he turned to me, meowing in disappointment. Melba wasn't there.

"Come on, boy. We'll catch her later." I started up the stairs, and he trotted quickly ahead. I glanced at my watch. We had arrived only seven minutes late.

Tara Martin stood at the door. She flashed a quick scowl at me before averting her face as she usually did. She rarely looked directly at me. "Now I can't put in my full two hours," she said before I could greet her and apologize for arriving late. "I can't stay to make up the time, either, because I need to get to the bistro to help get ready for lunch."

Suppressing the irritation I felt at her abrupt tone, I said, "I'm sorry we're late. I'll see that you don't lose your time because I overslept this morning." I pulled out my keys, inserted the correct one, and unlocked the door. Diesel paid no attention to Tara and scooted into the office. He made a beeline for his usual spot in the window ledge behind my desk.

Tara made no response to my remark as I flipped the light switches to illuminate the office that contained my desk, a desk for another worker, and shelves containing a small part of the rare-book collection. The rest of the books resided on shelves in other rooms, along with the archives, here on the second floor of the old mansion.

Tara marched straight to her desk, set her bag and her backpack down on the floor beside her chair, and removed her coat, a rather shabby trench coat at least an inch too long for her short, squat body. I could see streaks of dirt and mud along the hem.

I took my place at my desk, shedding my jacket onto the back of my chair. I woke my computer, wondering whether Tara would remain in a huff or deign to speak to me. After all, I had offered an apology.

"Thank you," she said as she approached my desk. "I appreciate it, especially since it's your responsibility to be here and unlock the door."

"Yes, it is." I kept my tone even, though her graceless words annoyed me further. She could easily have stopped at *appreciate it*, but that wasn't her style.

Diesel meowed suddenly, but Tara paid no attention. By now I had a full view of her clothing that her coat had concealed. Today she was wearing wrinkled drab-brown leggings, the rusty-looking black skirt, and the dowdy, slightly stained gray shirt. This was the worst I had seen her appearance yet, and I felt sorry for her. Evidently most of her clothing was old and without much style. She wouldn't be able to work in the main library looking like this. Even student workers had to be better dressed. I supposed she couldn't afford new clothes, despite her part-time job here and her part-time work at the French bistro of my soon-to-be wife, Helen Louise Brady.

The important thing was that she was a good worker, adept enough at the computer for the tasks I set her, and a remarkably accurate typist. She had been working for me for only a couple of weeks now, but I had quickly been impressed by her work ethic. For that I was willing to put up with her personal quirks, chiefly her tactlessness. I didn't know her well enough to try to coach her out of it, but if she was to work for me on an ongoing basis, I had little doubt I would give in to temptation to talk to her about it. If I didn't, I figured either Helen Louise or her partner at the bistro, Henry Hollister, probably would. They couldn't afford to let Tara alienate customers.

When I made no further comment, Tara settled at her desk and readied herself to continue her current task. The first week of December, the archive received a large donation of books from an alumna of the college, amounting to twenty-three good-sized boxes. Since it was politic to accept such gifts, particularly, as with this one, when they came with substantial donations to the college, I had no choice but to inventory the collection. We reserved the right to dispose of any items not suitable to our rare-book collection, especially if there were duplicates of titles we already owned.

Tara, who had proved adept with spreadsheets, was going through each box, checking every book for damage, such as mold, mildew, or stains, along with unstable hinges. She recorded author, title, publication information, and condition for each title. She had also numbered each box and included the box number for each book. Later, when the collection had been completely entered into the spreadsheet, I would check for duplicates against the items already cataloged. At some point afterward, I would begin cataloging the items selected for inclusion. I had quite a large quantity of books from other donors that had to be dealt with first, however, so it might be a year or more before I could accession any of these. Unless, of course, someone higher up decided this collection should take priority.

We worked quietly for a good quarter of an hour before a loud, jarring ringtone disturbed me. I looked up to see Tara grabbing her cell phone from beside her computer. She muttered, "Excuse me," before she hurried out of the office into the hallway.

She neglected to close the door behind her, however, and at first all I heard was the murmur of her voice. Then suddenly her volume increased, and I heard her clearly.

"I told you, I don't know who you think you're calling, I never heard that name." Then, seconds later, I heard a loud crunching sound.

Tara came back into the office, her shattered phone in her hand.

TWO

She looked at me, a ferocious glint in her eye, as if she dared me to speak to her. She shoved the remains of her phone into her backpack and resumed her seat at the desk. Then I heard the tapping of the keys as she continued her work.

That was an extreme reaction to a wrong number, I thought. Was she mentally unstable? I hadn't witnessed such an outburst from her, if I could call it that, in the brief time I'd worked with her. I wanted to ask whether she was okay, but after studying her body language for a moment, I decided the better course of action was to ignore the episode.

I felt a paw on my shoulder and turned to see Diesel staring at me from the window next to my chair. He meowed softly, and I patted his head to reassure him. He always picked up on tension, and even I could feel it emanating from Tara in the aftermath of her destruction of her phone.

Diesel pushed his head against my head briefly before settling back into his resting position in the window. I turned back to my computer and tried to focus on my work. Thoughts of the odd behavior of my assistant continued to intrude, however, and I finally decided that I would talk to Helen Louise about it. I wondered whether Tara had done anything weird like this while working at the bistro. She might have been more likely to confide in Helen Louise if she was worried about something.

My office phone rang. "Good morning. This is Charlie Harris. How may I help you?"

"It's me, Charlie," Melba Gilley said. "Would you mind coming down here a minute?"

"Sure, be right down." I cradled the phone and pushed back my chair. "Come on, Diesel, let's go downstairs."

Diesel knew what that meant. Melba. He jumped down from the window and headed to the door. I followed him, pausing only long enough to let Tara know I would be downstairs if she needed anything.

All I received in response was a shrug.

By the time I reached Melba's office, she was already engaged in showering my cat with affection. She greeted me without looking up, and I dropped into the chair beside her desk.

After a few seconds I interrupted her cooing at Diesel to ask why she wanted to see me. "Just for Diesel?"

She chuckled. "No, though that's always a bonus." She kept a hand on the cat's head as she sobered. "I witnessed something really odd, and I wanted to ask you about it."

I suspected she must have seen, or at least heard, Tara destroy her phone. I waited for her to continue.

"What is it with that girl?" Melba asked. "I say *girl*, but she's got to be in her late thirties, I reckon. I actually saw her stomping on her phone. I happened to be passing the foot of the stairs, and I heard her talking. Then she dropped her phone on the floor and stomped it real hard." She shook her head. "That's way past strange."

I shrugged. "I agree. I have no idea why she did it, although from what I heard, she was really upset over the call she got. Did you hear what she said?"

Melba nodded. "That's a pretty extreme reaction to a wrong number, wouldn't you say?" She didn't give me a chance to answer. "That girl either has some serious anger issues, or else she's just plain weird. Maybe both."

"I agree. Definitely an excessive reaction. She made it obvious when she came back into the office that she didn't want to talk about it, though, so I left her alone."

"Probably better not to know," Melba said. "Though I sure am curious about her. I haven't spoken to her that much, because frankly she's put me off. She's got about as much tact as a rubber duck."

I chuckled. "You're right about that. I think she's simply socially inept. She doesn't understand how she comes across."

"I don't think she cares," Melba said.

"You could be right," I said. "I'm not sure what her career goals are, but if they involve dealing with the public, she's going to be in trouble."

"If she hasn't learned by now, I reckon she's not going to change any unless somebody takes her in hand." Melba eyed me speculatively.

"Don't look at me," I said. "My charm school has been closed for decades."

Melba giggled, and Diesel warbled, as if he understood the joke.

Melba sobered and regarded me with an intent expression. "It's odd, though."

"What do you mean?" I asked, puzzled by the abrupt shift in tone.

"She was definitely upset, angry even," Melba replied slowly. "I'd swear, though, she was also frightened."

I considered that for a moment before I shook my head. "I didn't get that impression."

Shrugging, Melba said, "I could be wrong. It's just a feeling I had."

"She's due to go to the bistro when she puts in her hours here," I said. "Once she leaves I'll call Helen Louise and tell her about it. If Tara's really bothered by the call, maybe she'll talk to Helen Louise about it."

"Maybe," Melba said, her tone doubtful. "Tara seems pretty much a loner to me. I feel kind of sorry for her."

"I doubt she'd thank you for that," I said.

Diesel warbled loudly, and both Melba and I looked at him. He gazed back and forth between us. I could only wonder what was in his brain at the moment. Had he picked up on something that neither of us humans had? It was entirely possible with my empathetic boy.

"If only you could tell us," I murmured.

Diesel butted his head against my knee.

I rose from the chair. "We'd better get back upstairs to work."

"I'd better get back to work, too," Melba replied as she gave Diesel one last head rub. "Let me know if anything else happens with her."

"Will do. Come on, boy, back upstairs."

Diesel followed me out of Melba's office and hurried up the stairs ahead of me. When I entered my office I saw him already in his spot in the window embrasure. Tara's head was bent over her computer, and her fingers worked busily on the keyboard. She did not acknowledge my return. I refrained from the superfluous remark I was tempted to make and went to my desk.

Diesel chirped occasionally at either birds or squirrels he spotted in the trees he could see from his vantage point. Otherwise, the only noise in the office came from the tapping of keys on a keyboard. I worked on cataloging a collection of books from an earlier donation. Most of the items were obscure Southern novels from the nineteenth century. I doubted many of them were of much particular literary merit, but they fitted the guidelines for the college's rare-book collection: Southern fiction, especially by Mississippi writers. Novels often provided insight into the mores and customs of a particular time, and I'd had several graduate students working on theses or dissertations who had worked with these materials.

Time passed quickly when I was absorbed in my work, and Tara startled me by clearing her throat loudly. I looked up to see her standing by her desk, backpack and bag in hand. "I'm leaving now. Don't forget what you promised about my time sheet." She turned and walked out of the office.

"Yes, Your Highness," I muttered, annoyed by her peremptory tone. Really, the woman had all the grace of a dead hedgehog.

Diesel meowed loudly, as if in response to my comment. I turned to grin at him. "Yes, that was rude," I said. "But she was rude first."

The cat meowed again, louder this time. Now I laughed. When Tara first started working in the office, Diesel had made overtures of friendliness to her, but she had not encouraged him. He quickly realized she wasn't a cat person, and since then he had ignored her. She hadn't been actively hostile to my cat, but she had made it clear she didn't want him near her. Diesel was happy to oblige and keep his distance.

I picked up my cell phone and speed-dialed Helen Louise. The lunch rush at the bistro wouldn't start for at least an hour, so she ought to have a minute to talk to me.

She answered after three rings. "Hi, sweetheart. How are you?"

"I'm fine, love. Are you busy? How's your morning going?" I asked.

"Fine so far. How about you?" she asked. I could hear sounds of activity in the background. I thought she was in the kitchen.

"Fine, except for dealing with Miss Graciousness herself."

Helen Louise laughed. "Tara's in fine form today, is she?"

"I overslept and was seven minutes late this morning, and she of course let me know she wasn't pleased," I said. "Her usual charming self."

"Don't let her ruffle your feathers, love," Helen Louise said, a hint of laughter still in her voice. "We're used to it here. That personality is why I keep her in the kitchen most of the time. Henry has an iron hide, and he doesn't put up with any of her attitudes."

"Good for Henry," I said.

"I hope it's not going to be a problem that she's going to be one of the servers at Sean and Alex's housewarming party at the farmhouse," Helen Louise said. "If you'd rather, I can get someone else, but I think she could use the extra money."

"Hopefully she'll be too busy to be rude to anyone." I quickly felt ashamed at the cattiness of that remark. "Don't pay any attention to me. I'm sure she'll be fine. There was one odd thing this morning, though."

"What happened?" Helen Louise asked.

I told her about Tara smashing her cell phone. "Has she ever exhibited that kind of behavior around you or Henry?"

"No," Helen Louise replied. "She can be a bit testy sometimes, but she's never had an outburst like that."

"That's good. Hopefully it won't happen again."

Renovations at my grandfather's farmhouse had finally finished, and my son, Sean, and his wife, Alex, had scheduled a party for tonight to celebrate and show off the completed work. Sean had bought the house from me because he wanted to keep it in the family. I hadn't been to see the final product yet and was looking forward to the party.

"Henry will be there, seeing that everything runs smoothly," Helen Louise said. "I'll be keeping an eye out, too, but the advantage of having a younger, hardworking business partner is that he's willing to deal with catering parties himself."

Helen Louise had struggled for a few years with the idea of taking on a partner, because the bistro was her pride and joy. After a short but successful law career, she had gone to Paris to study French cuisine. She returned to Athena and opened the bistro, quickly becoming prosperous. She'd had a hard time letting anyone else be in charge, but now that we were soon to be married, she had become much happier to have Henry shoulder his share of the burdens of management.

"Henry is a jewel," I said, and she quickly agreed. "Would you like me to pick you up tonight? No sense in taking two cars."

"Yes, that would be great. Around six?"

"I'll see you then," I said.

We chatted briefly for a few moments; then I ended the call and went back to cataloging.

I decided to work through my usual lunch hour. I called Azalea to inform her. I knew she hadn't planned a hot lunch for me, and I gave Diesel a few treats to tide him over until we reached home.

We left at two o'clock and drove home. Ramses greeted us enthusiastically when we came into the kitchen from the garage. Anyone would have thought he hadn't seen us in weeks the way he carried on. Diesel tolerated the hopping and batting for about fifteen seconds. He pushed Ramses aside and stalked into the utility room. Ramses transferred his attentions to me. I forestalled his attempt to climb my pants leg and scooped him into my arms. I let him nuzzle the side of my face as I stroked his back. After he seemed to calm a bit, I put him back on the floor, and he trotted after Diesel.

I scrounged in the fridge for my lunch, and I found slices of chicken breast for a sandwich. I made one with mayo, lettuce, and sliced red onion. I poured myself a glass of sweet tea, and I also took out another slice of chicken breast in order to give Diesel and Ramses bits of it.

After I finished the sandwich and the boys finished their chicken, we headed upstairs. I intended to take a nap to recharge my batteries. I had no idea how late the housewarming party might run, and I didn't want to fade out too early on a Friday night.

After I disrobed and put my clothes away, I stretched out on the bed in my shorts and T-shirt. Diesel stretched out next to me, and Ramses scrunched himself up against my stomach. As I finally started to doze, I was thinking about the evening to come. I hoped it would be a success. I was sure it would all go off smoothly, and I smiled. I was so happy for Sean, Alex, and my granddaughter, Rosie. Then I drifted off.

If I'd had any inkling the night would take such a strange turn, I wouldn't have been able to fall asleep.

THREE

|||||||||||||||||||||||||||||||||||

I arrived at Helen Louise's house a couple of minutes after six. She met me at the door with a kiss. I waited while she locked up, and then, arm in arm, we walked to the car, where I held the door open for her.

She glanced into the backseat, illuminated by the streetlight under which I had parked. "No Diesel tonight?" She slid into the seat.

"No, I figured there would be too many people," I said before I shut her door.

When I got in the car, and while I was fastening my seat belt, she asked, "Who's keeping him and Ramses company tonight?"

"A history student at Athena named Carly Everett," I said. "She earns extra money by pet-sitting. I saw her flyer pinned to the bulletin board in the main library building a few days ago. She has excellent references."

"I'm glad you found someone," Helen Louise said.

"The boys took to her right away when she came to interview with me," I said. "She grew up with cats and dogs, and she seems kind and responsible."

"Good. What year is she?"

"Sophomore. So she should be around for a few more semesters, in case we want to travel somewhere that Diesel can't go."

"Does this mean I might finally get you to Ireland?" Helen Louise laughed gently.

"Perhaps. If I can get you to take two weeks away from the bistro." I was teasing, and she understood that.

"Perhaps," she responded laughingly. "Maybe for our honeymoon."

"That would be great."

For the remainder of the drive out into the country—not actually that far away from Athena—where the old farmhouse was located, we talked about our upcoming nuptials, scheduled for the first Saturday in February. That was only three weeks from tomorrow, I realized.

Everything was set. The wedding itself would be held in Helen Louise's church. Melba was serving as matron of honor, with my daughter, Laura, as an attendant, along with Sean's wife, Alex. Sean was my best man, and my son-in-law, Frank Salisbury, would be an attendant. Azalea had agreed to sing. Neither of the grandchildren was old enough to serve as a ring bearer or flower girl, so we had opted to do without. There was brief talk of Diesel serving as the ring bearer, but there would be about fifty guests at the wedding. Too many, I thought, to make it easy for him to accomplish the task without getting skittish.

The reception, catered by Henry and the bistro staff, would be held in the church hall. I had given some input into the menu, but Helen Louise and Henry knew far more about such things than I. Their taste and expertise were sufficient for the task, and I looked forward to a hearty meal after the ceremony.

I turned the car into the farmhouse driveway. The porch lights shone in the darkness, but there were also Japanese lanterns set along the walk from the driveway to the porch to illuminate the way. Guests weren't expected until seven, but Helen Louise and I had come early in order to help, if necessary. I spotted Laura and Frank's car already parked, and I pulled in behind it. Ahead of their vehicle I spotted the van the bistro used for catering events.

"I'm sure Henry has everything well in hand," Helen Louise said as we made our way onto the porch.

"I'm sure he has." I rang the bell, and the door opened almost immediately to reveal my daughter-in-law, Alex.

"Good evening." She hugged us each in turn. "I'm so glad you're here early so we can give you the private tour."

"Hi, Dad, Helen Louise." Laura, too, greeted us with hugs.

"You're both looking extremely chic tonight," Helen Louise said.

"So are you," Alex said, casting an admiring look at Helen Louise's emerald silk dress. Laura's choice of deep blue and Alex's crimson set off their respective complexions beautifully.

"I have to get a picture of the three of you." I pulled out my phone, and they obligingly posed, Helen Louise in the middle.

"Perfect." I showed them the two photos I'd made, and they professed themselves happy.

"Where are Sean and Frank?" Helen Louise asked.

Alex shook her head. "They're out back on the new porch, finishing their cigars. Sean assured me they'd be done in plenty of time to greet our guests."

Sean had become a cigar enthusiast during his years in Houston as a corporate lawyer, and my son-in-law, Frank, had recently joined him. As long as they didn't smoke around my grandchildren, I didn't fuss much. I'd rather they didn't, but I supposed they could have far worse habits.

"I'm going to spray Frank down with odor-canceling stuff." Laura grinned.

"Save some for Sean," Alex said.

Helen Louise and I laughed.

"Where is Henry?" Helen Louise asked after the mirth had spent itself.

"He's in the kitchen with his crew," Alex said. "Everything is fine. Henry shoos us out anytime we go into the kitchen."

"That's Henry," Helen Louise said. "He's a mini tyrant on occasions like this, but things always run smoothly because of it. He's on top of everything."

"That's exactly why Alex and Sean hired him," Laura said. "You picked an awesome partner, Helen Louise."

"Which one?" I asked, feigning affront.

"Both of them," Laura retorted, and punched me in the arm. "Big goober."

Helen Louise and Alex laughed.

"Come on, now." Alex turned and led the way to our left, into the formal parlor. The house was one of the old shotgun-style dwellings, with a long hall from the front of the house straight back. Rooms opened on either side of the hall.

Alex had received some fine antique pieces from her family, and my late great-aunt Dottie had inherited most of the furniture from this house when her brother, my paternal grandfather, died. Most of the family antiques had been in the attic in my house since well before Aunt Dottie died, and I had allowed my children to take what they wanted for their own homes.

I recognized various pieces as we made our way through the house. There had been only one bathroom when my grandparents lived here, an addition made when my father was a boy. Sean and Alex had added two more, including one for their master suite. Rosie, their daughter, had her own bathroom, as did the guest room. The builders were able to take a second parlor and divide it between the two bedrooms in order to make the new primary bath and Rosie's bathroom.

"The fixtures for the bathrooms are gorgeous," Helen Louise said. "I love the style, a mixture of modern and antique, too. You made excellent choices, Alex."

"Sean and I made them together," Alex said. "He really does have a good eye for design."

As we walked through the house, I felt a bit emotional after seeing it brought back to such a beautiful state. I had memories of the way it had been before my grandparents died. It was probably shabby back then, but I had always loved coming here. My grandmother gave me so much love and attention; all my memories of this place seemed touched by a golden glow.

Now, seeing fresh wallpaper and paint with shiny fixtures in every room, I knew my grandmother would have loved to see the house looking so restored and renewed. My grandfather, on the other hand, would be worrying about what everything cost. I had to smile at that thought.

"It's really beautiful," I said, my voice husky.

Helen Louise put her arm around my waist. She understood what this house meant to me.

"Thank you, Dad," Alex said. "Sean wanted to make you proud of the place."

"He succeeded," I said after clearing my throat.

"Is someone taking my name in vain?"

My handsome son walked into the hall from the back porch he had added to the house. Frank was right behind him. I caught a whiff of the cigars they'd been smoking. Laura curled her nose and grabbed Frank's arm. She towed him away, barely giving him time to greet Helen Louise and me.

"I was telling Dad that you wanted to make him proud of the place," Alex said. "He loves everything."

"I do," I said. "My parents and my grandparents would be so happy to see the old place so beautiful."

"Thanks, Dad," Sean said. "I really appreciate that."

The doorbell rang.

"And so it begins," Sean said. "Excuse me, Dad, Helen Louise. Time to start greeting the rest of our guests." He held out an arm for Alex. She took it, and they proceeded to the front door. Helen Louise and I stepped out of the way.

I didn't expect to recognize many people tonight, because I knew most of the guests would be friends of Sean and Alex or business acquaintances. I did know the first person through the door, however. Melba Gilley.

After greeting Alex and Sean with hugs, she made a beeline for Helen Louise and me. "Doesn't the house look beautiful?" she said, a wistful note in her voice.

"It does," Helen Louise said.

"I'm real jealous that Alex, Sean, and Rosie get to live in such a historic old house. Especially the way it's been restored," Melba said.

"Let's have a closer look while they're greeting more arrivals," I said, gesturing toward the front parlor.

While the three of us toured the house, with Melba exclaiming over various pieces of furniture, rugs, and other decorative items, the guests arrived in a steady progression. By the time we reached the back of the house, I heard a constant hum of conversation from the other end.

Helen Louise excused herself to slip into the kitchen to check in with Henry and the staff to see how things were going. After a moment, she came out with Henry, and they went into the dining room, which was the prime catering spot for the party.

Melba spotted someone she knew and darted forward into the growing crowd. I stood by the dining room door to wait for Helen Louise to finish her inspection. Tara came out of the kitchen carrying a stack of plates, and I moved aside to give her plenty of room to enter. She uttered not a word as she moved past me, and the greeting I had intended to offer never got voiced.

She deposited the plates on the sideboard and came back to the door. She glanced up at me and muttered a greeting. Then she looked down the hallway at the swelling numbers of the guests. Suddenly she turned, her face sickly pale now, and darted down the hall, past the kitchen, and onto the back porch.

I thought perhaps she had been taken ill somehow, and I followed after a few frozen seconds, thinking she might need help.

When I stepped onto the back porch, however, I couldn't see her anywhere.

FOUR

I called out, "Tara. Are you okay?"

No response.

I went to the edge of the steps down into the backyard and called again. Though there was light from the porch shining into the darkness of the yard, I didn't see even a flash of the white shirt Tara was wearing.

I tried again, even louder. "Tara. Where are you? Answer me."

Still no response.

After a brief hesitation, I thought she might have gone to the van to retrieve something and climbed inside it. I picked my way through the semidarkness over to where the van was parked and knocked on the door before I opened it. I stuck my head inside and called Tara's name again.

I listened but could detect no sound inside the van. Puzzled, I shut the door and walked back to the porch. I stood there looking out into the yard, wondering where on earth the woman had gotten to. Surely she hadn't run off into the woods.

I called out loudly again, but it was in vain. Thoroughly aggravated now, I went back into the house and almost ran over Helen Louise.

"I'm sorry," I said.

"What's going on? I thought I heard someone yelling back there." She waved her arm to indicate the porch.

"You did. Me." I explained what I was doing and why.

Helen Louise frowned. "How extremely odd, even for Tara. Could she have slipped back into the house while you were checking the van?"

I shrugged. "I suppose it's possible."

"Let's check the kitchen," Helen Louise said.

I followed her the few steps into the room. No Tara, though two other members of the staff were busy working there. Helen asked whether they'd seen Tara in the last few minutes, and they both answered in the negative.

"How about the dining room?" I asked.

We found a number of people in the room, helping themselves to the various hors d'oeuvres on offer. Henry stood chatting to Melba and a man I didn't know, but again, no Tara.

"Maybe she's in one of the bathrooms," Helen Louise murmured in my ear. "Let me check."

I nodded.

Helen Louise returned shortly and reported that all the bathrooms were empty. "You go look in the kitchen again, in case she's come back," Helen Louise said. "I'm going to have a word with

Henry. If she's ill, we really need to find her and get her proper medical attention. I spotted a doctor I know among the guests."

"That's good." I turned and walked back to the kitchen. No Tara. I was beginning to think she had run off into the woods after all, because when I looked out on the porch, she wasn't there, either.

When I turned back, I saw Helen Louise and Henry only about three feet away. I reported that I hadn't seen Tara.

Henry frowned as he shook his head. "She seemed perfectly fine while we were setting up. We've been here about two hours, and she never said anything about feeling unwell." At six foot four, Henry was a big man, with wide shoulders, a thick ginger beard, and massive arms. I wouldn't ever want him aggravated with me as he currently appeared to be with Tara. He had a temper, but he would never hurt anyone.

"Has she ever done anything this odd before?" I asked.

Henry started to shake his head, then stopped. "Come to think of it, one time recently she was busy arranging desserts in the display case at the bistro during the lunch rush, and she disappeared abruptly into the kitchen. She had just handed someone a piece of cake, too, and almost caused the customer to drop it."

"Did she explain why she did that?" Helen Louise looked annoyed.

"She said she had a stomach virus and had gone into the bathroom to throw up. She did look really pale. It wasn't convenient, but I told her to go home if she was sick. I also told her she shouldn't have come to work if she had a virus."

"She certainly shouldn't have. What a careless thing to do." Helen Louise was now visibly disturbed. "How long ago was that?"

"A week or so ago," Henry replied. "Unless she's had a relapse, she should have been over that bug by now."

Suddenly I recalled the incident this morning, when Tara destroyed her phone after a call that had upset her. I wondered whether this was something similar. "Maybe something, or someone, frightened her," I concluded.

Helen Louise shook her head. "I suppose that's possible, but running out of the house seems a bit extreme to me. If she were a teenager, I could just about understand it. But she's a mature woman and generally a really good worker."

"I agree," Henry said. "There's something awfully strange about this."

"We really need to find her," I said. "I'm going to get Frank and ask him to help. Sean needs to remain in the house with his guests, because we don't want to attract too much attention to this situation." After nods from Helen Louise and Henry, I went in search of my son-in-law.

I found Frank in the front parlor, talking with a couple I didn't know. I begged their pardon and drew Frank aside and quickly explained the situation.

"I'll be glad to help," Frank said. "What's the plan?"

I had been thinking about it and had decided that we would start from the front porch and each go in a different direction around the house until we met at the back. If Tara was hiding somewhere on either side, we should be able to find her.

Frank nodded, and we moved through the guests until we made it to the front door. There were a couple of people out on the front porch, despite the chill in the air, and they were smoking. We nodded at them and went down the steps into the yard. Frank went to the left and I to the right.

I used the flashlight app on my phone to help light the way, though illumination from the front porch and rooms inside the house helped with the process. As I walked along, shining my light in different directions, I called out Tara's name. Occasionally I stopped to listen, hoping to hear her if she was anywhere nearby.

All I heard were the usual nighttime sounds, along with faint noise from inside the house. It took me only about five minutes to reach the back of the house, and Frank arrived moments after me. I shot him a questioning look, and he shook his head.

"Not a sign," he said. "Do you think we ought to search the woods back here?" His outstretched arm indicated the area directly behind the house.

"Probably," I said, "but we're going to need stronger light and at least a couple more searchers. I hope Tara isn't hurt or ill, but if she's not, I'm afraid she's going to be in big trouble with Helen Louise and Henry. She came with Henry, so she couldn't have gone far."

"It's certainly a bizarre thing to do," Frank said. "I know a couple of guys that are here for the party we can count on to help. Stewart and Haskell ought to be here by now, too. If you want to stay here, I'll see whom I can round up."

"Thanks," I said, and Frank disappeared into the house through the back door.

I stood and listened intently for sounds coming from the woods, but I heard nothing that I could identify as produced by a human being. What on earth had got into Tara? If she hadn't suddenly taken ill, had she perhaps been frightened by someone or something? If so, what or who did that?

I didn't think it likely she would have run off into the woods. The night was chilly, and the temperature was still dropping. I decided to check the van again. Perhaps she had hidden herself in there. It would at least be a bit warmer than it was outside. This time I went to the back doors of the van and opened them both. I shone the light from my phone app into the interior, but Tara wasn't there. I looked in the front of the van also, but no Tara.

Where else could she be?

I was walking back to the porch when I remembered there was another part of the house we hadn't searched. The root cellar. I didn't know whether Tara knew about it, but on the chance that she did, I figured I ought to check.

The entrance was off to the side of the porch, and as I approached it, I noticed that the door wasn't completely shut. I pulled it open and stepped down the short flight of stairs to the beaten-earth floor.

As I shone my light around, I called out Tara's name.

I listened for a response, and I felt the chill of the place. The root cellar had been dug into the ground over a century ago, if not longer. My ancestors had kept food down here to preserve it for later use, and if I felt cold in my jacket, I knew Tara must be feeling it much worse in her work clothes.

There was no response to my call, but I waited a few seconds. I caught a brief sound, as if someone inhaled quickly. She must be here somewhere. The root cellar wasn't large, maybe ten feet by eight. There were cases of champagne and white wine stored on shelves here for tonight's event, as well as some of Sean and Alex's own wine and other food items. I moved slowly to the shelves that stood to the left of me and shone the light behind them.

Tara sat huddled on the floor, her arms over her head. She was shivering.

"Tara," I said softly, "you need to come out of here. You'll make yourself ill if you stay in the cold."

Her body stiffened, and she unbent slowly to look up at me. "I'm okay." Her voice faltered.

"What's wrong?" I asked. "Are you sick? Are you frightened of something? Or someone?"

She remained sitting on the floor as she shook her head. "No, I get panic attacks sometimes. The only thing to do is find a dark, quiet place so I can recover from it."

That was a reasonable explanation for her behavior, I supposed, but it didn't ring quite true.

"What triggered this panic attack?" I asked.

"I don't know, I just started feeling it, and I knew if I didn't get out of the house, away from all those strangers, I'd be in big trouble," she said, her tone a bit resentful.

"Are you okay now?" I asked. "Do you think you are recovered enough to come back in the house? I think you need something warm to drink, like coffee or hot tea."

"Charlie, are you in there?"

I heard Frank calling from the doorway into the root cellar. I stepped back a few paces and shone my light in that direction. "Yes, I'm here, and so is Tara. You can go back to the party. I can take care of things from here."

"If you're sure," Frank said.

"I am. Go back to the party." I turned and walked to where Tara now stood behind the shelves.

"Are you ready to go back?" I asked. "Henry and Helen Louise are really worried about you."

Tara frowned, then said gruffly, "Sorry I made them worry."

"How long have you had these panic attacks?" I asked, sensing she wasn't quite ready to go back in the house.

She shrugged. "Off and on for a few years now. I guess maybe I'm a little claustrophobic when there are a lot of strangers around."

"I can understand that," I said. "I get claustrophobic myself sometimes."

She shot me a quick upward glance before her gaze turned downward again. She shivered.

"Come on, let's get out of here, it's getting really cold. You don't want to get sick." I started to reach out and take her arm, but something in her stance warned me that would be the wrong thing to do.

"Come on, now," I said again, gently.

"All right."

I started for the door, and she came along behind me, but slowly. When we reached the porch, Tara balked, her right foot on the bottom step. "I can't go back in there." She sounded breathless.

I really didn't know quite what to do. I couldn't force her inside, but I was concerned that she had been down in the cold of the root cellar for a good quarter of an hour.

"Okay, you wait right here. Did you bring a jacket with you tonight?"

She nodded. "It's black flannel. I left it in the kitchen."

34

"I'll get it for you and let the others know you're okay. Stay right here on the porch."

Tara climbed the remaining steps and stood with her back to the door.

Suppressing a sigh, I went into the house. Helen Louise was hovering not far from the door.

"How is she?"

"Okay, I suppose. She told me it was a panic attack, probably because of the crowd of strangers. She doesn't want to come back in the house, though. She left a jacket in the kitchen. Let me get that for her, and then we can talk about what to do."

Helen Louise nodded, and I went into the kitchen to retrieve the jacket. Tara still stood with her back to the door. I handed her the jacket and urged her to put it on. I waited while she did so, her face averted.

"Hang out here for a minute while I talk to Helen Louise," I said.

Tara nodded. "Okay."

Back in the house, I told Helen Louise that I thought someone ought to take Tara home. "I don't think she's going to come back in the house. Something, or someone, has really spooked her."

"If she truly had a panic attack, then I'm really sorry for her," Helen Louise said. "With her out of commission, Henry needs help. I guess I'll have to pitch in. Would you mind taking Tara home?"

"No, I don't mind," I said. "Maybe I can get her to open up to me some and find out if there was something more specific than a crowd of people that brought on the panic attack."

"Thanks, sweetheart." Helen Louise kissed my cheek. "I'll let Sean and Alex know what's going on. You don't have to come back to fetch me if you don't want to. I can ride back in the van with Henry and the others." She knew I wasn't fond of crowds, either, especially when I didn't know most of the guests.

"If you're sure you don't mind," I said, trying not to sound too relieved.

Helen Louise smiled. "I'll be too busy to be with you, love, so go home."

"Okay, will do. If I can get the car out without having to get guests to move their cars out of the way."

Helen Louise grimaced. "I hadn't thought of that. Well, we'll do what we have to do."

"I'll let you know if cars need to be moved."

She headed for the kitchen, and I returned to the porch. Tara hadn't moved from her position.

"I'm going to take you home," I said.

"I guess I'm probably fired," Tara replied.

"Not necessarily, but you'll have to discuss this with Henry and Helen Louise tomorrow. Are you scheduled to work tomorrow?"

"Yes," she said.

Tara followed me around the house to where I had parked my car. To my relief I discovered that most of the guests had parked away from the driveway, so I had a clear path out to the road.

I tried to engage Tara in conversation on the drive home, but her responses were mostly monosyllabic, and after a few minutes I gave up. I didn't speak again until we were approaching the city limits. I asked her for directions to her home, which turned out to be an apartment in an area of town that was a bit run-down.

She directed me to her building, and I pulled to a stop.

"Are you going to be okay?" I asked when she opened the door.

"I've got pills I can take." She got out of the car. A moment before the door shut, I heard her say, "Thank you." The door closed.

I watched her until she was inside the building. Pondering the whole strange episode, I drove home.

FIVE

||||||||||||||||||||

I was in bed reading when Helen Louise called me that night. Ramses and Diesel lay on the bed with me. I glanced at the time on my phone before I answered the call. Only a few minutes past ten-thirty.

"Hello, love, I'm home now." Helen Louise sounded tired. "Henry insisted on dropping me off at home first, and he and the others went on to the bistro to unload the van."

"I'm glad. I felt guilty not being there with you," I said. "Are you worn out?"

"Not quite," Helen Louise said, "but I must say I'm glad that I have someone younger at the helm for events these days. It didn't take me long to forget how exhausting they can be."

"Henry is a godsend, that's for sure," I said. "Were Sean and Alex annoyed that I didn't come back?"

"No, I explained the situation to them, and they understood,"

Helen Louise said. "They were concerned about Tara, naturally, but I told them I was pretty sure she'd be okay. How was she when you left her?"

"The usual Tara," I said. "She did at least thank me for taking her home." I paused. "I was a little concerned, though, when I saw where she lived. In a run-down apartment complex in a not-so-good part of town."

"Really?" Helen Louise sounded surprised. "Where exactly was this apartment complex?"

I gave her the address.

"That's really strange," Helen Louise said. "She told Henry she had a room in a house not far from campus. Really a studio apartment over someone's garage. I wonder when she moved."

"Maybe she told Henry, and he didn't think to mention it to you," I said.

"That's possible," Helen Louise said. "He has more than enough on his mind. No need to keep track of employees' addresses and report them to me."

"Still, it is a bit odd," I said. "But Tara is odd."

"She is, but generally she's a good worker," Helen Louise said. "With the exception of tonight."

"Have you and Henry talked about what happened?"

"We haven't really had time. Tara is due to work tomorrow, and he's going to talk to her then. She really can't run off like that without telling anyone."

"No, she can't. I can't help but wonder if there's something else going on. You remember what I told you about that phone call this morning, and her destroying her phone."

"We agree with you. Something's not right with Tara, but whether she'll confide in anyone is doubtful."

"I think you're right," I said. "Did you get a chance to talk to Melba?"

"Not really," Helen Louise replied. "She left not long after you did, I think."

"That's unusual for her," I said. "I hope she wasn't feeling ill." Melba loved parties, and she knew so many people; she was quite the party person. I decided I'd better call her in the morning to check on her. I mentioned that to Helen Louise.

"If she's ill, let me know," Helen Louise said. "She might simply have been tired after a long week at work." She paused to yawn. "Sorry about that. I suppose I'd better start getting ready for bed."

"Yes, you should, sweetheart. Sleep well tonight," I said.

"You, too."

I put the phone away and picked up my book again. I wasn't quite ready to turn out the light. I found it difficult to concentrate on my book, however. I kept thinking about Tara and her change of address. I simply found it odd. I supposed she might have discovered the room near campus was too expensive, and she decided to find a cheaper place to live. I didn't know whether she had any source of income besides her job at the bistro and her job at the archive.

I hoped Melba wasn't ill. I figured Helen Louise was right; Melba was probably just tired from the workweek. I knew she had stayed late a couple of evenings to wrap up a special project she was working on for the library director. That must be it.

At that point I turned off the light and settled down to sleep with my two furry bedmates.

When I went downstairs in the morning in search of coffee, I found Stewart and Haskell in the kitchen.

"You're up early for a Saturday," I said after greeting them. I poured myself a cup of coffee.

Stewart was at the stove, cooking eggs and bacon. Diesel and Ramses immediately went to him, hoping for handouts. Haskell sat at the table, drinking coffee. He wasn't wearing a uniform, I was pleased to see. He put in so much overtime some weeks I hardly saw him.

"Looking forward to a quiet weekend?" I asked him.

"I sure am," Haskell said with a slow smile. His gaze drifted to Stewart, who happened to turn at that moment. He smiled back at his partner.

"I hope nothing happens to interrupt it," I said.

Haskell was a deputy in the Athena County Sheriff's Department. He worked closely with the chief deputy, Kanesha Berry. She relied heavily on him, and he was a staunch supporter of hers in the department. Not everyone in the department was happy to have a Black woman as chief deputy. Kanesha had the record to back up her claim on the position and was more than capable of silencing her detractors. She also had the support of a number of influential citizens, like Miss An'gel and Miss Dickce Ducote, among others. Not many people in Athena cared to get crossways of the Misses Ducote.

"You and me both, brother." Haskell grinned. "Hey, how come we didn't see you at the party last night?"

"I was there early on." I explained what happened. "Frank was going to recruit you and a couple of other guys to help. I guess you hadn't made it yet when he was looking for you."

"I wondered why Helen Louise was working the party," Stewart said as he placed a plate of scrambled eggs and bacon before Haskell. "How about you, Charlie? Ready for breakfast? There's plenty."

"Thanks, I'd love some," I said.

"Let me get the biscuits out of the oven, and I'll fix you a plate," Stewart said.

After he put a plate piled with hot biscuits on the table, Stewart gave me my breakfast and sat down with his own. There was more than enough bacon to go around. Ramses went from chair to chair, begging, but Diesel stuck close by me.

"Where's Dante?" I asked, referring to Stewart's poodle.

"He's out in the backyard," Stewart said. "He's been cooped up a bit lately, so I thought I'd let him run around." He checked his watch. "He's been out there long enough. I'd better bring him in."

"Sit there," Haskell ordered as he pushed back his chair. "I'll let him in."

Stewart flashed a smile at his partner. "Thanks, babe."

Haskell returned shortly with the dog. Dante made a beeline for Stewart, but soon he started frisking around Diesel and Ramses. He loved playing with the cats. Diesel tolerated him most of the time, but Ramses loved to tussle with the dog. In between bites of bacon, the pets played with one another.

"You mentioned this Tara the other day," Stewart said. "I believe you said she's pretty awkward."

"Yes, she is," I said. "Her social skills are underdeveloped, I'd say."

"Too bad about the panic attacks," Haskell said. "I've heard they can be pretty nasty. People who have them sometimes feel like they're having a heart attack, don't they?"

"That's what I've heard, too," Stewart said. "I worked with a student some years ago who had them. He scared the whole lab one day when he started having one. We rushed him to the student clinic, and he was okay after a while. Scary few minutes, though."

"By the time I found Tara last night, I think the worst had passed," I said. "I don't think it was a good idea for her to run off like that by herself, though. What if she'd passed out in the root cellar or knocked herself out down there? It was dark. Sean really needs to get the electricity on in there so it can be illuminated."

"I'm surprised he hasn't done that," Stewart said. "Aren't they keeping wine in there?"

"They are," I said. "I'm going to remind him that it needs to be done. Going down there with a flashlight isn't really safe."

"I'd hate to find a snake in the root cellar," Haskell said.

"Me, too," I said. "I think they should keep it locked as well once Rosie gets a little older. I don't like the idea of her exploring and getting shut up there in the dark."

"Do you think Alex is happy now about the house?" Stewart asked.

My daughter-in-law had expressed reservations about living in the country ever since Sean bought the house from me. She agreed to the renovations, however, and was involved in the decisions about decor and so on, but she hadn't seemed completely committed to the project. In recent weeks, though, she had a change of heart.

"She's fine with it now," I said. "They've put the house here in town up for sale."

"It really is a showplace," Haskell said. "And it's not that far from town."

"No, it takes only about fifteen minutes," Stewart said.

"If they drive as fast as you do," Haskell observed in a wry tone.

"Eighty miles an hour isn't *that* fast," Stewart retorted. Then he grinned. "Especially with a deputy sheriff in the car who can get me out of a ticket."

Haskell rolled his eyes.

I couldn't help laughing. Stewart was, as ever, irrepressible. "I've done it in twenty without speeding," I said.

Stewart shot me a glance of disbelief.

"Well, not much," I said with a grin.

Haskell snorted. "If you get caught—either of you—don't expect me to fix the ticket."

"You see how it is with Mr. By the Book, Charlie." Stewart sighed loudly.

"Somebody needs to rein you in," I said.

Stewart threw a towel at me. He missed, and it fell to the floor. Dante immediately grabbed it and started savaging it, as if it were a deadly animal. We all laughed, and Stewart firmly but gently wrested the towel away from the poodle.

"I'll clean up the kitchen since Stewart so kindly made breakfast." I pushed back my chair and carried my dishes to the sink.

"I won't argue," Stewart said.

"Thanks, Charlie," Haskell said.

"Come on, Dante, let's go back upstairs." Stewart pointed toward the door, and Dante started running out of the kitchen.

"See you later," Haskell said.

Diesel and Ramses hovered near me, no doubt hoping for more tidbits, but I resisted. I wrapped the leftover bacon in paper towels and put it in the refrigerator. Useful for salad or baked potatoes later.

While I unloaded the dishwasher and reloaded it with the dirty breakfast dishes and utensils, I thought about the events of last night. Tara's odd behavior still bothered me. I wasn't exactly doubting her explanation of the panic attack, but I wanted to know what triggered it. Was it really because there were so many people in the house?

Or was it because one of the guests frightened her?

SIX

ıııııııııııı

Since I knew only a few of the guests at the housewarming party, I had no clue who, if anyone, could have frightened Tara. For some reason, I couldn't help linking her behavior yesterday morning with her cell phone to the panic attack last night. She was obviously unsettled over something, but what could it be?

She had an off-putting personality, and for the first time, I began to wonder if that was deliberate. If it was deliberate, why was she doing it? Why didn't she want people to get to know her? The way she generally behaved, she wasn't making it easy for anyone to get close to her.

As I closed the dishwasher door, I decided I was being fanciful, looking for a mystery where there probably was none. That was part of my problem with being so curious about my fellow human beings. Or, as Kanesha Berry would no doubt say, my confounded nosiness.

Later in the day, I thought I might drop by the bistro and see whether Tara had reported to work. I wanted to observe her dealing with the customers. Saturday was generally a busy day at the bistro. People came in and lingered over their coffee and croissants in the morning, then later over their quiche and other popular dishes during the lunch rush. How would she handle all those people?

That decision made, I headed up the stairs, my two faithful companions scooting up ahead of me, and took a shower and shaved.

Thirty minutes later, dressed and refreshed for the day, I came back downstairs. I had realized, midshower, that I had left my cell phone on the kitchen table. When I picked it up, I saw that I had a missed call. I checked, and Melba had called a few minutes ago. It was now nearly eight-thirty.

I called her back. "Good morning. How are you?"

"I'm fine, and how are you?"

"Same," I said. "What's up?"

"I want to know what went on last night, and why you disappeared from the party." Her tart tone amused me. She hated not knowing things, especially if it involved people close to her.

"I heard you left the party early, too, by the way."

"I was pretty tired before I even got to the party," Melba said. "So for once I did the sensible thing and went home to bed instead of staying up way late and drinking more than I should."

"You're getting smarter in your old age," I said, and promptly heard a snort from the other end of the conversation. "Anyway, Tara had a panic attack last night, and I took her home. Helen Louise had to work in her place, so I came home when I had dropped Tara off at her apartment."

"Panic attack?" Melba said. "Do you know what triggered it? Did she say?"

"She did. Said it was all the strangers. She turned tail and ran out to the back of the house. It took us about twenty minutes to find her."

"Where was she?" Melba asked.

"In the root cellar, of all places. Sean hasn't gotten electricity installed in it yet, and this time of year it's pretty chilly down there."

"Why didn't she simply stay on the back porch?"

"I don't know. To me, that would have been the logical place," I said. "The guests were staying in the house, so she would have been by herself back there."

"That girl is plain peculiar," Melba said. "Wonder if she saw somebody who scared her. Somebody she didn't want to see *her*."

"I wondered the same thing, but then I decided I was being a little too imaginative. I don't really know all that much about panic attacks and how rational a person is during one."

"I suppose so," Melba replied. "I don't really know much about them, either, other than that they can be frightening."

"By the time I found her, she seemed over it. She was calm but not very communicative."

"Back to normal, then," Melba said with asperity.

"Yes, and under the circumstances, it seemed best for her to go home. She's supposed to work a shift at the bistro this morning, and I thought I'd go by later on and see how she's doing."

"And if she showed up for work," Melba said.

"That, too. Got a question for you, since you're the person who keeps the records for the library staff," I said.

"Yes, I do," Melba said. "What is it?"

"It's about where she lives." I told her about dropping Tara off at the run-down apartment complex last night.

"I don't remember what her address is," Melba said. "I'll check on it and call you back."

"Okay, thanks." I realized this was an invasion of privacy, but I was concerned about Tara, however. Melba could access her work computer from home and should be able to find out the address pretty quickly.

Melba called me back three minutes later. "What was the street that complex is on?"

"Baxter Avenue."

Melba exhaled a breath. "That's not the address in her record. According to that, she lives in a complex on the other side of town. Better area, for sure."

"This is getting really odd," I said. "According to Helen Louise, the address Tara gave at the bistro is for an efficiency apartment near campus."

"Three different addresses," Melba said. "Definitely weird. Sounds to me like she's trying to hide from someone."

"Now I wonder whether she stayed where I dropped her off last night," I said. "It could have been a blind because she didn't want me to know where she really does live."

"I think you're probably right. Maybe she's paranoid."

"I don't know what's going on with her, but I'm even more worried about her now. It's clearly not normal behavior."

"No, it's not. What are you going to do about it?" Melba asked, obviously concerned.

"Talk to Helen Louise and Henry, for one thing," I said. "I wonder whether they've observed any other odd behavior." I recalled the incident Henry had related of a couple of weeks ago when Tara abruptly disappeared into the bathroom in the kitchen area and her explanation for that. I recounted it to Melba.

"What time are you planning to be there?" Melba asked. "I think I'll join you."

"That would be great," I said. "How about eleven?"

"Fine. See you there," Melba said. "With Diesel, of course."

"Of course." I chuckled as I ended the call. Melba didn't want to miss a chance of loving on my cat, and he would certainly be happy to see her.

At ten-forty-five, Diesel and I were ready to go. I left a note on the kitchen table for Stewart and Haskell to let them know we would be out of the house for an hour or two. I put Ramses in the den and turned on the television to keep him company. I didn't like leaving him on his own, but he liked the animal channel. My young cousin, Alissa Hale, who currently boarded with me, was in California visiting friends and her mother, but she wasn't due back for a few more days yet. Otherwise she would have been happy to keep Ramses with her.

Melba was already at the bistro, sitting at the table we usually occupied in one corner of the room near the cash register. Diesel went straight to her, and she lavished attention on him. Melba already had a glass of tea, so I figured she had been waiting for several minutes. I checked my watch, and it read two minutes to eleven.

Melba saw me. "No, you're not late, but I was feeling restless and left the house early."

"Have you seen Tara yet?" I asked, glancing around to see if I could spot her in the crowded room.

"Not yet," Melba replied. "I haven't had a chance to ask Helen Louise about her."

I spied Helen Louise chatting with a table of four women, a couple of whom I recognized as her fellow church members. Probably talking about our upcoming wedding, I guessed. When Helen Louise came over to our table a couple of minutes later, she confirmed my supposition.

"Everything is set for the church," Helen Louise said. "Now, what can I get you to drink?" She rubbed Diesel's head with the back of her hand.

"Iced tea," I said.

"Right. Back in a minute." She walked away to get my beverage.

"Do you know what you want?" Melba asked, glancing at the day's menu on the blackboard behind the cash register.

"Quiche," I said. "I had a good breakfast, so I'm not all that hungry." Today's quiche was spinach, mushroom, bacon, and Gruyère cheese. I couldn't resist that.

"I skipped breakfast, but quiche sounds good. Along with a salad," Melba said. "I might still have enough room for dessert."

"I'll have to wait and see." I loved Helen Louise's pastries, but I really didn't need the extra calories. I was mindful of the upcoming wedding, and I didn't want to have to have my tux let out for the occasion. It fit fairly snugly now.

Helen Louise came back with my tea and took our orders. "Easy enough. I'll be right back with the food." She glanced down at Diesel. "Perhaps a couple of tidbits for *le chat* as well."

I nodded. If he didn't get something, Diesel would pout.

Before she left the table to get our food, though, I asked Helen Louise quickly about Tara. "Is she here today?"

Helen Louise nodded. "Let me get your lunch, and we'll talk more then, if I'm not needed elsewhere for a few minutes." She headed for the kitchen.

"They must have her working in the back today," Melba said. "At least she can't get frightened by the crowd out here."

"No, that's true. She's probably best out of sight of all these people."

Helen Louise came back with our food and set it before us. After a quick glance around the bistro, she slipped into a chair across from me.

"Tara's working in the back today," Helen Louise said. "She seems none the worse for her panic attack last night."

"That's good," I said before tasting the quiche.

"This is heavenly," Melba said, pointing to the quiche with her fork.

"Thank you. I'll let Henry know. It was his choice for the menu today," Helen Louise replied.

"Has Tara said any more about what set off the panic attack?" I asked.

"Only that the crowd of guests in the house really bothered her. I've noticed before that she seems uneasy when she's working out front here and we're busy." Helen Louise frowned.

"We checked up on her address," Melba said. "Or addresses, I should say. Her address in her work application at the college is for an apartment on the other side of town from where Charlie took her last night."

"And that's obviously not the address she gave us." Now Helen Louise looked both disturbed and irritated. "Is she a habitual liar? Or does she not want anyone to know where she lives?"

"Could be both," I said. "I'm beginning to think she's afraid of something or, more likely, someone. But the question is who?"

"Maybe she's hiding from an abuser," Melba said. "That would explain her behavior."

"She told us that she moved from Memphis because she was tired of living in a big city," Helen Louise said. "I suppose an abusive partner or spouse could have somehow followed her here."

"I haven't heard her say anything about where she was before she showed up at the college," I said. "Melba?"

Melba shook her head. "Nope. She barely talks to me anyway."

"She doesn't say much to me, either," I said. "Let alone confide in me about anything personal."

"She's definitely an enigma," Helen Louise said. "I do feel rather sorry for her, because she seems so friendless. She almost seems to work to put people off."

"That could be a result of abuse," Melba said. "Maybe she's afraid to trust anyone."

Helen Louise said, "Excuse me." She got up to go to the cash register. Her church friends were ready to pay.

"I don't know what we can do for Tara," I said. "Other than remain friendly and be willing to help if she needs anything."

"That's fine with me," Melba said. "But I'd lay odds she won't ever ask."

"Maybe not, but if we allow her to feel more comfortable around us, it could help."

"True." Melba addressed herself to her salad, and I doled out a few of the tidbits of boiled chicken Helen Louise had brought for Diesel. He seemed satisfied, so I worked on my quiche. It was delicious, but then I expected no less of Henry and his culinary gifts.

Tara made no appearance while Melba and I were there. People started streaming in the closer to noon it got, so we finished our meal, paid our checks, and bade goodbye to Helen Louise.

Diesel demanded more attention from Melba before he would get in the car for the drive home, and Melba naturally obliged. I noticed a couple of cars circling the town square, obviously hunting for parking spaces. One, an expensive make, came around the second time and stopped briefly. I could see the driver, a man in his thirties, glaring at me. I looked straight at him, giving him my best stone face. He moved on.

I knew, though, it was time to move on and give up my parking space. I said as much to Melba, and she nodded. "People get so impatient," she said. "And I'd be impatient, too, in their situation." She gave me a quick hug, and we went to our cars.

When we reached home, I went straight to the den to let Ramses out. He meowed at me several times, though when I first opened the door, he was so focused on the TV he didn't hear me right away. There were lions on screen, and I wondered if he thought they were house cats like him.

After going upstairs to change into comfortable Saturday leisure clothes, I went back to the den to check my email. I scanned the contents of my inbox, but I didn't see anything that demanded immediate attention. I picked up my phone and called Sean.

"Hey, Dad," he said after several rings. "How are you doing this morning?"

"I'm fine. How about you and Alex? Have you recovered from last night?"

"We're fine, too. We did sleep in a while, but we were anxious to pick up Rosie and bring her home." Rosie had spent the night at Laura and Frank's house, along with baby Charlie and the nanny.

"How is my favorite granddaughter?"

"Full of energy and running around the house." Sean chuckled. "Trying to keep up with her is going to wear Alex and me out before lunchtime."

"Sounds like you at that age," I said. "Were you happy with how the housewarming went?"

"It was great," Sean said, "though I hated that Helen Louise had to work. What is wrong with that woman Tara? Helen Louise mentioned a panic attack."

"That's what Tara told me. Apparently it was triggered by the sight of so many strange people."

"Sorry that she was affected that way. She was okay, though, when you took her home?"

"As far as I could tell," I said. "I'm sorry I had to miss so much of the festivities."

Sean laughed. "No, you're not. I know you hate crowds, too, although not to the level of panicking. Alex and I were so busy talking to people that we wouldn't have had much time to spend with you anyway. Everyone loved the house, and I could tell some people were trying to figure out how much everything cost."

"There are always people like that," I said. "Pay them no mind."

"We don't," Sean replied with some asperity. "I invited a number of people I felt obliged to for business reasons, but that's probably the last time they'll get an invitation to our house."

"Good for you," I said. "As long as it doesn't hurt your business."

"It won't," Sean said, and I admired his confidence.

I was struck by a sudden idea. "Do you by any chance have a guest list that I could look at?"

"Yes, I do," Sean said. "What on earth for? I don't mind your having it, of course."

"It's just a crazy notion," I said. "This niggling thought that it wasn't the crowd of people that spooked Tara. What if it was one person? I didn't know most of the people there last night, but Melba can go through it and tell me who they are. Especially if anyone is relatively new to Athena."

"You're sticking your nose in again." Sean sounded partly amused and partly annoyed. "Is this woman Tara going to thank you for getting involved in her business?"

"No, she probably won't, but while she's working with me in the archive, I want to know that she's okay," I said.

Sean sighed into the phone. "All right, Dad, I'll send you the list, but promise me you won't do anything crazy with it."

"I promise," I said. I never did anything crazy, as far as I was concerned, so I didn't mind giving him my word I wouldn't.

"Hold on a moment, Rosie wants to say hi," Sean said.

Moments later I heard my granddaughter gabbling into the phone. She hadn't quite mastered actual words yet, but I figured it wouldn't be long before she did.

"Hello, sweet girl, Grandpa loves you."

More gabbling ensued before Sean took back his phone. "I'll send the list in a few minutes. Someone needs a diaper change, so I'll talk to you later."

"Thanks, son," I said, and ended the call.

With a toddler involved, I knew it might be more than a few minutes before Sean was able to send me the list, so I moved to my recliner. Ramses hopped into my lap right away, and Diesel stretched out beside the chair. I switched the channel to an old sitcom and settled back to relax.

The ringing of my phone some time later woke me from my unintended nap. In a bit of a haze, I moved Ramses out of my lap so I could get up and retrieve my phone. I had left it on the desk. I saw with a shock that it was a few minutes past two-thirty. I'd been asleep for nearly two hours.

Helen Louise greeted me when I answered the call. "Hello, love, did I wake you?"

I suppressed a yawn. "Well, yes, but that's okay. I hadn't meant to take a nap." I settled down in my chair again, and Ramses jumped back into my lap. He made a few biscuits on my legs before he settled down. I tried not to wince when his claws penetrated the fabric of my pants.

"Wish I could have taken one with you," she said.

"Me, too. What's up?"

"I got a little information out of Tara," Helen Louise said. "About where you dropped her off last night."

SEVEN

||||||||||||||||||||||||||||||||||

That statement brought me fully awake. "What did she say?"

"I confronted her, in a friendly way, about the address issue," Helen Louise said. "She said a good friend lived in that complex where you took her. She said she didn't want to go home to her empty apartment last night. She still felt a bit shaky after the panic attack."

"That's reasonable, I suppose. Did she tell you where her *empty apartment* is?" I asked.

"She said it's in that complex on the other side of town. She moved there recently because her landlord at the efficiency apartment near campus was too nosy. Kept showing up at her door at odd times asking questions and wanting to talk."

"That would certainly be enough to put a tenant off, particularly a person as private as Tara appears to be," I said. "Was the landlord male or female?"

"Female," Helen Louise said.

"All reasonable," I said. "I'm happy to know that Tara has at least one friend she can go to. As odd as she can be, I frankly wondered whether she had any friends."

"I've done my best to let her know that she can talk to me if anything is worrying her," Helen Louise said. "I'm not sure whether I really got through to her, though. I've never dealt with anyone as self-contained as she is, or as socially unaware."

"Same here," I said. "I think we've spent enough time on the subject of Tara Martin. The weird thing is, that name rings a faint bell, but I can't remember where it comes from."

Helen Louise laughed. "There was a soap-opera character named Tara Martin. Did you ever watch *All My Children*?"

"Yes, I did. No wonder the name was familiar." I spent many a weekday afternoon during the summers of my adolescence glued to the television set, waiting to find out what was happening with the residents of Pine Valley. Tara was one of my favorite characters. "I haven't thought about that show in years."

"She told me she was named Tara after the plantation in *Gone with the Wind*," Helen Louise said. "Said she'd never heard of the soap opera."

"Okay, enough about her. Anything about wedding arrangements that we need to discuss?" I asked.

Helen Louise mentioned a few details, wanting my input. We talked a couple of minutes longer; then she said she needed to get back to work.

Only three short weeks until we would be married. For a moment my heart skittered in my chest. I thought I'd only ever be married once, to my dear Jackie. But fate, in the form of pancreatic cancer, had decided otherwise. I found love a second time with a friend, who had been a friend of my first wife as well. I suspected I would feel Jackie's presence in the church three weeks from now as Helen Louise and I exchanged vows. I believed that those we loved most never truly left us. They lived in our hearts and in our minds, always.

Enough of that, I told myself. Time enough to get sentimental on the day itself. I remembered that Sean was going to send me the guest list for the housewarming party. I got up from the chair, dislodging Ramses again, to go to the computer. As I waited for the new messages to download, I thought about that guest list. What was I going to do with it? I could show it to Tara and ask her whether she knew any of the people on the list.

For one thing, I doubted she would answer me. I didn't think I would know many of the people on the list, though I might recognize the names of people I'd heard about. After I shared it with Melba, I would ask her about any strangers on the list. If Tara was frightened by one of the guests, I figured it could be someone who was a relative newcomer to Athena. Like Tara herself, from what little I knew.

The messages had finished downloading. I clicked on Sean's, and I scanned the list. I knew, or at least was slightly acquainted with, ten of the guests, not including Melba, of course. Kanesha Berry was on the list. I hadn't seen her there, so I figured if she made the party, it was after I left.

A few of the other names sounded vaguely familiar, but the majority I didn't recognize. I was sure that Melba would do much better. I had sworn more than once that Melba knew everyone in town, and she had rarely proved me wrong.

I thought about what I was doing. Was I working on instinct in this instance, believing that there was more to Tara's story of a panic attack than she had explained? Or was I looking for a mystery where there was none?

I had always admitted that I was nosy, especially where people were concerned. Tara puzzled me. I had never been around anyone like her. That alone piqued my curiosity. I doubted she would welcome my interest or any attempts to help, but her actions had aroused not only my curiosity but also my sympathy. She just seemed so *alone*. I knew there were people who appeared to prefer that, but I admitted that I found it hard to understand.

I focused on the email from Sean again. I forwarded the message to Melba and asked her to look over the list to see if she knew everyone on it. If she didn't, I wanted the names of the people she didn't know. I wasn't sure what I would do with the information, but it might give me a place to start. I might come up with some way to put those names to the test with Tara and see if she reacted to any of them in any way.

Looking at the list again, I stuck on Kanesha Berry's name. On impulse I picked up the phone and called Melba. She answered immediately.

"Afternoon, Charlie. What's up?"

"I just emailed you the guest list from the party last night," I said.

"What do you want me to do with it?"

I explained that I was curious about the many names I didn't recognize.

"I'll go through the list and let you know whom I know and whom I don't. That's it?"

"Yes," I said.

"What exactly are you looking for?"

"I'm not really sure, to be honest. I've been wondering if Tara's panic attack was caused by her seeing someone she didn't want to encounter for some reason. Perhaps the abuser we were talking about."

"That's possible, I suppose," Melba said. "But how are you going to figure who it was if you're right about her being upset by somebody?"

"I don't know yet," I said. "I'll figure it out after I hear back from you."

"I'll work on it, but I've got a lot to do around the house this weekend," Melba said. "So don't be sitting by the computer, waiting for an email."

"I won't," I said, though I knew I'd be impatient until I heard back from her. When I got these nosy spells, I wanted quick results.

Melba bade me goodbye, and I set the phone aside. I needed to occupy my mind with something besides Tara Martin and her odd potential problems. I had plenty of books to read. In fact, I had so many books I hadn't yet read, I'd have to live to be two hundred to read them all. But I wasn't in the mood for reading at the moment. Rare for me, but it did happen occasionally.

I heard the doorbell ring, and I hurried out of the den to answer it, accompanied by both Diesel and Ramses. They knew what the sound meant, and both of them enjoyed visitors.

I opened the door and found my daughter, visibly pregnant, on the doorstep. Beside her stood my grandson, Charlie, my little namesake.

He immediately reached up to me, saying, "G'anpa."

Naturally I picked him up and stood aside for Laura to enter. She shut the door behind her, stopping Ramses at the last moment from darting outside. "Bad kitty," she said. "You know you're not supposed to go out the front door."

Ramses uttered a plaintive meow while Diesel rubbed against her legs. She bent slightly to scratch his head.

"I thought we'd surprise you, Dad," Laura said. "I hope it's not inconvenient for us to drop by like this without calling first."

Charlie, now that I had held him for nearly a minute, wanted down to play with "kitty." He meant Diesel, although he liked Ramses, too. Charlie and Diesel had a special bond, and had since my grandson's birth. Diesel took it upon himself to watch over Charlie whenever my grandson was present in the house.

"Come in the kitchen," I said, offering Laura my arm. Ramses was liable to dart between her feet, and I didn't want her to stumble. "How are you feeling?"

"Fine, Dad," she said with a smile. "Just a couple more months to go, thank the Lord."

I pulled out a chair for her, and she sank into it with a barely suppressed sigh.

"I will admit I like getting off my feet whenever possible," Laura said.

"How about something to drink?" I asked.

"Do you still have some of that decaf tea?" she asked.

"I do," I said. "Hot tea?"

"Please."

I filled the kettle and put it on the stove; then I got out the teapot and the bags and poured some half-and-half in a pitcher. While we waited for the water to boil, I asked about Frank.

"He's using the time we're out of the house to have a cigar on the back porch." Laura wrinkled her nose. "I could wring Sean's neck for getting him into cigars, but as long as he doesn't smoke them inside the house, I'm not going to fuss."

"And as long as you can spray him down with that scent-remover stuff." I grinned.

"That, too." She grinned back at me. "He works so hard at the college; I think he deserves a hobby that helps him relax. He told me that when he's smoking a cigar, he calms down and lets whatever is stressing him at the moment just recede into the background."

As the head of the theater department at Athena College, Frank had plenty of responsibilities, as both an administrator and as a teacher, so I agreed with Laura in principle. I wasn't keen on either my son or my son-in-law smoking, but they did it only a couple of times a week, as far as I was aware. They didn't expose their children to it, either.

"Has Frank's semester started off okay?" I asked. Laura was on a sort of sabbatical this spring because of the baby's impending arrival.

"Just the usual aggravations, like students wanting to add and drop classes at the last moment, and dealing with pettifogging administrative stuff." She shook her head. "He takes it mostly in stride, but it would drive me bonkers to have to deal with it."

"Now you know why I was happy to retire from being a branch

library manager in Houston." The kettle whistled, and I turned the burner off. I poured some hot water into the teapot and sloshed it around. I poured that out, put in the tea bag, and added more hot water. I set the teapot on the table to let the tea steep.

"I do," Laura replied. "How is that woman, the one who works for you in the archive? Isn't her name Tara? I heard about the panic attack."

"By the time I found her, she seemed to be over it and pretty much back to her taciturn self," I said. "I dropped her off in town at the home of a friend. She made it to work at the bistro this morning."

"That's good," Laura said. "I had a friend in Los Angeles who had panic attacks. They could be pretty nasty. A couple of times we thought he was having a heart attack. One of the other cast members who had been in med school knew what was going on, however, and helped get him calmed down without his having to go to the emergency room. Did Tara say what set it off?"

"She said it was seeing all those people in the house while she was serving." I checked the teapot and decided the tea was ready. I poured for both of us, waiting until Laura had added cream and sugar to hers before I did the same for myself.

"Different things trigger people who have them," Laura said. "A sudden fear is one of them, and it sounds like what Tara experienced." She raised her cup and had a sip of the tea.

"Yes, according to her. One part of her problem is that, in my opinion, she's pretty antisocial. She appears to be uncomfortable around other people, even one-on-one." I related the incidents of yesterday morning, Tara's response to my late arrival and to the destruction of her phone.

"I wonder if she's seen a doctor or a therapist about it," Laura said.

"I don't know," I said. "I am willing to broach the subject with her, but I have no idea how she'll react. It might come better from Melba, though."

"Because that would be woman to woman?" Laura arched an eyebrow.

"Partly," I said. "And partly because I don't relish the idea of trying to talk to Tara about anything that personal. I really know almost nothing about her outside her work at the archive. She's an excellent worker, and she's accurate, too, with data entry."

"You're a kind man, Dad," Laura said. "I think you should be the one to talk to her. You know Melba can be a little impatient with people, not that she's unkind, but you know how she can be. You'd probably handle the situation better. You're less likely to get annoyed with the woman."

Laura was right about Melba. I annoyed her on a regular basis, but I'd known her since childhood and could overlook it. Tara probably couldn't, or wouldn't.

"I give in," I said. "I'll talk to her on Monday morning. And I won't be late this time."

Laura chuckled. "You've always been early to everything, so I'm getting a kick out of knowing you were actually late once in your life."

A howl of rage interrupted our conversation. Charlie was toddling around the room, trying to get away from Ramses, who was chasing and jumping at him.

"Ramses, you stop that now."

Ramses knew that tone of my voice, and he halted. Then he slunk under the table. Charlie's rage dissipated immediately, and he crawled under the table to pat Ramses. Diesel joined them, pushing Ramses aside. Charlie chuckled.

Laura and I shook our heads. I doubted that Ramses had actually hurt the baby. He simply wanted to play. Diesel much of the time ignored the younger cat's attempt at fun, so Ramses went for every opportunity.

We chatted through two cups of decaf tea apiece and watched Charlie play with the cats. Laura at last glanced at her watch. "We'd better get going, Dad. Frank will be expecting us back by now."

Charlie insisted on G'anpa carrying him out to the car, so of course I had to give in. I got him situated in his seat and helped Laura into the car. I stood on the sidewalk and watched them drive away. I loved every moment I spent with them and wished I could spend more, but I was happy with what I had.

I thought about Tara later on that night, telling myself that talking to her on Monday morning wouldn't be so bad.

As it turned out, I didn't have the opportunity. Tara didn't show up for work.

EIGHT

On Monday morning I made a special effort to be in the archive office early. Diesel and I arrived at ten minutes to eight. Tara was due in at eight, but eight o'clock came without Tara walking through the open door. I had left it open because I wanted her to know right away that I was at work.

Five minutes passed, then ten, then fifteen. I called Melba. "Have you heard anything from Tara?" I asked. "She hasn't come to work yet, and it's not like her to be late."

"No, I haven't," Melba said. "I can try calling the number I have on file, but since she destroyed her phone, I don't know if it will be any good."

"Did she list any kind of emergency contact?" I asked.

"If she doesn't answer the number on file, I'll see if there's someone else to call. I'll let you know."

I thanked her and hung up the office phone. Given the events of the past few days, I felt uneasy about Tara. When Helen Louise and I had discussed Tara briefly yesterday, taking a few minutes out of our talk of the wedding and the honeymoon after the regular Sunday family dinner, she hadn't said that Tara seemed unduly worried about anything while at work on Saturday. Could something have happened yesterday?

Melba called me back a couple of minutes shy of eight-thirty. "No luck," she said, sounding annoyed. "The number she gave for herself says no longer in service, and the emergency contact number she gave is for a plumbing supply business in Memphis. Nobody there has ever heard of Tara Martin."

"Why would she give a number like that for an emergency contact? Such an obvious fake," I said.

"I don't know," Melba said. "I can't think of anyone else to call, except Henry at the bistro. I hate to bother him this early because I know he's busy baking and preparing for the day."

"I don't think he'll mind in this situation," I said.

"Okay, I'll call him. I'll let you know if he's heard from her."

Diesel could obviously tell that I was worried, because he reached out from his spot in the window and placed a large paw on my shoulder. He warbled as if asking me what was wrong. I turned to him and scratched his head. "I'm okay," I told him. "A little concerned about Tara, that's all."

That appeared to satisfy him, and he turned to look out at the window again. He chirped occasionally at either a squirrel or a bird that he could see outside.

I tried to focus on work, but my concern for Tara kept my mind occupied. I realized I wouldn't be able to accomplish anything until I knew where she was, and how she was.

I heard hurried footsteps on the stairs, and moments later Melba appeared in the doorway. She paused for a moment to catch her breath. Her pale face alarmed me. She advanced into the room and dropped into the chair in front of my desk. Diesel slid down from his perch in the window and went to her. He put a paw on her thigh, and she stroked him.

"Must be something bad," I said. "I don't think I've ever seen you so pale."

Melba nodded. "It is bad. Henry was about to call me. He was apparently listed as Tara's emergency contact. She's in the hospital in a coma."

"Oh my lord," I said, appalled. "What happened?"

"Hit-and-run last night," Melba said. "No witnesses, as far as they know. Someone found her in the street and called the ambulance. Police are investigating, but no leads yet."

"Where was she found?"

"Near that apartment complex you took her to Friday night," Melba said. Color slowly returned to her face, and she seemed calmer now.

"Was Henry her only emergency contact?" I asked.

"Yes, and that is really odd," Melba said.

"I'm beginning to think that she was trying to hide from someone," I said slowly. "I'm also wondering whether Tara Martin is her real name."

"You mean because it's also the name of a soap-opera character?" Melba asked. "I thought about that, too."

"Things simply don't add up, given what we know now," I said.

"Maybe she's in the Federal Witness Protection Program."

"Maybe," I replied. "But in that case, I think there would have been a better background story, and a reliable emergency contact number. I'd like to think that the feds are more thorough."

"You're probably right." She shook her head. "What the heck is going on here?"

"I'm wondering now if the hit-and-run was deliberate," I said. "Maybe the person she was afraid of tracked her down and tried to kill her."

"We could sit here all day and speculate," Melba said. "We don't really know what's going on. Maybe the hit-and-run was an accident and the driver got spooked and drove off and left her. Lord knows there are plenty of cowards in this world."

"Yes, there are, and leaving somebody lying in the road is despicable," I said with some heat. "I hope there's some way they can find out who did this."

Melba gave Diesel a few last rubs of the head before she pushed herself up out of the chair. "I'd better get back downstairs, but the Lord only knows how I'm going to be able to concentrate on work now."

"Same here," I said. "Let me know if you hear anything at all. I think I'll run over to the hospital at lunchtime to check on her."

"If they'll tell you anything," Melba said. "You know they have to be careful about that since you're not family."

"True. It would be a wasted trip most likely." I frowned. "I imagine at some point the police will get in touch with us since she works here."

"See you later." Melba headed out the door.

I opened the messaging app on my phone and found Kanesha Berry in my contacts. I composed a text about Tara and the hit-and-run and sent it to her. If Tara should happen to die, this would become a murder case. As chief deputy, Kanesha was the designated homicide investigator. The police department didn't have a homicide squad.

About five minutes later I received a response in the form of a text. *Aware of the situation,* Kanesha replied. *Someone will be in touch with you and the bistro to investigate victim.*

That was it. Typical Kanesha. Blunt and to the point. I knew better than to respond to her message. She had said all she was prepared to say, and now I simply had to wait until the police department sent an officer around.

I hated not knowing more about Tara's actual condition. That she was in a coma didn't tell me much. Was it natural, or was it medically induced? How severe were her injuries? What were her chances of survival? Had she sustained any brain damage?

I put those thoughts aside and prayed for Tara. When I finished, I decided to go downstairs to the staff lounge and get some coffee. I thought about any contacts I might have at the hospital who might be willing to give me any information about Tara, but I concluded there wasn't anyone I could really ask. I knew how strict the privacy rules were, and I couldn't in all conscience ask someone to breach them on my behalf. I had only a tenuous connection to Tara, after all. It was up to the college to stay in contact with the hospital.

Melba would, I knew, do her best to glean information from the college whenever possible, and I would have to be satisfied with that. Perhaps before the workday ended Melba would get an update.

There was no coffee in the lounge, and I debated whether to make a fresh pot. I decided I would. Diesel watched as I rinsed the carafe, changed the filter, and added grounds to it. I turned the machine on, and I seated myself on the sofa to wait for the coffee. It normally took only about five minutes, and I decided there was no point in going back upstairs during that time.

Diesel crawled onto the sofa with me and laid his head and front paws on my lap. He knew I was still perturbed about Tara, and he did his best to comfort me. As always, having him with me made me feel better. I stroked his head and down his neck and back. He purred in gratitude.

"You can't settle down to work, either." Melba had appeared in the doorway, coffee cup in hand. She gestured toward the coffeepot. "I hope you made enough for me, too."

"I did," I said. "Should be ready in a few more minutes. Have a seat."

Melba chose one of the chairs at the small table. "This is so frustrating."

"I texted Kanesha about this," I said. "She is aware of the situation and said that someone from the police department will probably be in touch with us and the bistro at some point."

"I'm not sure what we can tell them," Melba said.

"I'm going to tell them about the phone incident Friday morning and about what happened that night at the party. I can't help but think those incidents might be related to the hit-and-run."

"You're probably right," Melba said. "I pray Tara can recover and isn't brain damaged."

"Me, too." I demurred from expressing the idea that she might die from her injuries, but Melba knew that was a possibility as well as I did.

We both watched the coffeepot for signs that it was done. Neither of us spoke during the couple of minutes that followed.

"Finally." Melba got out of the chair to pour herself coffee.

I urged Diesel gently aside and poured my own coffee, adding powdered creamer and sugar. "Back to work," I said.

Melba preceded me and Diesel out of the lounge. "Talk to you later," she said as the cat and I headed up the stairs.

Lunchtime came, and Diesel and I drove home, the weather still too chilly for walking to work. I had given up my notion of going to the hospital, because I realized it would be useless trying to find out more about Tara's condition. I hated waiting, but I had little choice.

When Diesel and I walked into the kitchen, I found a large chef's salad at my place on the table. Beside the salad sat a container with Azalea's homemade Thousand Island dressing. Ramses wasn't in the kitchen, nor was Azalea, and I assumed they were busy somewhere in the house. I poured myself a glass of sweet tea and settled down to my meal.

Azalea and Ramses appeared by the time I finished the salad. Ramses immediately pounced on Diesel, wanting to play.

"Good afternoon," I said to Azalea. "Great salad, as always."

"Glad you enjoyed it. I made a caramel cake this morning," she said. "Would you like a piece now?"

I was sorely tempted, because I loved Azalea's caramel cake. "I think I'd better save it until later," I said. "That salad filled me up."

"It'll be here for after dinner," she said as she took my salad bowl to the sink.

"I received some horrifying news this morning at work," I said. "My assistant, Tara, was the victim of a hit-and-run last night. She's in the hospital in a coma, and I'm really worried about her."

Azalea turned to face me, her expression one of great distress. "May the Lord watch over her," she said in a quiet tone. "Did they catch the person who did it?"

"No, it was late, and there were no witnesses. Whoever did it went off and left her to die."

Azalea shook her head. "What an evil person to do something like that." Her eyes closed, and her lips moved, but no sound came out. I knew she was praying for Tara, and I joined her. When I next looked up, Azalea was regarding me with an odd expression.

"Are you going to get involved?" she asked.

"Not planning to," I said. "This situation is beyond anything I can help with. It's up to the law enforcement divisions."

"Kanesha will have to handle it if this poor woman dies," Azalea said.

"She will," I said. "No better person to run the investigation." Azalea nodded.

"They're going to have to find out who Tara is," I said.

"What do you mean?"

"She's been incredibly secretive about any family or friends she might have," I said. "She's given three different home addresses here in Athena, and the emergency contact that she gave the college turned out to be a business where no one had ever heard of her."

"Why would anyone do that?" Azalea said. "What is she afraid of?"

"We don't know. Perhaps she's hiding from an abusive partner or spouse," I said.

"Lord bless her soul," Azalea said.

"Yes," I replied. After a glance at my watch, I pushed back from the table and stood. "It's early, but I think I'll head on back to work. I want to check through Tara's desk to see whether I can find any kind of clue that could help us find family or friends for her."

Azalea nodded. "I'll be praying you do."

Diesel and I arrived back at the administration building a few minutes later and entered through the back door from the parking lot. I paused to pull a soft drink—diet, of course—from the refrigerator before we went up to the office. Melba's door was closed, and I figured she was still out to lunch.

The moment I unlocked the door, I heard the office phone ringing, and I hurried inside to answer it.

I picked up the receiver and sat at the desk. After I identified myself, I asked, "How may I help you?" Diesel climbed into the window behind me.

"Good afternoon, Charlie." I recognized Haskell Bates's voice. "Are you available to talk? In person, that is."

"Sure, come on by," I said.

"Thanks. I'll be there in about ten minutes." Haskell ended the call.

Haskell had been brisk and businesslike, so I figured this was not a social call. Probably related to Tara Martin's accident. My heart skipped a beat. With Haskell, and therefore the sheriff's department, involved, did it mean that Tara had died?

I fretted over this until Haskell walked into the office.

"Afternoon, Charlie," he said. "Mind if I sit?" He indicated the chair in front of my desk.

"Of course not, go ahead," I said. "Look, how is Tara? Has she died?"

Haskell leaned back in the chair and regarded me, his expression unreadable. "No, she hasn't, but the doctors aren't giving her much hope of surviving this. She was in bad shape when they brought her in. They're doing tests now to determine the extent of her injuries."

I felt sick at my stomach. I had feared as much, but I had been holding on to a bit of hope. Now that disappeared. "Oh my lord" was all I could say.

Haskell nodded. "It's one of the worst cases I've ever seen. We think it wasn't an accident."

"Why?" I asked, still struggling to cope with the news.

"Because she was found on the sidewalk, and there were tracks to indicate that the vehicle came up on the sidewalk to run her down."

If anything, my stomach felt sicker. To run down a defenseless person in cold blood was hard to understand. Someone must really have hated Tara. Or feared her.

"Are there any leads in the case?" I asked.

"We have the marks of the tires," Haskell said. "But there are no witnesses. A man in the apartment complex heard a commotion, but by the time he went out to investigate and found Ms. Martin, there was no sign of the vehicle."

"I guess this means that y'all are treating this as potential homicide," I said.

"More or less," Haskell said. "We're working the case with the police department, but we'll take it over when the victim dies. Unusual, but as I said, the doctors think her chances of surviving are pretty much nil. We need to find a next of kin."

He didn't need to explain why. "I don't think I can help you with that," I said. "Melba checked, but the contact information Tara gave was bogus."

Haskell pulled out a notebook and a pen. "Can you tell me what it is?"

"I can't give you the exact address," I said. "Melba can get the information for you. Helen Louise has a different address. Friday night I gave Tara a ride home from Sean and Alex's party, and Tara directed me to an apartment complex. I gather that's where she was found."

"Is there anything else you can tell me about her?" Haskell asked after he had finished making his notes.

I told him about the odd incident with the phone on Friday morning. "She didn't make any explanation, although I'm sure she knew that I had heard her stomping on the phone. She was a private person and socially awkward. She sounded angry, and perhaps a bit afraid, according to Melba. She overheard the incident, too."

Haskell nodded. "What about at the housewarming party?"

I told him all I knew about that. "You'll need to talk to Helen Louise and Henry. There was a similar incident at the bistro a couple of weeks ago. I believe she said she had some kind of virus and abruptly left the dining room and stayed in the back. Henry sent her home."

Haskell rose from the chair. "Thanks, Charlie."

"I hope y'all can catch the scum who did this," I said. My tone was heated, and I heard Diesel warble behind me.

"We'll do our damnedest," Haskell said. "I'll let you know about Ms. Martin."

"Thanks."

I watched him walk out of the office before I turned to my cat. I patted his head and told him everything would be okay. If he detected my lie, he didn't let on.

NINE

|||||||||||||||||||||||||||||

A quarter of an hour later, I was absorbed in cataloging when I heard a knock at the door. I looked up to see a scruffy-looking individual hesitating in the doorway. After a quick perusal I decided the person was a youngish man, perhaps thirty, give or take a few years. Dressed in ragged jeans, a ratty leather jacket, dirty sneakers, and sunglasses, he had a raffish appearance, including short beard stubble.

"Good afternoon," I said. "Can I help you with something?"

He took that as an invitation to enter the office, and he walked closer to my desk. "Yeah, I'm looking for Tara. I think this is the right place. Archive, right?"

"Yes, this is the archive, and Tara does work here," I said.

"Well, man, is she here? Got something for her," he said, his voice low and raspy.

I wondered if he was attempting to make a drug delivery. I knew

I shouldn't judge by appearances, but he reminded me of such characters I had seen on TV.

"She's not here today," I replied. "She wasn't able to come in to work." I was not going to share with this individual Tara's actual condition or anything about what had happened to her. She was in no shape to talk to him or anyone else, as far as I knew.

He frowned, then reached into his pocket. I tensed, and behind me I heard Diesel growl. He was as suspicious of this guy as I was.

When I saw what he withdrew from his jacket, however, I relaxed. He held out a cell phone.

"She needs this," he said. "Can you get it to her if I leave it with you?"

I hesitated, and he laughed. "It ain't a bomb, dude. It's just a phone. She broke hers."

"Sure, I'll see that she gets it," I said. Silently I added, *If she's ever able to use a phone again.*

He set it on my desk and turned to leave.

"Will she know who it's from?" I asked. "You haven't told me who you are."

He turned back to face me. "She'll know who I am." Then he strode from the room.

I looked at the phone. He hadn't brought a charger with it. I figured it was probably the same kind of phone as the one she had destroyed.

The whole encounter seemed rather strange to me. I decided to call Haskell and tell him about it. I picked up my phone, and Haskell answered right away.

"It's Charlie," I said. "Something odd just happened." I gave him the details and waited for his response.

"Hang on to the phone," Haskell said. "Either I'll come pick it up, or another one of the deputies will. It's probably completely innocent, but we'll hold on to it in case Ms. Martin does somehow recover."

"Thanks," I said. "I'll keep it here."

"Got it," Haskell said. "Later."

I put down my phone and turned to Diesel. He was watching me intently, I discovered. "Nothing to worry about, boy," I said, though I wasn't entirely convinced of that myself. He responded to a brief head rub and went back to looking out the window.

Before I could go back to cataloging, Melba appeared in the doorway. She advanced toward the desk and sat in the chair in front of me. Diesel came forward to greet her and accept the usual tributes.

"Who was that ratty dude who came up to see you just now?" she asked without preamble.

I pointed to the cell phone the guy had brought. "He asked for Tara, said he had a phone for her. Did he talk to you?"

"No, he didn't. I heard the front door open, and when I looked up he was at the stairs. Only caught a brief glimpse of him, and I was wondering what on earth he was doing here." She frowned. "Did you tell him anything about Tara's present condition?"

"No, I didn't. He could be a friend of hers, or merely a guy who sells phones," I replied. "I didn't think it was any of his business. I did call Haskell, though, and told him about the incident."

"Did you get his name?"

"No, but he said that she'd know who he was," I said. "Then he left."

"Too bad you couldn't get his name," Melba said.

"Short of locking him in the office until he told me his name, I'm not sure what else I could have done," I said, slightly nettled.

"Don't get huffy with me," Melba said. "It wasn't criticism, just an observation."

"Okay. I figure Haskell can find out who the guy is."

"True," Melba said. "What I'm curious to know is whether they can figure out where Tara really lives. Is one of those addresses the truth, or was there somewhere else she didn't tell anyone about?"

"I wouldn't be surprised if there was," I said. "What is behind all the mystery? Is she simply overly paranoid about people knowing anything about her private life?"

"Maybe she's on the run from someone," Melba said. "Suppose she could be an escapee from prison somewhere?"

I shrugged. "Anything is possible, but if she escaped from prison, the police and the sheriff's department probably get information about people like that. If that's what's going on, they'll figure it out."

"Her fingerprints should tell them something," Melba said.

"I'm sure they'll be checking them," I replied. "As fascinating as all this is, I don't think we're going to solve anything ourselves. It's up to the authorities to find out who she is."

Melba rose from her chair with a faint grin. "Hint taken. I need to get back downstairs anyway. You be a good boy, Diesel, and don't let Charlie work you too hard." Diesel meowed, and she gave him an affectionate pat on the head before she walked out the door.

I tried to focus on cataloging, but I was too restless, worrying about Tara. I thought about her condition, and I realized there was one thing I hadn't asked Haskell. Was Tara intubated? If she was, I knew that wasn't a good sign.

I reached for my phone and texted Haskell that question. I had hardly put the phone down again before I had an answer. Tara was on artificial respiration. My heart sank further.

Who had done this to her? And why? What could she possibly have done that someone would want her dead?

None of it really made sense to me, because there were so many pieces missing to the puzzle of Tara Martin. I wondered whether anyone other than Tara herself knew the complete truth.

Suddenly I felt the need for some fresh air and a change of scenery. "Come on, Diesel, let's go downstairs for a bit." I picked up his harness and put it on him, then clipped the lead to it. We headed downstairs, where I hesitated a moment before I decided we would go out the back way. The front of the building faced a busy street, and that was the route to the house. I didn't want Diesel to think we were going home.

We went out the back door. The sun was out and had warmed up the day enough to make it comfortable to be outside for a while. I let Diesel sniff around the parking lot before we headed down the sidewalk. While we ambled along, I focused my thoughts on the upcoming wedding and the changes that would ensue. Besides being married again, I knew the biggest change would be our living arrangements. I was used to sleeping alone—barring my feline companions, that is—and used to having a bathroom to myself. It had been a long time since I had shared a bathroom with a wife, and I would have to be a lot neater from now on. I knew Helen Louise kept things tidy at her house, and in my years as a widower, I had grown a bit sloppy.

I knew Azalea and Helen Louise had already talked about the running of the household once my bride moved in. Azalea would continue to look after the boarders' spaces, and they would split responsibility for the rest of the house, so Helen Louise had told me.

After about fifteen minutes of these and other thoughts, I decided we had better head back inside. I figured I would check Tara's desk to see if she had anything personal in it that could help the police find any friends or relatives. It was a complete long shot, but I thought I at least ought to try. Haskell or some other officer would probably do the same thing. I decided I would also look at her computer, if I could get into it, to see if there was anything on it that might provide a clue.

When we gained the back door and entered, I unhooked the leash from the harness. We headed for the stairs, and Diesel as usual started scampering up ahead of me, but he stopped suddenly midway. He looked back at me and made a rumbling noise. He obviously smelled or otherwise sensed something that disturbed him. I moved more cautiously upward at the right side of the stairs, my keys in my hand in a defensive hold.

I stepped onto the second-floor landing and paused, alert for signs of danger. Diesel stood beside me, still giving that rumbling growl. I could see that the door to my office was open, and I heard faint sounds coming from within. I knew I had locked the door when we left for our walk, but someone had got in somehow.

We moved slowly closer to the open door. I wondered whether I should go back downstairs and call the campus police. That was probably the smart thing to do. I didn't think that whoever was poking around in my office had heard us. Diesel had stopped growling, and I had been careful to make as little noise as possible.

I started to back away, but Diesel growled again and lunged forward. Before I could stop him, he was inside my office. Terrified for his safety, I went after him.

TEN

IIIIIIIIIIIIIIIII

I stopped abruptly three steps into the office. Diesel had stopped, too, and stood hissing at the man in the office. I grabbed my cat and pulled him back.

I yelled a question at him. "How did you get in here?"

He turned suddenly and threw up his hands. "Chill, dude, the door was open. I came back for the phone."

I recognized him then. The man who had come by this morning to drop off a cell phone for Tara. I thought he had to be lying about the door being open, but I didn't feel like turning my back on him at the moment in order to examine the lock.

"I locked it up before we left for a walk," I said as evenly as I could while I stroked Diesel to calm him down.

The man looked at my cat, and I could see he was nervous. "What is that thing?"

"He's a cat, an ordinary house cat," I said. "He comes from a big breed."

"Well, don't let him loose. I don't want him clawing me." He backed up against the front of my desk.

"If you don't answer my questions, I may let him come after you," I said, my tone hard. Diesel helped me by hissing again at the stranger.

He threw up his hands again. I could see him, however, glancing toward the open door behind Diesel and me. I figured he was gauging the odds of his being able to run past us and down the stairs before I could sic Diesel on him. I wouldn't, actually, because I didn't want anyone hurting my boy. The stranger didn't know that, though.

"Don't try it," I said. "Tell me your name."

He glanced sideways for a moment; then his eyes met mine. "Uh, I'm Ryan Jones."

"What do you do for a living, Mr. Jones?" I asked.

"All kinds of sh . . . um, stuff," he said, still eyeing Diesel warily. "Deliveries, mostly, like I'm a courier. For anybody that wants to hire me."

"So somebody hired you to bring that phone here?" I asked.

Jones nodded. He licked his lips. "Yeah. Little business that sells refurbished old phones."

"Why did you come to get it back? Is there something wrong with it?"

"I dunno. I was just told to pick it up and bring it back to the store." He was looking down at his feet as he spoke, and I took that as a sign that he was lying.

"You're too late," I said, lying in turn. "I gave it to the police. Ms. Martin hasn't shown up to work, and no one knows where she is."

He looked up at me. He didn't seem shocked by my news. "That's too bad," he said. "Guess I'll have to tell the guy that sent me. If he still wants the phone back, he can talk to the police."

"Yes, he'll have to," I said. "Now, I suggest you get out of here before I release my cat."

He didn't wait. He ran around me and out the door. I heard the slam of his feet on the steps as he rushed down. Moments later, I heard the front door bang open when it hit the wall.

I released Diesel and breathed a little hard while I walked to my desk. I sank into my chair, and Diesel put his front paws on my leg. He warbled, and I rubbed his head. After a few deep breaths, I pulled out my cell phone and called Haskell.

He answered after a few rings. "What's up, Charlie?"

"You or someone needs to come pick up that cell phone," I said. "I came back from my walk to find the office door open—and I know I locked it before we left—and the guy who brought the phone was inside looking for it."

"Did he get it?" Haskell broke into my narrative.

"No, I don't think so. I locked it in my desk. Let me check real quick. I told the guy the police already had it." I put the phone down, set it on speaker, then retrieved my keys. The drawer in which I had stashed the phone didn't appear to have been messed with, and I sighed in relief when I unlocked it and found the phone inside.

"It's here," I said. "He didn't manage to break into my desk. I still don't know how he got into the office. He claimed it was unlocked."

"I'll be over in a few minutes," Haskell said. "Lock that phone back in the desk until I get there."

"Will do."

I ended the call and shoved the object of Jones's quest back in the drawer. The desk locked again, I extracted my water bottle from my jacket pocket, opened it, and took a long drink of it. Diesel, no longer worried about me, rested comfortably in the window behind my chair.

I picked up the office phone and punched in Melba's extension. After four rings, the call went to voice mail. I left a message asking Melba to call me or come upstairs as soon as she could.

I thought about the encounter with Jones. I realized quickly that I had forgotten to ask him the name of the seller of the phone. That was a stupid omission on my part. I was sure, though, that Haskell or the Athena police would be able to trace the man.

If Jones had told me the truth about finding the door open, that meant someone else had been in my office before him. Melba sometimes retrieved items for archive users if I was not available, but she would never have left the door unlocked. She would have locked it behind her when she escorted the person downstairs and into a room reserved for researchers. Archive items weren't allowed to leave the building.

Melba also would have left me a note.

There wasn't one.

If Jones wasn't lying, then I had a disturbing quandary. Who had gained entrance to the office? And what did the person want?

I eyed Tara's desk. From where I sat the desk appeared undisturbed. Tara kept it neat and free of clutter, and that meant there was very little on the desktop except the computer, a stapler, and a couple of folders related to her work. The box of books she'd been working on sat in the chair by the desk.

I got up to examine the box, and as far as I could tell, nothing was missing. I sat in the chair and tugged on the central drawer. It was locked, as were all the drawers. I had a spare key for it in my desk. Should I wait until Haskell arrived before I examined the desk?

I decided it couldn't hurt to have a look now. I put on a pair of the cotton gloves I used when I handled fragile or rare materials. It had occurred to me that if someone had entered the office before Ryan Jones, that person might have been interested in Tara's desk. If that was the case, I certainly didn't want to mess up any fingerprints, though if someone was that stupid these days, that person surely deserved to be caught.

Desk key in hand, I sat and carefully inserted it in the lock and turned. The lock clicked, and I pulled the drawer out. I didn't touch anything, and all I saw at first glance were the usual supplies. Pencils, pens, a pair of scissors, a box of staples, and the plastic fasteners we used instead of metal clips. I moved objects around with care but found nothing else in the drawer.

I closed that drawer and started on the three to one side of the first one. All I found in them was a supply of scratch paper and paper for the printer attached to the computer. I riffled through both stashes of paper, but that yielded nothing.

The second and third drawers were empty, except for a crumb or two in the second one. I remembered that was where Tara occasionally stowed snacks, though she rarely ate them while at work. That was strictly forbidden while she worked with archival materials or books for the collection.

I couldn't see that anyone had broken into the desk, because the lock appeared intact, with no noticeable scratches on it. I decided that Ryan Jones was the one who had opened the office door somehow. I figured that the phone he dropped off must be the object of his break-in, but thankfully he hadn't found it. I had told him the police already had it, but I doubted he had believed me. I was not a good liar, even for a good cause.

I locked Tara's desk and went back to my own. Diesel offered an interrogative-sounding meow when I sat. "No luck," I said. He gazed at me for a moment before turning back to stare out the window. He was the self-appointed squirrel monitor, and he took his duties seriously. He never knew when the squirrel army might decide to launch an attack through his window.

Haskell arrived two minutes later. I looked up from my work to see him bent, examining the lock on the office door. He took a picture of it with his phone; then he apparently manipulated the picture somehow. He greeted me and advanced to my desk.

"I enlarged the picture, and I can see some scratches on the lock." He handed me the phone, and I examined his photo. I, too, saw the scratches, faint as they appeared. I gave him back the phone.

"Mr. Jones's work, I presume. He told me his name is Ryan Jones, by the way," I said. "I haven't found any evidence of a second intruder, so he must have been the one who opened the door."

"Looks like it," Haskell said. "Did he give you any reason for coming to get the phone back?"

"He said he was supposed to take it back to the store." I opened the drawer and extracted the phone.

Haskell held out a bag for it, and I dropped the phone inside. He sealed the bag and wrote on it with an indelible marker before stowing the bag and its contents in a pocket.

"I looked through Tara's desk," I said. "It was locked, but I have a key. I checked, but I couldn't see any signs that someone tried to force it."

"Did you find anything useful?" Haskell asked.

I shook my head. "Not a thing, unfortunately. Have y'all made any progress on finding out where she lives?"

"Not a thing." Haskell echoed me. "Except that apparently she doesn't live at any of the three addresses she gave."

"That's so bizarre," I said. "Why is she being so secretive?"

"We don't know yet," Haskell said. "Kanesha has contacted the MBI and the FBI office. She's hoping to hear something, even if it's negative, in the next day or so. If or when Ms. Martin dies, that will escalate everything."

"She's still hanging on," I said.

Haskell nodded. "So far, but the doctors are still not giving her much, if any, chance of surviving this. I think machines are doing most of the work at the moment."

I had to suppress a shudder. I had a horror of being hooked up to a ventilator. I had seen a friend in the condition some years before, and it was heartrending. His only chance for survival was to remain hooked up to a machine permanently, and that was no way to live. His family had the ventilator removed, and he died a few hours later.

I knew that was what he would have wanted, and I believed his family had done the right thing.

But where was anyone that close to Tara who could make that decision? Who would even know what her wishes were in a situation like this?

"If you can't find any family or a close friend, what will happen?" I asked.

"It will be up to the medical team," Haskell said, his tone somber.

For a moment, I was too choked up to respond. I felt profound pity for Tara. Who hated or feared her so much that they did this to her? I prayed to find out so that justice would be served. Tara didn't deserve this.

"I'll take the phone in to be examined." Haskell turned toward the door. "I doubt it will tell us much, but we can always hope it will yield something. Maybe a contact or two survived from the previous phone."

"I hope to God that you get some lead from it," I said.

Haskell waved a goodbye and departed.

I leaned back in my chair and tried to get a grip on my emotions. Yielding to sorrow right now wouldn't help anyone, least of all Tara. I had really hoped to find a clue in the desk, no matter how small, that could help in this situation. In the hundreds, if not thousands, of detective stories I had read in my life, someone had always hidden something in a desk. Why hadn't Tara done that? Maybe when the cops finally tracked down her actual address, they might find something hidden there.

I stared at my computer for a few minutes, lost in a maelstrom of thoughts that confused me.

Detective stories.

Desks.

Hidden clues.

Once those three items emerged out of the chaos in my brain, I sat up straight and stared hard at Tara's desk.

Of course. Why hadn't I realized it before?

Key in hand, I headed back to Tara's desk for another look.

I found a clue in under two minutes.

ELEVEN

What I had remembered from so many detective stories in which similar searches were carried out was that there were often secret cubbyholes or items taped to the back or underside of drawers.

Since the desk was a standard-issue metal office desk, I knew there would be no special cubbyhole in it. But I did find, systematically checking the undersides and backs of each drawer, that Tara had secreted something on the back of the bottom drawer.

I had to pull the drawer completely out in order to retrieve the taped object I had felt with my probing. Tara had used duct tape and had covered it thoroughly. I spent several minutes getting the duct tape off, and when I did, I found a key stuck to the last strip.

I pulled the key free and examined it closely. Diesel stood right by me, until he got distracted by the tape I had balled up and dropped on the floor. Then he decided to play with the tape, and I was able to look at the key.

As far as I could tell, it was an ordinary padlock key.

The fact that Tara had taken the trouble to hide it in such a fashion obviously meant that it was important to her to keep the key out of reach of someone. But who?

Where was the padlock that this key would open?

I figured that maybe Tara had hidden it here because the archive office wasn't as accessible as other places. The building did have a security system, and there were hidden cameras in various spots, including in the archive.

Perhaps Tara also thought that the person or persons from whom she was hiding wouldn't think to look in her workplace for the key.

But Ryan Jones had been looking in the office. Was he trying to find the key? That was something that Haskell and the other officers would have to sort out. I doubted I would see Mr. Jones again anytime soon.

I texted Haskell about the key after I had replaced all the drawers and locked the desk. Where should I hide the key? I decided after brief cogitation to put it on my own key ring. It should be safe there until Haskell or a fellow officer could collect it.

If they could ever figure out where Tara was actually living, they might find the lock to fit the key there. If they didn't, I couldn't imagine how they would find the lock that it fit. It might not even be in Athena. It could be anywhere.

Diesel was still occupied with the balled-up tape, batting it around on the floor. I watched him for a moment, happy to see him enjoying himself. My phone alerted me to an incoming message.

The message came from Helen Louise. We rarely texted each

other, since we preferred talking. The message was simple. *Can you come to the bistro as soon as you get a chance?*

I responded with a *yes* and set my phone back on the desk.

I wondered what was up. There was no point in sending back a question. I texted Haskell again to say I would be at the bistro and would have the key with me. He still had not responded to the previous text.

"Come on, boy, let's go see Helen Louise," I said to Diesel. He immediately left off with his game and came eagerly to me. He knew seeing Helen Louise meant nice, warm chicken, his favorite treat at the bistro.

I called Melba to let her know we were leaving for a little while, but it went to voice mail. I wondered where she could be. She hadn't mentioned being out of the office today. I left a message, made sure I locked the door behind us, and went downstairs to the car. My good parking karma held. I found a spot almost in front of the bistro. I had Diesel in his halter with the leash attached, so there would be no incidents of his darting away from me. He rarely ever did that, but one should be prepared.

Helen Louise looked up from behind the counter when we entered. She had a slightly harassed expression, and I immediately felt worried. What was wrong?

Diesel and I went to our usual corner table. Helen Louise came over after dealing with a customer. We exchanged a quick kiss before she slid into the chair next to mine.

"What's wrong?" I asked.

"Shorthanded," Helen Louise said. "With Tara out of the picture, Henry is going to have to find someone else quickly. I'm here only because of the shortage."

"I'm sorry, love, I wish I could help."

Helen Louise smiled. "I appreciate it, but we'll cope. I'm worried sick about Tara. Is it true that the doctors aren't giving her much chance of survival?"

"It is," I said. "She's on a ventilator, which is never a good sign."

"No, it's not. My father refused to have one when he was in the hospital for the last time." She turned her head away for a moment. When she faced me again, I could see her fighting to hold back the tears. "He was struggling so hard to breathe, but he wasn't going to live on a machine."

"He had congestive heart failure, didn't he?" I asked.

She nodded. "He was too far gone for them to do much else. So he struggled until his heart finally just stopped."

I pulled out my handkerchief and handed it to her. She gave me a grateful smile and dabbed at the tears. She took a deep breath. "I get emotional every time I talk about it," she said softly.

"I understand completely," I said gently. "Why did you want us to come over?"

"Other than spending a few minutes with you?" Helen Louise smiled. "Yes, but I'll have to tell you more about it in a few minutes. Just a moment." She rose from her chair after nodding to three people at the cash register.

Diesel meowed in complaint. I knew he was bothered because Helen Louise hadn't patted his head or addressed him at all. That she hadn't was a measure of her stress at the moment. She wouldn't forget his chicken, I was sure, and that would soothe his feelings.

When Helen Louise returned, she brought sweet tea for me and boiled chicken for Diesel. After serving us, Helen Louise returned to work. Diesel tucked in.

When Helen Louise joined us again, Diesel meowed his thanks, and she gave him a quick pat on the head. This evidently satisfied him, for he stretched out beside my chair and fell asleep.

"I wanted to tell you about something," Helen Louise said. "I'll tell Haskell, or whoever else comes, but I wanted you to be first."

I was definitely intrigued. "So what is it you have to tell?"

"A man came in with two others, another man and a woman. I had seen this man a couple of times before here. Both times, I saw him speak briefly to Tara, who had served his food. She was working out front for a while that day while Debbie had a doctor's appointment. Nothing strange occurred as far as I could tell," Helen Louise said. "He came in again this morning, and I had the vague feeling I'd seen him somewhere else. I'm just not sure where."

"Did he ask for Tara?"

"Not exactly," Helen Louise said. "Debbie served him this time, and she mentioned to me after he left that he'd asked about that other girl he'd seen before. Debbie doesn't know that Tara's in the hospital." She paused. "Henry and I thought it best not to tell anyone. Debbie simply repeated to him what we had told her, that Tara wasn't feeling well and hadn't come in today."

"That seems ordinary enough," I said. "I'm not sure why you think you need to tell Haskell about it."

"It wasn't completely ordinary," Helen Louise said. "His response when she told him Tara wasn't well was that it was probably her IBS acting up. I thought that was odd, that he would know Tara well enough to know she has irritable bowel syndrome."

"That is odd," I said. "Do you know if Tara really suffers from IBS?"

"She's never mentioned it. She hasn't missed work until lately," Helen Louise said.

"Was that the extent of the conversation Debbie had with him about Tara?"

"I asked Debbie if he'd said anything more," Helen Louise replied. "She said that was all."

"How was Tara usually with customers? Did she usually chat with them?"

"No, she didn't, which is why I think this is a bit odd. Maybe this man knows Tara and might be able to help in some way," Helen Louise said.

"It's a slender lead," I said, "but Haskell might as well know about it."

I told her about the key I had found hidden in Tara's desk and that I had texted Haskell about it. I still hadn't heard from him.

"How mysterious," Helen Louise said. "No pun intended, but if they find what the key unlocks, it could unlock the mystery surrounding Tara."

"I think you might be right," I said.

Helen Louise looked up as the bell on the door tinkled. "Here comes Haskell now," she said.

I turned to look and saw him striding toward the table. He pulled off his hat before he sat and placed it on the only empty chair at the table.

After greeting Helen Louise and an awakened Diesel, he turned to me. "Sorry I couldn't respond to your last two texts, Charlie, but I was tied up. I needed a break, so I just came here hoping you'd still be here."

"That's fine," I said.

"What can I get for you?" Helen Louise stood.

"Sweet tea and whatever you recommend," Haskell said promptly.

Helen Louise laughed. "Be right back." She headed for the kitchen.

Haskell turned to me. "So tell me about this key."

I pulled my key ring out of my pocket as I started telling him how I found it. I had to pause for a moment while I freed the key from the ring. I handed it to Haskell as I finished my story.

Haskell regarded the key now lying on his palm. "Nothing really distinctive about it." He turned it over. "Same on this side. No telling what it goes to, other than probably a padlock of some kind. Maybe a storage unit."

"I hadn't thought of a storage unit," I said, feeling a faint touch of excitement. "That could be it."

"Possibly," Haskell said. "Don't get too excited, though. Are you sure that Ms. Martin put it there? Could anyone else have done it at some time in the past?"

That made me frown. "I really hadn't thought about it. I just assumed Tara had done it because of her secretive nature."

"That's an indication, certainly, that it belongs to her, but it's not proof. And unfortunately, we can't get a fingerprint from it now."

"That's true." I now regretted my haste in freeing the key from the duct tape. I probably should have left it intact and let the officers deal with it.

Helen Louise arrived with Haskell's lunch. He took one look at the plate of chicken casserole and sighed happily. Before he began eating, I asked whether he needed me for anything else.

"Not at the moment," he said.

"I have something to tell you," Helen Louise said. "It's somewhat tenuous, but it could be of some help." She resumed her seat at the table after casting her glance around the bistro.

"Tenuous is better than nothing," Haskell said.

While he ate, Helen Louise related what she had told me earlier. He remained silent until she had finished. After a long sip of his tea, he wiped his mouth with his napkin. "Can you describe this man?"

"Tall, dark, pretty good-looking, wearing a nice suit." Helen Louise paused. "Nothing particularly memorable, really, other than good looks. I'd certainly recognize him if I see him again."

"If you do, try to get a name," Haskell said. "And a picture, if you can do it discreetly. We'll take any lead we can get." His expression turned grim. "I don't think it's going to be long now before this becomes a homicide investigation."

TWELVE

"So there's no hope at all?" I asked.

"No, she's completely unresponsive now," Haskell said. "I think they'll be taking her off the ventilator sometime this afternoon or evening."

"That will be it, then." Helen Louise turned away briefly to dab at her tears with my napkin. I felt like crying myself. Poor Tara. What a sad end for her.

"We're going to do everything we can to find out who was responsible for this," Haskell said, his tone hard.

"I know you will," I said.

Haskell nodded and pushed back his chair. He grabbed his hat from the other chair. "I need to get back. Thanks for the key, Charlie. We'll see if we can figure out what it will unlock."

Helen Louise also rose and slipped behind the counter to operate the register. I couldn't hear their brief exchange, but Helen Louise was back quickly. "I'm going to have to get back to work, love," she said. "Is there anything else I can get you? Some dessert, perhaps?"

"No, I'd better not," I said, though I wouldn't have minded a piece of her delicious chocolate cake. "Diesel and I need to get back to work, too." I pushed out my chair and took hold of Diesel's lead. He yawned and stretched.

Helen Louise and I shared a quick kiss, and Diesel and I left the bistro.

When Diesel and I arrived at the library administration building, I went to check Melba's office. The door was still closed. I was getting a little worried. It wasn't like her to be gone this long without any word. I pulled out my phone and texted her to find out what was going on. I started climbing the stairs, phone still in hand. Melba hadn't responded by the time Diesel and I were back in our accustomed places in the office. I debated whether to call her. After a moment or two of dithering, I called.

The call went to her voice mail. I asked her to call or text me ASAP to let me know she was all right. I put the phone down on the desk and stared at it, willing it to respond with some kind of message from Melba.

Nothing came.

My gaze strayed toward the office phone. A light was blinking. I frowned. That light usually meant voice mail. I pulled out my helpful cheat sheet for the office phone system and double-checked how to retrieve voice mail. I didn't use it often, because I generally received email messages instead.

To my relief, when the message began to play, I heard Melba's voice. "Sorry I couldn't call your cell phone, Charlie, but my phone was stolen. Couldn't remember that number, so I called this one. Once I'm finished with the police and get myself another phone, I'll be in. See you soon."

I felt relieved but at the same time horrified. I prayed that Melba wasn't hurt during the theft. I also wondered where it had happened. Had someone broken into her house and taken it? She didn't mention that anything else was taken, so perhaps it happened away from her house.

All this speculation was useless, I realized. I needed to occupy my brain until Melba came back to work. Then I would get all the details. I was looking blankly at Tara's desk, and my gaze finally concentrated on the box she had been working on before the attack. I supposed I might as well find out how far she had got with the books and pick up where she left off.

Before I retrieved the books, I logged in to my computer to access the shared file in which she had listed the books. I clicked on it, and after a few seconds' hesitation, it opened. I went to the end of the file, and I saw that it had 107 lines in it. Tara had accomplished a lot in a short time.

She had set up the spreadsheet according to my specifications. There were columns for author name, book title, publisher, date of publication, date of data entry, and box number. A quick scan revealed to me that Tara must have regularly re-sorted the list to keep it alphabetical by the author's surname.

I did a special re-sort on the list in order to put all entries together by the date of data entry, most recent first. That would let me isolate the latest work. I could have sorted by box number instead, but either way would get me what I wanted.

According to the list, Tara had added fourteen books from the latest box. I went over to her desk and counted the books in the pile atop the desk. There were fourteen. I matched a couple of the titles on her desk to those in the list to be certain that these were the ones, because there appeared to be a good dozen or more books still in the box.

The box was what I wanted. I took it over to my desk, removed the books, and stacked them near my computer. I grabbed the book on the top of one of the two stacks, opened it, and began to enter its information in the spreadsheet. I had to concentrate because I didn't want to make any typos.

I was absorbed in my task when, at some point later, I heard a knock at the door. I surfaced from my computer and looked up to see Melba entering the office. I immediately saved my work. Then I got up and went to her to give her a hug.

"Thank you, Charlie," she said, pushing me gently away after a moment. "I'm okay. I wasn't hurt."

"Thank the Lord for that." I escorted her to the chair and waited until she was seated before I went back to my desk. In the meantime, Diesel had come to greet her. He sat beside the chair and gazed into her face with the usual adoring glance. She obliged by rubbing her hand up and down his head and upper spine.

"So, what happened?" I asked.

"I had stopped at the pharmacy during lunch," Melba said. "I was going in to get some aspirin, and I had my phone in my hand. I was about to call you, and this person on a motorcycle came out of nowhere. Grabbed the phone out of my hand and was gone before I realized what had just happened."

"Were you able to see anything that could help identify the thief?"

"Not much," Melba said. "It happened so fast, and I was so shocked I didn't take in much. The motorcycle zipped away out of sight before I could see the license plate or much detail about the rider. Except that he was wearing all black leather with a black helmet."

"Are you sure it was a man?" I asked.

"I'm pretty sure," Melba said. "The figure on the bike was large. Either a big woman or a man, but I think it was a man."

"I'm so glad you weren't hurt," I said.

"I was confused; then I got really angry. I screamed a couple of times. Rage, not fright," Melba said. "Then I got in the car and drove to the police station to report it. I was there a couple of hours. Turns out there have been similar crimes, and all anybody has been able to say about the thief is pretty much what I told them."

"Don't they have any leads?"

"I don't think so," Melba replied. "As soon as I finished at the police station, I went to the place where I got my phone and reported it stolen. They did whatever it is they do in such cases, and then I bought a new phone. They were able to transfer most of my information, like texts, pictures, and contacts from the cloud. Whatever that is. I've never really figured it out."

"I'm glad they were able to do that," I said. "I wish they had the power to make the phone self-destruct so that it's no use to the thief."

"Me, too," Melba said. "I had to get a new number." She delved into her purse and pulled out a piece of paper. She read out the number; I jotted it down. I would put it into my phone later.

"Did you store any financial information on your phone?"

Melba shook her head. "Absolutely not. I never did business stuff with my phone. I barely do any on my home computer." She sighed. "And now I have to update my phone number all over the place." She rose with one last pat for Diesel. "I'd better get downstairs and see what mess has collected while I was out."

"If I can do anything, let me know," I said.

"Thanks. Talk to you later." She exited the office. Diesel came back to his place in the window.

As I tried to focus my attention once again on the spreadsheet and the books I needed to enter into it, I found my thoughts wandering back to Melba's story. For some reason, Ryan Jones kept intruding into my thoughts. I wasn't sure why, because I had nothing to connect him with the cell-phone thefts. I couldn't really pinpoint why I was suspicious of him. The connection with Tara bothered me. Plus the fact that he apparently worked for someone who sold recycled phones.

I was wasting time with these fruitless speculations. I wasn't equipped to solve the cell-phone thefts. I forced my thoughts back to the work for which I earned a salary. I returned to where I was when Melba had come in, and within twenty minutes I had finished entering the remaining books. I packed them all back into the box and set the box on the floor by Tara's former desk.

Though it pained me to think about it, I wondered whether I would be able to get a student to take over the project that Tara had been working on. I realized that I simply couldn't think about this right now. The project wasn't high priority so far, so I could make a decision later after I knew what would happen to Tara.

I hated this. As odd and antisocial as she was, Tara deserved to be able to live her life how she deemed best for her. Some unknown person had decided Tara needed to die and had run her down with the intent to kill. It was taking longer than the killer intended, but the outcome would be death.

Why?

That was the question that would haunt me until the killer was caught.

Diesel must have sensed my frustration and anger. He suddenly warbled behind me, and I turned to see him regard me anxiously. I put my head to his and tried to center myself, to rid myself of these feelings. They did me no good, nor did they do Tara any practical good. Slowly, I calmed, and Diesel relaxed. I felt it as I stroked his back.

"I'm okay now, you sweet boy," I told him. Indeed, I did feel better. He had that effect on me, as he did on others.

"Good afternoon."

A cool, assured voice coming from behind me startled me, and I whirled around in my chair to see a woman dressed in a business suit and high heels two feet inside my office. I had been so caught up in my thoughts that I hadn't heard her approach. The woman advanced to my desk and extended a hand as I rose to greet her.

"Hello, I'm Millie Hagendorf," she said in that same cool tone. Sharp blue eyes appraised me, and for a moment I felt pinned by her gaze. She had red hair, cut in a fashionable bob, and she wore pearls around her neck and a pearl brooch on her dark-blue jacket.

"I'm Charlie Harris," I said. "What can I do for you, Ms. Hagendorf? Please have a seat."

The manner of her dress, and her manner in general, made me think of a number of Athena alumni who wanted to donate to the college. Perhaps she was interested in the rare-book collection or the archive and wanted to give money or a collection of her own. I awaited her reply with some eagerness. Diesel remained in his spot in the window. Evidently he was not attracted by the visitor. Not a good sign, frankly.

"I'd like to find out more about the archive and the collections, Mr. Harris." She set what looked like a Louis Vuitton purse on my desk. I had learned about Louis Vuitton from Laura and Alex. She was a woman with expensive tastes.

"Anything in particular?" I asked. "That's a broad question, and I could sit here and talk about the archive and its collections for several hours. They're quite extensive, and we have over a thousand rare books as well."

Millie Hagendorf, instead of answering immediately, looked around the office. "Do you work here alone? Aside from your cat?"

"I do have occasional student and part-time workers," I replied. "My current one is out sick today. I work three days a week."

"It's not a full-time job?" she asked.

"No, and I don't particularly want one," I said frankly. "The college funds this position as twenty-four hours per week. I get benefits, prorated, of course, but I don't really do this for the salary. I love cataloging rare books and processing collections. I'm an alumnus of Athena. Are you an alumna?"

"No, I'm not," she said. "I went to college in Georgia. So I suppose there's no access to the archive outside of your working hours?"

"No other access, and there are rarely emergencies that would require me to come on campus during the off times to let someone work here."

"This is all interesting, Mr. Harris," she said. "I have little knowledge of how such an enterprise works. I'm a writer, and I'm thinking of including an archivist and an archive in my next book." She flashed a smile that was not reflected in her eyes, which remained chilly and remote. "I'm doing some preliminary research."

"I see. What kind of books do you write?" I had never heard her name before, and I didn't remember seeing any of her books at the local bookstore.

"I don't have anything published yet," Ms. Hagendorf replied smoothly, "but I'm hopeful this project will be the one that will sell. I think I need to do more in-depth research into this in order to have the authenticity it needs." She paused for a moment. "Do you accept volunteers in the archive? I think that would help both of us."

I had some experience of volunteers, not all of it good, in my public-library days in Houston. They mostly meant well, but they could be erratic in actually showing up to help. Ms. Hagendorf looked like a purposeful woman, one who would show up for work and get the job done.

"I do accept volunteers," I said. "There's paperwork you'll have to deal with before we can finalize any kind of work arrangement."

"Where can I do that?"

"Online, if you prefer, via the college website." I explained how to find what she needed. "Or you can go to the human resources office on campus and do it there." I gave her the directions to the building that housed these services.

She rose. "Thank you. I think I will go right to the HR office to get the process going. I'm eager to start." She smiled again, a little more warmly this time.

"I hope it all works out for you." I rose to shake the proffered hand. "I'll look forward to talking with you further."

She nodded and left the office.

I sat again and swiveled the chair to be at face level with Diesel. "What do you think of her, boy?"

The cat regarded me for a moment, then gave me a low growl.

"I agree," I said. "There's definitely something odd about this."

But what? I couldn't quite put my finger on it.

THIRTEEN

On the way home later that afternoon, I thought again about Millie Hagendorf. What was it about her that bothered me?

For one thing, I decided, there was an air of coldness about her. Or maybe simply aloofness. She expressed interest in archives, but I couldn't detect any real enthusiasm behind that. In my experience, people interested in archives and rare books exhibited more passion when discussing the subject. Archives were not to everyone's taste, nor were rare books.

Over the many years of my working life, I had grown to trust my initial impressions of people like Ms. Hagendorf. If she really followed through on her alleged interest in helping with the archive by filling out the necessary forms, I would question her further before accepting her as a volunteer. If I did accept her, she would be on probation for three months.

I had the uneasy feeling she was after something during our talk, but I couldn't determine what that might be. I supposed that the attempt on Tara's life had made me suspicious of any stranger who came into the archive office asking questions. I couldn't imagine a connection between Ms. Hagendorf and Tara's tragedy. There probably wasn't one, so I tried to put Ms. Hagendorf out of my mind.

Azalea and Ramses greeted us in the kitchen when Diesel and I reached home. Ramses immediately wanted to play, and Diesel allowed him to gambol along to the utility room with him. I smiled at their retreating forms and asked Azalea how the day had gone.

"Fine, except for that scamp and his messing around with anything he could get his paws on," Azalea replied without rancor. "He is just a mess, and that's all there is to it."

I had to laugh. "As long as he doesn't get in your way or destroy things, it sounds like you don't mind putting up with him."

"He's all right," she said. "Keeps me entertained most days."

Azalea had come a long way from the first days when I had rescued Diesel and brought him home. She definitely had been anti-cat then, and it had taken her years to warm up to my sweet boy. She finally had begun to thaw, and when Ramses came along, she seemed to surrender completely, to the point of sometimes taking Ramses home with her for the weekend. Ramses adored her, and he seemed to enjoy his weekends away with Azalea. In turn, Diesel appeared to enjoy being an only cat on those occasions.

I pulled a cold can of diet soda from the fridge and headed to the den. Azalea called after me to say that dinner would be ready at six, and I called back my thanks. In the den I brought up the calendar on my computer. I had several tasks to perform in advance of the upcoming wedding in a few weeks, and I didn't want to forget anything. I had trouble keeping track of such things without some kind of aid, and keeping the calendar on the computer, which I could get to on my phone, was a big help.

One thing I knew was coming up soon, and that was having a fitting for my tuxedo. I had a tuxedo, but it was old and a bit shabby now. I decided to rent one for the wedding, and there was a store on the square downtown that rented tuxedos and other formal wear.

That fitting was tomorrow, I was surprised to discover. For some reason I had thought it was next week. It was a good thing I checked. I set the appointment to remind me tomorrow two hours ahead of time. I got sidetracked rather easily at work, and at home, and without a reminder I might forget it completely by tomorrow. I made sure I put the reminder in my phone calendar as well.

On the day itself, I might be a bundle of nerves, but this far out, I was perfectly steady, no misgivings or concerns about marrying Helen Louise. I adored her, having known her much of my life. She had grown up beside my late wife, Jackie, and me, and we had always been friends. I'd never had eyes for anyone but Jackie, but I had always been fond of Helen Louise. Those feelings deepened over time, and now I looked forward to a happy marriage with Helen Louise.

Those were the happy thoughts I needed to stick to, I decided. I could do nothing for Tara and her situation other than pray, and that I did. Barring a miracle, which I did pray for, she hadn't any real hope. The sheriff's department, with aid from the appropriate other law enforcement agencies, would investigate and come up with an answer. I hoped that they would, and soon.

My cell phone rang. Haskell was calling. I had a bad feeling about the call. He usually texted.

I greeted him. "What's up?"

"I'm sorry to have to tell you that Tara passed away," Haskell said. "They took her off the ventilator about thirty minutes ago, and she was gone soon after."

"Thank you for letting me know," I said, my heart sinking. "I can only hope that she's at peace."

"Amen to that."

"Have you let Helen Louise know yet?" I asked.

"I have," Haskell replied.

"I'll let Melba know, if that's okay."

"Sure," he said. "I've got to get going. It's officially a homicide investigation now."

"Catch the bastard who did this," I said.

"We're going to." Haskell sounded grimly determined. He ended the call.

I put my phone down and found that I had a lump in my throat. Tara hadn't been friendly or even, truth be told, likable, but I felt sorrow at her passing and the manner of it. I hoped she would receive the justice she deserved.

I picked my phone up again and called Melba. She answered after a couple of rings.

"Hi, Charlie, what's up?"

"I've got sad news about Tara," I said. "She passed away a short time ago."

"They took her off the ventilator, I guess," Melba said.

"They did, and she died not long after," I replied.

Melba, in a fierce tone, said a few things about the perpetrator behind Tara's death that I wouldn't say in front of anyone. I understood her feelings and shared them, though, so I didn't scold her for the awful language.

"Yes, and much more in the same vein," I said.

Melba gave a shaky laugh. "You're always such a gentleman, Charlie. I'm not as nice as you are. I guess I'm not that much of a lady."

"Don't be ridiculous. You know you can say anything to me, and I'll still think you're a true Southern lady," I said. "Southern belles have been known to swear on occasion, with just cause. And I think this is certainly the occasion *and* the cause."

"God bless you, and God bless poor Tara." Melba sighed into the phone. "I hope they can find some family or friends. I hate to think of her dying all alone like that with nobody with her."

"I hope somebody will claim her and take her home, wherever that might be."

I made a sudden decision. If the authorities were unable to trace any family or close friends who were willing to see that Tara was properly buried, then I would take care of it. I knew that Helen Louise would help me and that Sean would take care of any legal issues involved.

I said as much to Melba, and she replied, "You're a good man, Charlie Harris." After a brief pause, she said, "I need to get back to work. Thanks for letting me know."

I could hear the sorrow in Melba's voice, and I knew she had been affected as well by Tara's death. We knew so little about her. I had no idea how old she was. In fact I rarely saw her face clearly. She hardly ever looked directly at me. Even during her supposed panic-attack episode, she didn't look directly at me.

I went to the kitchen to tell Azalea the news. She was there, preparing dinner. I told her, and she immediately bowed her head in silent prayer. When she finished, she looked at me. "She's at peace now."

I nodded, and she turned back to her work. She began to sing softly. I recognized the melody and the words immediately. "Swing Low, Sweet Chariot."

After listening to a couple of verses and their choruses, I tiptoed away. Ramses was sitting rapt near Azalea's feet, staring up at her. Diesel seemed mesmerized as well, because he didn't follow me back to the den like he usually would.

Wiping my eyes with my handkerchief, I entered the den alone. I sank into my recliner and put the footrest up with the lever. Suddenly I felt exhausted. I closed my eyes and willed myself to sleep.

I was drifting when I heard voices from somewhere. I hadn't closed the door to the den to allow the cats to join me. It sounded like the voices were coming from the kitchen. I lowered the footrest, shoved myself out of the chair, and went to see who was here.

As I got closer to the kitchen, I quickly recognized the second voice. I almost turned around and headed back to the den. I wasn't sure I was up to dealing with Chief Deputy Kanesha Berry right now. Perhaps she was here only to see her mother. I did turn this time but had taken only three steps when I heard Kanesha's voice much closer behind me.

"Charlie, I need to talk to you."

Suppressing a deep sigh, I faced her. "Is this about Tara?"

She nodded. "Now that she's dead, this is a murder investigation.

There was obvious intention behind this hit-and-run, and she was the target."

I nodded wearily. "I don't think I have any information that can help you. I barely knew her, even though she worked with me at the archive."

"That may be," Kanesha said. "I'd like you to come back to the kitchen with me, though, and talk about her." She didn't wait for my verbal response. She walked back to the kitchen and disappeared through the door.

I followed, feeling even more exhausted now.

Azalea had placed another can of diet soda at my seat at the table, and I saw a full coffee cup at the place to my left. Azalea was no longer in the kitchen, and I had no idea where she had gone. Both Diesel and Ramses were there, and they greeted me as I took my seat. I petted them briefly before opening my soda.

Kanesha regarded me as she took a sip of coffee. "You seem upset. Is it about Ms. Martin's death?"

I set my can down. "Yes. Even though I really didn't know her, I'm horrified by the manner of her death."

"We all are," Kanesha said, her voice cold and hard. "This was a particularly brutal murder. The killer was ruthless. I'm surprised she survived as long as she did."

"Did she ever regain consciousness?"

"No, she didn't," Kanesha said. "If we had been able to talk to her, we might have something to go on. The killer either feared her for some reason or hated her enough to run her down."

I pushed the can of soda away. I felt nauseated by the picture that was trying to form in my mind. I didn't want to visualize the actual running down of a helpless human being by a determined killer.

After a deep, steadying breath, I asked, "Were there any usable clues at the scene? Like tire tracks and so on?"

"We did get tire tracks," Kanesha said. "But finding the actual vehicle is the trick. By now the car could be five states away. Or it could have a set of new tires, with the old ones scattered anywhere."

She actually sounded a bit depressed. That was unusual for her. I could tell she really cared about tracking down this killer and was not happy with the lack of information.

She leaned closer to me, cup in hand. "I need you to think about the time she spent with you. See if you can dredge up *anything* she might have said to you that could give us even a hint of a clue to who she was."

"I'll try," I said, "but she was the most reticent person I've ever encountered. I tried to draw her out a couple of times, but she rebuffed me, and not politely. She obviously didn't want anyone knowing her business."

"That's what I heard from Helen Louise, Henry, and Debbie at the bistro." Kanesha leaned back against the chair. "She was determined to keep everything about herself private. We're trying to find the man that Helen Louise told us about, but we don't have much to go on."

"Did Haskell tell you about the phone guy? Ryan Jones?"

Kanesha nodded. "I think we can lay our hands on him. We're on the lookout for him, as are the city cops for several reasons. We'll find him and find out what he might know about her."

"Did you hear about the theft of Melba's cell phone?"

"I heard about it from the police. There have been several similar thefts, and we're cooperating with the city force to capture this person."

"Good." I thought about suggesting Ryan Jones in connection with this series of thefts, but I had no sound reason for believing he was involved.

"We've been doing whatever we can to trace Ms. Martin," Kanesha said. "We still don't know where she was living. She covered her tracks really well, like a professional in fact."

I hadn't thought about that angle. "Are you thinking she's a police officer or government agent of some kind?"

"It's possible. She certainly knew how to hide herself. We'll crack it eventually, but she hasn't made it easy." Kanesha drained her coffee and set the mug on the table. She stood, pushing her chair back. "Please do what I asked and let me know if you come up with anything."

"I will." I rose to accompany her to the front door. Diesel and Ramses came with us.

The moment before she stepped onto the stoop, Kanesha turned to me and said, "We haven't found a Tara Martin that matches this woman in any regard. We're waiting on information on her fingerprints. If we don't get something from them, it will be as if she doesn't exist at all."

I was too stunned by Kanesha's final remark to react right away and call her back. By the time I did, she was getting into her departmental car and driving off.

If Tara Martin wasn't really Tara Martin, then who was she?

FOURTEEN

||||||||||||||||||||||||||||||||||||||||||||||||||||||

I had wondered if Tara was hiding under a name not her own. The fact that the name matched that of a soap-opera character had intrigued me. I hadn't watched soap operas in several decades now, so I had no idea if the character still existed in that universe.

What was her real name?

Surely they had tried to see if her fingerprints matched any person in one of the available databases. Mine were in a database somewhere, and I'd never been convicted of any kind of crime. I had been fingerprinted, for the sake of elimination, in the course of an investigation. It was therefore not unusual for ordinary persons to have fingerprints on record.

I thought about Kanesha's request when I returned to the kitchen. Diesel and Ramses stretched out together under the table while I sat and considered. I tried to recall conversations that I had had with Tara. I couldn't remember one that hadn't been focused on work.

She had told me about her experience with databases in our first meeting, but she hadn't mentioned any particular locations where she gained her knowledge. Only that she had tried college once before but had run out of money after a year and had to quit. Since then she hadn't been able to afford college.

I hadn't pressed her for details, though I had tried, in a friendly manner, to tease out tidbits of information. I met a stone wall every time. Because of her ability, easily demonstrated when I showed her what I needed, I had decided not to force the matter. I wished I had. Any clue, no matter how slender, could help now.

She had rarely asked me a question. In fact she rarely talked unless I spoke to her first. During her interview, I had managed to see her face a couple of times, but her features were ordinary. Not a face that would stand out anywhere. Perhaps that was deliberate on her part. I knew from Laura's experience as an actor that persons skillful with makeup could make themselves unrecognizable even to people familiar with them.

That was another question for Haskell. Had they discovered that Tara was made up when they took her to the hospital? Surely they would have noticed and would have cleaned her face. If she had worn makeup, I wondered what she looked like without it. At some point, probably very soon, they would release her picture to the public in an effort to find people who knew her. I doubted she was anyone I knew from the past, but you could never tell.

I hoped Haskell would make it home before I went to bed tonight. I might have to stay up until he came in to get answers to my questions.

Somewhere there had to be a clue to Tara's real identity. Perhaps the key I had found in her desk would be that clue, if the authorities could find the lock it opened. That search would take a while, I figured. Even now, the killer could be far away.

Unless he or she was after something that Tara had in her possession. What could it be?

How desperate would this person be to get hold of whatever it was?

Had the killer run down Tara to keep her from using information only she possessed? Or had the killer found what he or she was looking for and wanted Tara dead to keep her permanently silent? Had Tara's existence itself been a threat?

I felt a bit dizzy from the questions running around in my mind. It really was up to Kanesha and her fellow officers to figure all this out, and they had many more resources at hand in order to do it. But my nosy self couldn't stop being intrigued by it all.

Azalea returned to the kitchen, and Ramses promptly went to her and meowed in a minatory tone. He was no doubt once again on the point of utter starvation and wanted sustenance. Azalea looked down at him and shook her head.

"No, sir, mister, ain't time for dinner yet. You have to wait just like everybody else." Azalea's tone brooked no nonsense.

Ramses gazed up at her, gave a pitiful meow, and went back under the table with Diesel. I tried not to laugh, but a couple of chuckles escaped. Azalea raised an eyebrow at me.

"Why don't you go off to the den and relax? I'll call you when dinner's ready," she said.

I took the hint. Azalea preferred to cook without company most of the time. "Come on, boys, let's go."

Back in the den, I made myself comfortable in the recliner. Ramses stretched out on the extended footrest, and that forced me to spread my legs until my feet almost hung off the edges. He would never be as big as Diesel, but he was a good-sized cat at fourteen pounds. Diesel opted for the sofa this time.

I tried to force my thoughts away from Tara. I could think about the upcoming wedding, but Helen Louise had everything so well organized, aided by Laura and Alex, that I really hadn't much to do. I had nixed the idea of a stag party, and Helen Louise and I asked that, in lieu of gifts, anyone who wished to commemorate the occasion should donate to their favorite charity instead. Between us we had two households of goods, especially china, serving dishes and implements, and the like. We certainly didn't need more. We were merging households, and there were decisions yet to be made about dishes and utensils, decorative items, and so on. We would be incorporating some of Helen Louise's favorite family antiques, but the rest she was leaving for Frank and Laura, who were happy about getting upgraded furniture. Helen Louise was giving her house to my daughter and son-in-law. With another baby on the way, they needed more room than they presently had in theirs.

Helen Louise planned to wear her paternal grandmother's wedding dress. The elder Mrs. Brady had been as tall as her granddaughter—Helen Louise was almost six feet in height—and apparently the dress fit my bride-to-be well. I had no clue what it looked like, but Laura and Alex both had assured me that I could look forward to a stunning bride walking down the aisle to join me.

This was Helen Louise's first trip down the aisle, and I wanted the wedding to be everything she desired it to be. She was an amazing woman, and I loved her very much. Her happiness was the most important thing to me, and whatever she wanted for the ceremony and the reception, I wanted.

I drifted off to thoughts of the wedding and was sound asleep when Azalea came to call me to dinner. I yawned and eased the footrest down. "We'll be there in a minute or two."

I had to stop by the downstairs bathroom to splash a little water on my face to wake me completely. The cats had followed Azalea back to the kitchen.

Stewart and Haskell were already in their places when I walked in, and Stewart's poodle, Dante, frisked around them, hoping for treats. I greeted my friends and took my place at the table. Tonight's menu included fried chicken, mashed potatoes, green beans, biscuits, and cream gravy. Nothing more Southern than this meal, at least in my house.

The conversation remained general while we ate. I purposely refrained from asking Haskell any questions about the investigation into Tara Martin's death. Instead I listened while he and Stewart conversed about an upcoming long weekend that they intended to spend in New Orleans. Stewart had a ribald sense of humor, and Haskell did little to discourage him in his more outrageous flights of fancy. I found him too entertaining to try to rein him in, either. We laughed a lot, and I felt much better as a result.

Once we had finished the meal, and Stewart and Haskell had partaken of dessert—slices of Azalea's caramel cake—I broached the subject of Tara Martin. The mood instantly changed. I regretted that, but I couldn't suppress my curiosity any longer. Stewart backed me up, though, expressing his own curiosity about what steps had been taken in the investigation.

"You both realize I can't tell you everything," Haskell said.

"Yes," we said in chorus.

"Tell us what you can," Stewart said, and I nodded.

"All right, then." Haskell paused for a moment. "Why don't you ask me questions? I think that would work best."

Shrewd move, I thought. By making us ask the questions, he would likely not have to impart as much information.

"I'll have a go," I said. "Have her fingerprints yielded any leads?"

"No, they haven't," Haskell said. "They're not in any of our databases. We're trying to extend the search, but it takes time."

"What about her picture?" Stewart asked. "Are you going to circulate that?"

"There are plans to do that," Haskell said. "Kanesha is the one handling it. We'll get a lot of cranks responding, the same way we always do, but it can't be helped. Somebody out there knew this woman. We're hoping they respond."

"What picture are you going to use?" The only picture of Tara that I knew about was the one on her ID badge. Unless she had a driver's license, but I had never heard her mention driving. I supposed she walked or took a taxi.

"We have two," Haskell said. "Her ID card photo, and we can get a copy of it from the college so we have a clear image." He paused. "We also have a picture of her right after she was taken off ventilation."

"Had she died yet?" Stewart asked with a moue of distaste.

"No, but it wasn't long before. Her eyes were closed, of course, but it's a clear likeness, even though it's pretty morbid, in my opinion." Haskell shook his head. "I think they'll use the college ID pic first."

"Was she wearing any makeup?" I asked. "I wondered if she was made up to look different so she couldn't be easily recognized?"

"No, she wasn't," Haskell said.

"Have you made any progress in finding out where she's been living?" Stewart asked.

"Not yet," Haskell said. "It's real frustrating, too. She had to be living somewhere." He looked at me. "Do you think she could have been homeless?"

I thought about it for a moment before I answered. "It's possible, I suppose. She always seemed clean, even though her clothes were as drab as they could be. I'm sure Helen Louise will tell you the same, if she hasn't already. She and Henry couldn't afford to have someone working for them who didn't have good hygiene."

"Of course not," Stewart said, his nose wrinkling. "I saw her a couple of times at the bistro, and she appeared clean to me. Her clothes were shabby, but they always looked like they had been washed."

"We're trying to find traces of her around town," Haskell said, "but not much luck. Her picture and a story about her will be in the next issue of the paper. We're hoping to get it run in the dailies in the larger towns in the state and in Memphis."

"That's good," I said. "If she's from any of those areas."

"You heard her talk," Haskell said. "What kind of accent did she have? Did she sound like a Southerner?"

"I'm pretty sure she was a Southerner," I said. "I couldn't say she had a Mississippi accent, though. She didn't drawl, but she also didn't clip her words. Somewhere in between."

"Did she seem educated to you?" Stewart asked.

"I suppose. She came across as bright," I replied. "She certainly knew how to create and use spreadsheets. She was familiar with computers and the usual programs. I didn't talk to her about her education. According to her application, she graduated from high school about fifteen years ago, and she had a semester of college. I couldn't draw more out of her during her interview. She really didn't like to talk about herself."

"Maybe she was afraid to give something away without meaning to," Stewart said.

"I think you're right," I replied. "She was the most guarded person I've ever known."

"That's not going to make it any easier to find out who she really was," Haskell said. "Any more questions?"

"Was she robbed by the person who killed her?" Stewart asked.

"Hard to say." Haskell shrugged. "All she had on her was a backpack with a couple of library books in it, her college work ID, and a few dollars in bills and some change. Nothing else."

"She didn't have a necklace on?" I had a memory surface suddenly of a time when I had seen a necklace hanging outside Tara's shirt. I'd had only a brief glimpse of it, but it reminded me of a saint's medallion.

"No, she didn't," Haskell said. "You saw her with one?"

I nodded. "I think it was during my first talk with her. I saw it only for a moment. It was silver, or pewter, and it struck me that it was a saint's medallion. I couldn't see it clearly enough to say more than that."

"Maybe the killer took it," Stewart said.

"It's possible," Haskell said. "Did it look valuable?"

"Don't have a clue," I said. "I know very little about saints' medallions, other than what I've occasionally seen in books."

"Could you possibly make a sketch of it?" Haskell asked.

"No. I didn't see it closely enough, and my drafting skills are negligible anyway. You'd do better to ask Helen Louise and Henry, or even Debbie, if they ever saw it," I said.

"I will," Haskell said. "I'll let Kanesha know about it." He pushed back from the table.

"Going back to work?" I asked.

Haskell nodded. "Can't be helped. I'm glad I was at least able to come home for dinner." He bent to kiss Stewart; then he headed out of the house.

Stewart looked after him wistfully. "I hate that he has to work such long hours sometimes." Stewart had a busy schedule himself as a professor of chemistry at the college, but he didn't have to put in the hours that Haskell did during an important investigation like the current one.

"I understand that," I said, thinking of the many times that Helen Louise had worked late at the bistro. I'd had to be content with late-night phone conversations many a time, and short ones at that. Helen Louise would be exhausted from the day and needed her sleep, so I didn't keep her talking.

I helped Stewart clean up the kitchen, occasionally dodging a cat or the dog as we moved around. They were anxious for any possible leftovers, but they'd had enough tidbits during the actual meal. We spoiled them badly by letting them have people food, but we tried to keep it to reasonable portions. The cats were mostly interested in chicken and bacon, with the random green vegetable. Dante the poodle liked the same things.

Once we finished in the kitchen, Stewart took Dante to the backyard to let him run around and do his business. The cats and I went back to the den, where I read while they napped in their usual spots. Lately I had been in the mood to read vintage mysteries, and I had gone through the shelves of books my late aunt had collected. Thanks to her I had a treasure trove of mysteries from which to select. I was rereading Agatha Christie, Margery Allingham, and Georgette Heyer and having a good time with their detective stories.

By the time I finished the Heyer book I was reading, I realized it was bedtime. I roused the cats, and we went through the downstairs to make sure lights were off and doors were locked. We were halfway up the stairs when I heard my phone ping to alert me to a new text message.

I halted and pulled out my phone to check. Melba was the sender. Her message was brief.

Attempted break-in at the office. Can you meet me there?

FIFTEEN

||||||||||||||||||||||||||||||||||||||||

I responded to let her know I'd be on the way in a minute. I called Stewart to tell him what was going on and asked him to keep an eye on Diesel and Ramses until I got back. I stuck my phone in my pocket and hurried down the stairs and to the garage.

A few minutes later I pulled the car into the lot behind the administration building. There was no other car in the lot. Where was Melba? Where were the campus police?

I felt suddenly uneasy. Somebody ought to be here if an alarm had gone off. Had Melba texted me from home? Was she on the way here, too? I double-checked the message and saw that it was from her new cell phone.

I lived much closer than she did, so it would take her about ten minutes longer to get here. I stayed in the car, waiting for her arrival.

Why was there no alarm sounding? Had someone turned it off already?

To my great relief I saw headlights approaching then, and a campus police vehicle turned into the lot and pulled up beside me. I waited until the officer was out of the car before I rolled down my window, my ID ready.

"Evening, Mr. Harris," the officer said after he shone a light on the ID. "What are you doing here?"

"Melba Gilley texted me that there was a break-in," I replied. "She ought to be here any minute." The officer stepped back while I got out of my car.

"An alarm did go off about six minutes ago," the officer said. He looked familiar, but I couldn't recall his name, and I couldn't see his badge clearly enough to read it. "We checked it out, but we couldn't find any sign of an intruder when we went in. We were here within a minute and a half."

"That's strange," I said. "So you think it was a false alarm?"

"Not completely. We had to turn the alarm off, but we couldn't find any evidence that someone had broken in."

"The doors were locked?" I asked.

"The back door was unlocked," the officer said. "No sign of forced entry that we could detect. Who was the last person out? Somebody must have forgot to lock it."

"I don't know," I said. "If the door was unlocked and no sign of forced entry, what set the alarm off?"

He shrugged. "Not sure. When Ms. Gilley gets here, we'll all take another look around inside. Y'all will know if there's anything disturbed."

Another car pulled into the lot, and I recognized it as Melba's. She joined us quickly. After exchanging a greeting with the campus

officer, whom of course she knew—his name was Rusty Coleman—
we brought her up to date.

Melba gave a heavy sigh. "You know, I think I'm probably responsible for the unlocked door." She addressed Coleman. "I was
late to work today because my cell phone got snatched right out of
my hand, so I had to report it to the police." She related the rest of
her experience. She ended with "I worked late to make up for the
time I lost this morning. I had some reports that couldn't wait, so I
was here until nearly nine o'clock. I was in a hurry to get home, so
I guess I forgot to make sure the door was locked when I came out."

"Understandable," Coleman said. "Let's go in now and see if you
can find anything missing or disturbed."

We made our way slowly around the ground floor. Melba's office,
which led to the director's office, was locked, and we discovered that
other rooms on that floor were locked as well. Coleman couldn't
detect any signs that the locks had been interfered with.

I asked Melba whether the library director, Andrea Taylor, had
been notified about the break-in.

"Yes, she has. She's out of town at a meeting and won't be back
until tomorrow afternoon," Melba replied. "If we find anything
wrong, she'll come home as quickly as she can, but otherwise she left
it to you and me to deal with."

I knew that Andrea relied heavily on Melba. The associate library
director was a nice guy, but he dithered over the least little thing. We
didn't need him here complicating things with his erratic behavior.

Coleman led the way upstairs. We went first to my office. Coleman shone his light on the lock. He moved his head closer to get a
better look. He stood back and pulled a latex glove out of one pocket

of his uniform. Melba and I watched in silence. With the glove on his right hand, Coleman twisted the doorknob.

The door opened easily.

"I know I locked it," I said. "After what's been going on, I made sure it was locked before I left today."

"What's going on?" Coleman asked.

"The woman who was killed by that hit-and-run was a worker in this office," Melba told him somewhat tartly.

"Yeah, we were told about that," Coleman said. "Didn't realize she had any connection with you." This last statement was directed to me.

"She was working in my office," I said. "There have been some odd incidents since she was hit." I gestured with my hand. "Can we go in now? I'm anxious to see if anything was disturbed."

"I'll go first," Coleman said. With his gloved hand, he turned on the office lights. "Don't touch anything."

I stepped into the room, Melba at my heels. The first thing I noticed was that the drawers of the desk Tara had used were all pulled open.

"Those drawers were all closed when I left," I said. "Somebody was obviously in here."

"They didn't have much time after the alarm went off," Coleman said. "Otherwise they wouldn't have left them open." He walked over to the desk. "I doubt we'll find any fingerprints." He stepped away from us and made a call on his phone. Melba and I listened as he reported that an intruder had been in the archive office.

When Coleman had finished talking with the office, he turned back to us. "Any idea what they were looking for?"

"I believe so." I told him about finding the key. "I turned it over to a sheriff's deputy. I can't think of anything else someone would be looking for. The most valuable things a thief would be after would surely be computer equipment, don't you think? There's no money kept here."

Coleman nodded. "You're right, but check your equipment for me to make sure everything's here."

I made a quick survey of the room but could find nothing else disturbed. Nothing seemed out of place. I reported that to Coleman.

"I'm going to check the other doors on this floor, just to be sure everything is shut up tight. Once I've done that, I reckon y'all can go back home. We'll be keeping an eye on this building the rest of the night. Nobody's going to get in again."

"Thank you, Rusty," Melba said. "Should we wait here for you?"

"Yeah, wait till I can go back down with you." He vanished into the hall.

"You think he should check the attic?" I asked.

Melba looked startled. "I'd forgotten about the attic. You reckon anybody could be hiding up there until we're gone?"

"I think it's unlikely," I said. "But you never know. Let's mention it to him when he comes back." We moved closer to the door to the hall to wait for him.

Coleman returned a couple of minutes later. "No sign of any monkeyshines anywhere else."

"There is an attic, Rusty," Melba said. "But if all the doors on this floor are locked, then the attic is probably okay."

Coleman nodded. "Probably, but you'd better show me the way into it so we can be sure."

137

I waited where I was while Melba showed the officer the attic entrance. I could hear them talking as they walked down the hall. Melba was asking him about his wife, but I couldn't make out his reply.

They were gone for several minutes, and I was beginning to worry that they had found that someone had attempted entry to the attic. When they came back into my office, they were chatting normally.

"All clear," Melba said. "No signs that anyone tried to get into the attic. Not that they'd find much. I told Rusty that it isn't climate-controlled up there, so we don't store anything there."

"I'm glad to hear that no one got into the attic. It would be a cold place to hide this time of year," I said.

Coleman escorted us downstairs and out to our cars. "Y'all don't worry about anything. We'll liaise with the city police department and the sheriff's department and let them know what happened."

We thanked him, and Melba and I bade each other good night. On the short drive home, I thought about the key Tara had hidden in the desk. Obviously it was important enough for someone to get into the building and break into the office to try to find it. Once Kanesha heard about this incident, I knew it would spur her on to find out what the key unlocked.

I hoped it would unlock the mystery of Tara's real identity.

The longer it took to unravel this particular mystery, I feared the less likely it was that the investigators would find Tara's killer and the motive behind her death.

When I entered the kitchen, I found Stewart at the table, drinking coffee. Ramses and Diesel greeted me, the latter expressing his displeasure at being left behind. Stewart grinned at me when he set his cup down.

"He's been grumbling like that ever since you left."

I gave both cats some attention, and Diesel's meowing ceased. "Is that decaf by any chance?"

"It is," Stewart replied. "I made a full pot. Haskell should be on his way home soon. So what happened at the workplace?"

I gave Stewart an account of what had transpired while I poured myself coffee and stirred in cream and sugar. I paused for a sip of coffee before taking my place at the table. Stewart listened intently until I finished telling him the story.

"It's a good thing whoever did this didn't get angry and throw things around," Stewart said.

"I don't think there was time," I said. "The campus police respond pretty quickly when these alarms go off."

"Is the archive office hooked up to the alarm system?"

"Yes, and the rare-book room, too," I said.

"Does it sound in the building itself?" Stewart asked.

I frowned. "You know, I'm not sure. I think it does, but I could be wrong."

"The main thing is, the intruder didn't accomplish anything," Stewart said. "He didn't get the key you found, if that's what he was looking for."

"No, he didn't. I can't imagine anything else he might have been after," I said. "A random thief wouldn't break into a building like that unless he was after antiques or old books, surely."

"I wouldn't think so," Stewart said, "though there are some beautiful pieces there that could tempt an antiques thief."

"I suppose we'd better double-check in case something like that is missing," I said. "Melba will know better than I what should be there."

"She probably knows every single stick of antique furniture there," Stewart said.

We both turned at the sound of a key in the front door. Haskell appeared in the kitchen moments later, and Stewart rose to greet his partner with a kiss. Haskell looked tired as he pulled out a chair and sat at the table.

"I'll get you some coffee," Stewart said. "It's decaf, so you shouldn't have trouble going to sleep."

"Thanks," Haskell said. "I wouldn't mind a snack, either."

Stewart turned and grinned at him. "Coming up. There's some chicken left. Want me to reheat it?"

"No, I'll take it cold," Haskell said.

Stewart put the coffee down in front of Haskell before he went to the fridge and pulled out the leftover pieces of fried chicken. "Want anything else with it?"

"No, a couple of pieces ought to do me," Haskell said. "I hear someone got into your building at work, Charlie."

"The intruder managed to get into my office, and we found the drawers of the desk Tara used pulled out. I didn't leave them that way, and I know for sure that I locked the door."

"The intruder was good at picking locks, then," Haskell said. "At least he didn't get that key. That's got to be what he was after."

Stewart set the requested chicken in front of Haskell, who picked up a leg and started eating. We let him eat without attempting to draw him into conversation. When he finished, he leaned back in his chair and patted his stomach.

"That chicken hit the spot," he said. "That'll keep me till breakfast." He had a sip of coffee.

"Any developments since we saw you last?" I asked.

Haskell shook his head. "No. We're working on that key and also trying to find out where she lived. Until we start getting responses to her picture, that's what we're focusing on."

"Sounds like a sensible plan," Stewart commented.

I had finished my coffee, and I suddenly felt the need for my bed. I checked my watch, and it was nearly ten. I pushed back my chair and took my cup to the sink to rinse it out.

"Gentlemen, I'm going to leave you to it. It's bedtime for me. Come on, Diesel, Ramses, upstairs. Good night."

Stewart and Haskell bade us good night, and the cats made a beeline for the stairs. They were already on the bed when I walked into my bedroom.

I started to undress, but I paused when my phone rang. I saw that Helen Louise was calling.

"Hello, love," I said. "I was going to call you."

"Charlie," Helen Louise said, "someone broke into the bistro tonight."

SIXTEEN

"Are you okay?" I asked. "Was anything taken?"

"I'm fine," Helen Louise said. "Mad as hell, and so is Henry. We've never had a break-in before, and we're both convinced it has something to do with Tara."

I told her quickly about the intruder in the library admin building. "I think you're right. Tara has to be the connection."

"This is so infuriating. Sorry you had the same issue. Now, to answer your other question," Helen Louise said, "as far as we know, nothing was taken. Unless Tara left something here that we weren't aware of, and the intruder found that."

"Were things disturbed?" I asked.

"Only in the office," Helen Louise said. "The intruder made a bit of a mess there, tossing some papers around. The safe wasn't touched, thank goodness."

"Don't you have some lockers there for staff?" I asked.

"Yes, and as far as we know, Tara never stored anything in one," Helen Louise said. "None of them are locked, so the intruder would have no trouble getting into them."

"I suppose the police responded quickly to the alarm?"

"Yes, they were there within five minutes," Helen Louise said. "Whoever got in was gone by the time they arrived."

"Are you at the bistro now? Should I come?" I asked.

"No, you sweet man, I'm at home now, and I'm really okay," she said. "I think we both need a good night's sleep. Rest well."

"You, too. I'm so glad you're fine and the safe wasn't touched." I ended the call, laid the phone on the nightstand, and finished undressing. I put on my nighttime attire and climbed into bed after moving Ramses gently to the other side of the bed. He invariably wanted to sleep on my side of the bed.

"Good night, boys," I said as I switched off the light. I made myself comfortable under the covers, and Ramses came back to snuggle against my stomach as I turned onto my left side. Diesel lay with his head on the spare pillow—one that Helen Louise would soon be using. I wasn't sure how happy Diesel would be when he was ousted from his accustomed spot. We would have to wait and see how he reacted. He loved Helen Louise, of that I was sure, but he'd had his spot on the bed for most of his life.

We all would have adjustments to make with Helen Louise moving in with us. Perhaps Helen Louise herself most of all. She had been on her own for many years, and coming to live in a primarily male household would be quite different for her. I had grown used to having my own way most of the time in the house, but once we were married, I would have to remember that I needed to adapt to change.

Thinking about the upcoming changes kept me from obsessing over Tara's death and the latest incidents for at least a little while, and I relaxed enough to drop off to sleep. Other than waking once during the night to visit the bathroom—an increasing occurrence the older I got—I slept well and woke feeling refreshed in the morning when my alarm went off.

Neither Stewart nor Haskell put in an appearance while I was eating breakfast, and Diesel and I left the house for work that morning without having seen them. Azalea would look after Ramses until Diesel and I were home for the day, as usual.

I inserted my key in the lock of the back door to the library admin building after testing to make sure the door was locked. Once inside, Diesel and I walked through the break room to the front of the building to bid Melba good morning. She greeted us and gave Diesel the accustomed—and demanded—attention. We talked briefly about the interlude last night, and I told her about the break-in at the bistro. She uttered a few uncomplimentary words about the person responsible for the incidents.

"Have you heard anything more from the campus police and your buddy Rusty Coleman?" I asked.

"Only that everything was quiet the rest of the night," Melba said. "Thank the Lord. I don't want to have to do that ever again."

"Me, either," I replied. "Let's hope Kanesha and her officers figure out who Tara really was and get to the bottom of these shenanigans. I want to see justice done for Tara's sake."

"Whoever she really was," Melba said. "I keep wondering if there was any way we could have helped her."

"She was determined to keep people away," I said. "You can't make someone open up to you and force help on them."

"You're right, I know, but it's still sad to me."

"We had no idea she might be in danger," I said. "I'm pretty sure *she* knew; otherwise she wouldn't have hidden that key in the office."

"What puzzles me is why she was killed before they found what they were looking for." Melba frowned. "With her dead, they've lessened their chances of finding whatever it is they're after."

"I hadn't really thought about that," I said with chagrin. "But you're absolutely right. I wonder what Kanesha is making of that, because you know she's already thought of it."

"She's too sharp not to have," Melba said. "Somebody made a stupid mistake."

"Unless Tara threatened someone with exposure," I said slowly as a new thought struck me. "Maybe she had to be silenced, despite the fact that she had hidden something the killer wanted."

"That's a possibility, I guess," Melba said. "Whatever secret Tara was sitting on must have been a ring-a-ding doozy."

"Probably so," I said. "We'd better get upstairs to work. If you hear anything more about the break-in, let me know."

Melba promised she would, and Diesel and I headed upstairs.

The door was locked, and I let us in with the key. I flipped on the lights, and I saw that the drawers in Tara's desk had been shut. I wondered if the campus police had tested for fingerprints. I stepped nearer to peer more closely at the drawers while Diesel went to his window ledge.

I couldn't see any traces of powder. Either they had tested and cleaned the drawers thoroughly, or they had decided that testing for fingerprints wasn't worthwhile. Mine would have been all over the drawers after my searching the desk, and of course Tara's would have been there. The intruder would surely have been smart enough to wear gloves.

Leaving Tara's desk, I went to my own and began checking my email. I was a little surprised to find a message from Millie Hagendorf, in which she thanked me for my time yesterday. She shared that she had gone directly to the HR office to fill out the necessary forms. She ended by saying that she was eager for the opportunity to volunteer in the archives and hoped to hear back from me soon.

I knew it would take a few days for the HR people to do a background check on Ms. Hagendorf, and she had looked so respectable and prosperous that I had no doubt that she would pass. I would deal with that when I received the actual approval from HR. In the meantime I wrote a brief, polite email, thanking her for her interest and saying that I would be in touch in the near future.

The news was out about Tara, I realized when I surveyed the other email messages I had received. Several news outlets wanted to talk to me about her. Frankly I was surprised they hadn't simply shown up here at the office and barged in to talk to me. I wrote back to each one and told them they would have to speak to the college's public-affairs department for any information. I was not allowed to speak to the press without their permission.

That was perfectly true, thank goodness. I hoped the public-affairs people would be able to keep the newshounds satisfied. I didn't want to have to deal with any aggressive reporters. During the past few years and my involvement in murder cases, I had managed to stay mostly out of the spotlight, and I wanted to keep it that way. My son and daughter had frequently expressed their concerns about my association, and I didn't want to alarm them over this latest case.

The office telephone rang, and I gave it a baleful look. I hesitated before I lifted the receiver and put it to my ear. To my relief, it was Melba.

"The campus police have posted officers at both the front and back doors to keep reporters out of the building," she said. "The news broke overnight, and apparently public affairs is getting a lot of requests for information."

"I had several emails from press persons waiting for me this morning," I said. "I didn't bother to look at the morning paper at breakfast like I usually do. I didn't want to deal with it."

"It was pretty lurid, although Kanesha's office hasn't given out a lot of details. They did publish a photograph though. Her ID picture, I think."

"I'll take a look at the paper when I go home for lunch," I said. "I hope no one will try to waylay me when I try to get to the car."

"Sic Diesel on 'em," Melba said.

"I may have to," I replied. "Thanks for alerting me." I replaced the receiver on its cradle.

My cell phone rang, and the caller ID revealed that Kanesha was calling.

"Good morning," I said.

"Good morning, Charlie," Kanesha replied. "I'm sure you've seen the news this morning. The story's out there, and the reporters are swarming."

"I know. I've got several emails from different press outlets wanting to talk to me," I said. "I assure you I have no plans to do so. The public-affairs group here at the college is dealing with them."

"I'm glad to hear you're not going to talk," Kanesha said. "There are certain facts that we want to keep out of the press, and the fewer people who talk to them, the better chance we have of keeping those facts secret until the appropriate time."

"You can count on me," I said, my tone firm.

"I know I can," Kanesha said. "I just wanted to make you aware and caution you to be careful."

"I will be," I said. Before I could ask her if there was any break in the case, she ended the call.

I realized that the less I knew about the investigation, the less likely I would be to let something slip without meaning to. I hated not knowing what was going on, but I realized it was for the best. Haskell might be able to tell Stewart and me a few things. He would never share anything without Kanesha's express permission.

Now I needed to focus on work and put all thoughts of Tara's murder out of my mind. That was going to be tough, but I had to do it. I managed to work through the rest of my unanswered emails, responding as needed, and had turned to my desk to resume cataloging when the office phone rang yet again.

"Good morning, this is Charlie Harris. How may I assist you?"

"Hi, Charlie, it's Lisa," the voice responded.

I relaxed. The caller was my colleague from the main library next door, Lisa Krause.

"Hi, Lisa, what can I do for you?"

"We've found something in the catalog that appears to be a rare book, but it's showing as available for checkout. It doesn't have a call number, so I'm assuming it's still with you. Could you check on it and let me know? We have someone who's interested in seeing the book."

"Sure. What's the title of the book?" I prepared to jot it down.

"*A History of the Yellow Fever: The Yellow Fever Epidemic of 1878, in Memphis, Tenn*," Lisa said. "Tennessee is evidently abbreviated in the title."

I frowned at the title. It sounded vaguely familiar, but I didn't think it was a title I had cataloged. "Let me check on it, and I'll get back to you."

"No rush. Thanks, Charlie," Lisa said.

I turned to my computer and opened the cataloging module of our library system. I typed in the title and brought up the bibliographic record for the book. I checked to see when it had been entered, and to my surprise I discovered that it had been entered only last week.

Then I checked the user ID of the person who had entered the record, and I received another shock. Tara had entered it. She had certainly done it without my permission or oversight. The record was a full one, uploaded from the international bibliographic database we used to find already-cataloged copies of titles. The record itself looked fine as I scanned the various parts of it.

One thing stood out, however. There was a local bibliographic note in it, but it was coded to be "nonpublic." This meant that the note would not display in the public-facing catalog. I scrutinized the note and found it odd. All it contained was cryptic: #10 TM.

The TM told me that Tara had added this note, but I wasn't sure what the #10 meant. I checked the item record for the book, and it was coded for the regular book stacks. There was no call number, however. According to the data in the record, the book had been published in 1879. This item shouldn't be in the open book stacks, and if Tara had handled it recently, then it had to be somewhere in this office or in the rare-book room next door.

I called Lisa back to give her an update and told her I would search for the book.

Looking at the record again, I realized what the number must mean. Tara had numbered each box as she entered the books in the catalog, and she had included the box number in the spreadsheet. I opened the spreadsheet and searched for the title.

Sure enough, there it was. I wondered if Tara had entered records for other books she had handled into the bibliographic database. I would have to check that. For the moment, however, I wanted to find box number ten and the yellow-fever book.

I checked the boxes near Tara's desk, but box number ten wasn't among them. I remembered we had moved a few of the boxes she had finished to the rare-book room, and I went next door to check. Diesel followed me as he always did if I left the office, even when I went to the bathroom. One thing about having cats was that you rarely were able to use the bathroom alone.

I unlocked the door and turned on the lights. Diesel stepped into the room ahead of me and started sniffing around. I found the boxes of the books that Tara had worked with on a large table at the back of the room. It took me only a moment to find number ten.

I started pulling out books and examining them. The book I sought was the last one I pulled out. Tara had no doubt put it at the bottom for reasons unknown to me. Yet.

"Come on, Diesel, back to the office," I said.

He met me at the door. I switched off the lights and locked the door. Back in the office, I set the book down on my desk and resumed my seat.

I looked through the book page by page to see if Tara had inserted anything inside. I reached the end of the book without finding anything.

Was I making a mystery out of nothing?

I leaned back in my chair and thought about several things that occurred to me.

First off, I had never shown Tara how to load records from the bibliographic utility into our catalog. She had somehow figured that out on her own.

Did Tara have previous library experience? If so, she hadn't ever mentioned it to me. Surely it would have been to her advantage to tell me that when I first interviewed her. This was something I needed to share with Kanesha, though I couldn't be absolutely certain that I was right about Tara's having previous experience.

Had Tara simply thought she was being helpful by doing this?

I went back to the spreadsheet and searched a few other titles at random in the catalog. No entries found. I would have to search them all to be sure, though.

I eyed the yellow-fever book again. Had Tara perhaps made some kind of notation on a page or two? I went through the book more carefully. This time I noticed the occasional mark by a certain passage, but after reading them, I decided someone else had marked them.

On a sudden whim I picked up the book and opened it far enough to be able to look into the binding on the spine.

Bingo.

I saw a thin piece of paper stuck in there. I took my letter opener and poked the paper to push it out of the spine of the book. It slid out.

Putting the book aside, I took the folded paper with trembling fingers and opened it up.

There was a string of numbers written on it, nothing more.

SEVENTEEN

||||||||||||||||||||||||||||||||||||||||||||||||||||||||||||||||

I looked at the numbers. There were too many digits to be a phone number, I thought, unless you were calling Jupiter perhaps. Some kind of code, I reckoned.

Examining the note under strong light with tweezers, I determined that it wasn't old paper. There were small flecks of the binding material on it, but otherwise the paper looked like contemporary stock. I was pretty certain that Tara had hidden the paper strip in the book.

Why had she done so? What information could this seemingly random series of numbers hold?

I looked at the way they appeared on the paper. They were written as one long sequence. There were no separate groupings of the digits.

This needed to be in Kanesha's hands. They could test the paper for Tara's fingerprints. Unless Tara had used gloves to handle it, her fingerprints would show she had inserted it in the book. I hoped that this was a lead that could help find some clue to her identity. Once we knew who she really was, it should be easier to figure out who wanted her dead and why.

I texted Haskell to tell him that I had found a potential clue in the archive. He didn't respond until a good ten minutes later. He would come by and pick it up in about half an hour. I texted back my thanks and set my phone down. I decided to copy the numbers onto another piece of paper. When I finished, I put the paper away in my desk drawer. This was a puzzle I thought I would have a go at solving myself.

Now was the time to do systematic searching of all the titles that Tara had listed in her spreadsheet. The yellow-fever book might be the only one she had also put into the library catalog, but I needed to make certain. I decided to search in the bibliographic section of our catalog, the part that was not visible to the public. This way I wouldn't have to search twice.

I had managed to search about a third of the books in the spreadsheet when Haskell turned up in the office. I greeted him and motioned for him to have a seat.

"This will take a moment to explain," I said. "I hope you've got a few minutes, because I think it could be important."

"I don't mind taking a few minutes," he said. "Go right ahead."

I explained about the call from my colleague in the main library, then went through the basics of what I did and what I found. Using the tweezers, I picked up the piece of paper that I had found in the spine of the yellow-fever book. At Haskell's request I laid it flat on my desk, the number side up, and he leaned forward to peer at it.

After a moment he shook his head. "Don't have a clue what it is," he said. "I'd better take it in so they can test it for fingerprints and to be sure it's recent and not something that's been in the book a long time."

He pulled out a bag, and I handed him the tweezers. He carefully put the paper inside, sealed the bag, then wrote on the outside of it with a marker. Once he had the bag safely stowed in a pocket, he regarded me with a questioning expression.

"Have you found any other papers like this?"

"Not yet." I told him I'd been searching the list of books Tara had put into the spreadsheet, but so far I hadn't found another one in the library's database. "I'll finish the list, but I'm beginning to think this might be the only one."

"Can you recall how many times she had access to the rare-book room?" he asked. "I presume that the door is kept locked unless someone has to get in there to find a book."

"Yes, it is, and Tara didn't have access to the key. I had to let her in and out of the room if she needed to go in there. Now, to answer your question, I can remember only two times that she went in there. The first time was to move boxes of books from there to in here, and the second time was to take those boxes back and bring in more."

"No way she could have gotten in there without you knowing about it?" Haskell asked.

"No, I have the only key. There is no duplicate here in the office. Andrea downstairs has a key, but it's kept locked in her desk in her office. Melba can access it, but she never mentioned to me anything about Tara wanting the key. Tara wasn't supposed to be here unless I was here anyway."

"That's all pretty clear. Thanks, Charlie. If you find anything else, let me know." Haskell rose, and Diesel roused from his nap to see Haskell to the door.

"Will do," I called after him. Diesel followed him out of the office, but he came back soon after. He went to the cat water fountain I had installed for him and lapped up some water before he climbed back into the window.

I went back to my task of checking the books from the spreadsheet. Another half hour and I finished it. I had found no other titles from the list with bibliographic records in the database. The yellow-fever book appeared to be the only one.

Had it really been the only one? I wondered. What if Tara had hidden slips of paper in other books on the list but hadn't yet added the records into the catalog? And why had she added this one title in the first place? I didn't understand her reasoning behind that act.

I decided to take a closer look at the record for the yellow-fever book. I called it back up again on my computer screen and went through each of the tags, or fields, in the record. I made myself proofread slowly, because I didn't want to skip over something by being too hasty. I read so quickly in the normal course of things that sometimes I did miss the occasional word.

I reached the end of the record without spotting anything unusual. The only addition Tara had made seemed to be the nonpublic note with her initials and the box number. This one book with its added strip of paper in the spine might be the only clue Tara had left in the archive.

I speculated on why she had chosen to hide the numbers in the rare-book collection. Maybe because she thought no one would think of looking for it there? That made sense to me. Especially since she hid the paper in the binding of the book. That wasn't a place someone would normally look for anything. Librarians would, of course, as I had done.

That led me to another question. Why had she done it? Had she needed a record, for some reason, of where she had secreted that piece of paper with the numbers? I thought that was entirely possible.

What about the person who had inquired about the book at the main library? Lisa Krause hadn't provided any details about this person, and I felt impelled to find out more now that I had checked all the books that Tara had listed on the spreadsheet. I would have to give Lisa a reason why I wasn't going to let anyone else have a look at this book until Tara's murder was solved. The sought object in the book was in the hands of the sheriff's department, but a ruthless person might well tear the book apart trying to find it. I didn't want that to happen.

Lisa wasn't immediately available to talk. I left a message for her to call me back as soon as she had a few minutes to chat. While I waited for the callback, I put the yellow-fever book in the safe where we kept our rarest materials. The safe was fireproof, and the average intruder wouldn't be able to get it open.

That accomplished, I went back to my desk. Diesel had been watching me, and he gave me an interrogative meow. "Just a precaution," I said. He yawned and turned back to the window.

When the phone rang I was halfway through checking the spines of the other books in box ten.

"Hi, Charlie, it's Lisa."

"Thanks for calling me back," I said. "I can't explain why at the moment, but I did find the book. I'm afraid, however, that I can't let anyone have access to it for a while."

"Interesting," Lisa said, drawing the syllables out. "Does this have anything do with another murder you're involved in?"

"I can't comment on that," I said.

Lisa chuckled into the phone. "You don't have to. All right, I'll let the person know you couldn't find it but will keep looking for it. How's that?"

"That should be fine," I said. "Before you go, however, could you describe this person for me?"

"Sure, let me think." There was a brief pause before Lisa spoke again. "Female, probably in her late thirties, not a student or faculty member, just a random person who came in to use the library."

The college library was open to the public. They weren't given library cards, but they could use any of the print resources the library had and some of the electronic databases funded by the state. The library staff saw a lot of these people throughout the year.

"Can you tell me anything more about her appearance?"

"As I recall, she was wearing jeans and a hoodie. Oh, and gloves, too. I think she had come inside a few moments before she came to the desk, and it was pretty cold outside. She had a pleasant-looking face, and I think she might have brown hair. Maybe five eight in height. Anyone you know?"

"No, the description doesn't ring any bells. You did get her name, didn't you, and a contact number?"

"I didn't." Lisa sounded regretful. "A couple of students came up then, and I was the only one at the desk. The woman said she'd check back in a day or two."

"Okay, thanks, I appreciate the information."

"You're welcome," Lisa said. "Good luck with the murder."

I didn't reply to that sally and put the phone back on its cradle. The description wasn't all that helpful, but I would relay it to Haskell or Kanesha anyway. Time to finish examining the remaining books in box ten, however.

When I was done, I felt frustrated. I found no additional slips of paper, or anything else that appeared to have been added to the books. Was this the only thing hidden? I had to ask myself again. I supposed I could go through boxes one through nine to check each book, but as Tara had entered only one bibliographic record in the database, as far as I knew, I didn't see the point. She had obviously entered the one record because of what she had placed in the book.

Had she done it for herself? Or had she done it for someone else to find? Like the woman who had requested to see the book? It was rather odd that someone had inquired about this particular book on the very day that I found the slip of paper in the book's spine.

After arguing with myself over my next proposed action, I decided to go for it. I called Kanesha Berry on my cell phone. As I more or less expected, the call went to voice mail after several rings. Kanesha had probably looked at the number and decided not to answer. This frustrated me because she ought to know well enough by now that I didn't call her on a random impulse. I didn't call her unless I had something I thought she really ought to know.

The message I left conveyed that sentiment, but I also told her I had more potential clues in Tara's murder. I urged her to call me back as soon as she could.

I spent nearly twenty minutes fretting because I hadn't heard from her yet, and I debated calling again. But I waited, and moments later I received a call from her.

"Yes, Charlie, what are these clues you've found?"

"Has Haskell shown you the piece of paper I gave him and explained where and how I found it?" I asked.

"Yes, he has. Is that all you're calling about?"

"No, there's more. A woman came into the college library and inquired about the book. Lisa Krause was at the desk and spoke to her." I shared Lisa's description of the woman with her. "I told Lisa to tell the woman, if and when she returns, that the book isn't available for public use."

"That's useful information," Kanesha said. "I appreciate it."

"This woman wasn't a student or faculty member. A member of the public who didn't leave her name. Don't you think it's odd that she asked for this specific book?"

"We can't afford to overlook any leads, no matter how tenuous they might be. I'll get the police department to assist with this and assign someone to hang around the library until this woman comes back."

"If she's eager enough, she ought to be back in a day or two," I said.

"Thanks, Charlie, I appreciate it." Kanesha ended the call.

Feeling satisfied that I had done my duty, I put my phone aside. Time to get back to work. The work I was paid to do, as my children would happily remind me. I hadn't spoken to either of them yet about Tara's murder. I was surprised I hadn't had calls from both of them by now. Particularly from Sean, because he fussed more over my amateur sleuthing activities than Laura did. Perhaps I had better call Sean and make sure that everything was fine on his home front. I picked up my cell phone and dialed.

"Hi, Dad, what's up?" Sean sounded much as he usually did when I called him at work, slightly distracted.

"Thought I'd check in and see how you're all doing," I said.

"Fine, Dad," Sean said. "Alex is working from home today, and Rosie is with Charlie and the nanny at Laura's. I brought her in with me and dropped her off."

"Glad to hear all is fine. That sure was some housewarming party," I said.

"We had a great time, although we were exhausted by the time the last guest left." Sean's tone changed when he continued. "I saw in the paper that the woman who was working with you at the archive died from injuries in a hit-and-run. The one you took home from the party."

"Yes, that was Tara," I said, wondering what was coming.

"I trust that you're not inserting yourself into the investigation this time," Sean said.

"How could I?" I asked. "I barely knew the woman. I've answered questions and given them everything I knew about her, which frankly wasn't much. She was a very private person who didn't share things about her personal life at all."

"I'm glad you're staying out of it," Sean said. "I don't want to have to worry about you, especially not after your most recent exploit."

I knew he was referring to the conclusion of the murderous activities surrounding the return of a local prodigal son a few months ago. That had been a harrowing adventure, and I wasn't eager to repeat it ever again.

"No, this is nothing like that case," I said. "This one is all in the hands of the authorities."

"Great," Sean said. "We'll be seeing you for Sunday dinner as usual. Now I've really got to get back to work. Love you."

"Love you, too, son," I said.

One down, one to go.

"Hi, Laura," I said when my daughter answered.

"How are you, Dad?" she said. "Rosie is here with us today. Alex is working from home."

"Are Rosie and Charlie getting along?"

"Most of the time." Laura chuckled. "Unless Rosie tries to take a toy from Charlie. Then he isn't happy, but he lets her have it. He's old enough to understand she's still a baby."

"So is he," I said indulgently.

"He's nearly nineteen months old now," Laura said. "Not really a baby. He's at the toddler stage the way he walks around. I caught him running a little yesterday."

"He'll be leading you and Frank all over the place," I said. "And the nanny."

"I'm getting slower by the day," Laura said, referring to her pregnancy. "Number two will be here before long."

"I can't wait, and I know you and Frank are anxious for baby to arrive."

"And how," Laura said. "I can't wait to see my feet again." She laughed.

"I remember your mother at that stage," I said. "We were both impatient."

I heard a wail erupt somewhere in the background. I thought it was Rosie.

Laura sighed. "I'd better go, Dad. Sounds like something happened, and Rosie isn't happy. See you on Sunday."

I bade her goodbye and put the phone down. Evidently she hadn't seen the paper or Frank had deliberately kept the news from her. He was protective of her, and this close to the baby's arrival, he wouldn't want her getting upset about anything, especially about me.

I felt relieved. The subject might come up Sunday when the family gathered for our weekly dinner, but perhaps with help I could keep the conversation away from anything to do with the murder of my former worker.

The office phone rang. "Hello, Charlie," Melba said. "There's a Ms. Hagendorf here to see you. Shall I send her up?"

Why had she come back so soon?

EIGHTEEN

IIIIIIIIIIIIIIIIIIIIIIIIIIIIIIIIIIIIIIIIIIIIIIIIIII

"Yes, go ahead. Send her up."

After the polite email message from the woman, I really hadn't expected to hear from Ms. Hagendorf again so soon. HR had hardly had time for a background check, I would have thought. I hadn't received any kind of notification from them, either.

While I waited I considered how I would handle the conversation with her. It all depended on the purpose of her visit, I realized. What was her objective in coming here today? She had given me her reasons for wanting to volunteer, and I understood the need that writers had to do research to make their work feel more authentic.

I had done a quick search on her name, however, and hadn't found her listed as the author of any books. In fact I saw nothing online about Millie Hagendorf at all. I found that really odd. Was this woman operating under an assumed name?

She appeared in the doorway, offering the same chilly smile I had seen before. I rose from my chair and beckoned her in.

"Good morning, Ms. Hagendorf. How are you?" I indicated the chair in front of my desk.

"I'm fine, Mr. Harris." Dressed less formally today in slacks, blouse, and jacket, she seated herself and set her bag—Gucci, this time, I noticed—on the seat beside her. "How have you been?"

"Fine," I said. Before I could say anything else, she spoke again.

"I read in the paper today about the horrible death of that poor woman who was working here with you. Was she a student?"

"No," I said. "She hadn't worked here long, only since the semester started."

"I believe she also worked at the bistro on the square," Ms. Hagendorf continued. "That's a charming place with such delicious food, don't you think?"

I would have bet she knew about my connection with the bistro and its founder, but I wasn't going to give anything away.

"Yes, she did, as I understand," I replied. Diesel stirred behind me, making a grumbling noise. Obviously this woman's presence in the room unsettled him. It unsettled me as well, although I couldn't pinpoint a reason why. Since I had adopted Diesel, I had learned to trust his reactions to people. He had a way of sensing people who were not who they appeared to be.

Millie Hagendorf was a fake, although I hadn't determined yet what kind of fake. Was she using an assumed name, like Tara, to hide her true identity? Was she trying to fake being a pleasant and helpful potential volunteer? I suspected the answer to both these questions was a resounding *yes*. Being as noncommittal as possible was going to be my strategy in dealing with her until I discovered her ulterior motive in seeking me out.

I saw a slight frown appear on Ms. Hagendorf's face, but it was quickly erased. She had expected more from my answer about Tara's employment at the bistro.

"Didn't I see a wedding announcement in the paper a week or so ago about you and Ms. Brady, the owner of the bistro?" she asked.

"Yes, there was one," I said.

"Congratulations," she said.

"Thank you." I felt she was becoming frustrated with my brief answers. I simply kept regarding her with what I hoped was a friendly, open expression.

"I heard from the HR department," Ms. Hagendorf said. "They're working on the background check and expect to have it completed the first of next week. I know they won't find any problems in my background." She essayed another cold little smile. "I hope to be working with you by midweek, then."

"I see. I looked you up on the Internet, Ms. Hagendorf, and apparently you don't exist. I found that rather odd."

That startled her, I could tell. Her body gave a minute jerk but quickly settled back into its state of calm repose. "I should explain that," she said. "Millie Hagendorf is the pseudonym I plan to use for my fiction writing. I'm getting used to using it in my everyday life. I want to *become* Millie Hagendorf. I think it will make my writing much more authentic. Millie is so imaginative and creative, and she loves romance. Don't you agree?"

It took considerable effort for me not to burst out laughing. The woman really must have thought I was an idiot, but I wasn't going to let her think I didn't believe her.

"That sounds clever," I said. "I don't know many writers, at least any who use pseudonyms, so it might be a common strategy."

I could see that she relaxed ever so slightly at that. I resisted the urge to blurt out, *Horse pucky.* I smiled. She no more intended to write a romance novel than I did. I was beginning to think that all this had something to do with Tara Martin. I had no evidence for it, but the feeling hit me and was growing stronger.

"Is there anything in particular I can do for you today?" I deliberately didn't press her for her real name. The HR people could handle that, and I would find out from them eventually.

"No, I simply wanted to drop by and ask if you had a few minutes to show me the archive and rare books," she said. "Is that possible?"

I shook my head. "I'm so sorry." I glanced at my watch. Eleven-forty-three. "I have an appointment at noon, and I have a long meeting this afternoon. One of the banes of being a department manager, I'm afraid. Meetings that seem to go on forever."

I was lying, of course, about having to go to a meeting this afternoon. I wasn't about to attend any meetings that seemed to go on forever. I had suffered through way too many of them during my career in Houston.

"I really should have called and inquired before I came," Ms. Hagendorf said. I wasn't sure she believed me, but I really didn't care. The more I was around her, the more sure I was that I didn't want her working in this office. I would find some excuse to turn her down if she passed the background check.

I rose to see her out, and she thanked me for my time. I simply smiled and nodded. Once I heard her going down the stairs, I shut the door and locked it.

I saw Diesel was watching me as I returned to the desk. "We don't like her, do we?"

He warbled loudly, and I chuckled as I sat down to resume work.

Normally I was fairly easygoing when it came to dealing with people I didn't know. I was willing to take them on their own terms and give them a chance. Occasionally, however, I met someone to whom I had an adverse reaction. Something about a person would make my hackles rise, so to speak, before I even realized it was happening. That was the case with Millie Hagendorf. I didn't trust her, and I wasn't sure exactly why.

If I was lucky enough, I wouldn't have to deal with her again.

An odd thought struck me. Should I mention Millie Hagendorf to Haskell or Kanesha? I couldn't escape the feeling that Millie Hagendorf might be connected in an unknown way to Tara Martin. The coincidence of her showing up in my office twice now so fast upon the heels of Tara's death made me think she had to be connected. I hadn't the foggiest notion how. Maybe she was a friend of Tara's. Maybe her enemy. I didn't know.

I didn't want to text Kanesha at the moment. It would take too long to explain, and I thought talking to her once today already was more than enough. Best not to go directly to the well too often. Instead I decided to wait until I next saw Haskell to mention Millie Hagendorf to him.

That decision made, I was finally able to focus on actual work. I pushed away nagging thoughts, such as whether I was coming up with wild ideas to be included in the investigation and whether I should really bother Haskell with this. Then I consoled myself with the thought that there were so few leads in the case that even a possibly false one was worth considering.

Diesel and I went home for lunch, where we found only Ramses and Azalea in the kitchen. Stewart was lunching at the college with some of his fellow faculty members. Haskell rarely ever made it home for the midday meal. Azalea and I chatted briefly while I consumed a delicious grilled chicken salad with Azalea's homemade Thousand Island dressing and fresh hot rolls.

Back at work, the afternoon passed uneventfully with no more interruptions from anything or anyone related to the murder case. By the time Diesel and I were ready to head home, I felt I had made up in productivity for the interruptions of the morning. Before we left the office, I moved the last boxes of books that Tara had worked on into the rare-book room. I debated putting them into the safe, but I thought it unlikely that an intruder would come back again. I hoped I wouldn't be proven wrong over the weekend.

As it happened, I didn't have a chance to talk to Haskell about Millie Hagendorf until after the family dinner on Sunday. He sometimes had to miss the gathering because of the pressure of work, but apparently the murder investigation was at a standstill for lack of leads. We had the usual enjoyable meal, and we talked mostly about the new baby on the way, the upcoming wedding, and the housewarming party. No one brought up the subject of murder, for which I was grateful. I saw no need to worry my family, particularly my son and daughter and their spouses, about my interest in the case and my rather slender connection to it.

After the others had left and I was in the kitchen with Stewart and Haskell tidying up—Helen Louise had left a few minutes before—I brought up the subject of Millie Hagendorf. Haskell and Stewart listened to the story of my encounters with her while we finished cleaning up. While I still talked, we gathered at the kitchen table and enjoyed decaf coffee. The cats and the dog, worn out from all the activity and attention from various family members, including the two grandchildren, napped under the table.

When I concluded telling my story, I sipped at my coffee while I waited for reactions from the other men.

"I think the fact that you had a negative reaction to this woman is pretty telling, Charlie," Stewart said. "I've rarely heard you mention reacting to someone this way. You're normally so easygoing. And the fact that Diesel wouldn't have anything to do with her is another indicator, I think."

"Yes, those are good points," Haskell said. "She might be one of those persons who just puts other people off without realizing that it's happening. They simply don't know how to be warm and friendly. Instead they can come off as cold and calculating, completely unaware that they're doing it."

"I agree with you," I said. "That could be what's going on with my reaction to this woman. And maybe I'm making a big leap in trying to connect her in some way with Tara and her murder. This is why I wanted to bring it up to you, and Stewart, of course, because I know I am sometimes too eager to scent out a mystery when there really isn't one."

Stewart snickered. "Yes, Nancy Drew, you are eager."

I shot him a pained look. "Please, Frank Hardy, though I do love Nancy."

Haskell snorted at the banter. "Seriously, you two. I should call you Frank and Joe Hardy, because Stewart's as bad as you are sometimes, Charlie." He set his coffee cup on the table with a light thump. "Look, I'm not saying you're wrong about this woman, but there's got to be more to go on than what you have so far."

"I know," I said. "I think it's there, but I simply don't know where."

"Kanesha told me about the yellow-fever book," Haskell said, perhaps in an attempt to change the subject.

"What's this about a yellow-fever book?" Stewart asked. "Which epidemic? There were a number of them, because yellow fever was endemic in the Mississippi River valley for a long time."

"The epidemic of 1878," I said. "The book is about Memphis."

"Is the book important for some reason?" Stewart asked.

"It's part of a collection the archive received recently," I replied. "The reason it could be important is because of what Tara did." I launched into the explanation I had given Kanesha, and fortunately neither Stewart's nor Haskell's eyes glazed over while I went over some of the technical details. I finished by telling them about the woman who had asked for the book in the main library. "I wouldn't have investigated the book at all, at least not for a while, if it hadn't been for that."

"That's intriguing. Certainly a whopper of a coincidence," Stewart said. "What are the chances?"

"Slim to none," I said. "I did find a clue in the book." I glanced at Haskell, asking permission to tell Stewart. He nodded. I then explained about the piece of paper with the numbers on it.

"What is the significance of the numbers?"

"I don't know."

"We're looking into them," Haskell said. "How long had the record been visible to the public?"

"Only a few days." I had checked that. "Tara entered it last Thursday."

"Even more of a coincidence." Stewart looked smug.

"Yes, it is." Haskell raised an eyebrow at his partner. "It's not evidence, however. Until the woman comes back to the library and someone gets her name and description, there's nothing we can do."

"But you're still going to try to identify the woman and talk to her?" I asked.

"We are. Maybe she'll turn up again tomorrow." He pushed back his chair and took his coffee cup to the sink. "I'm full as a tick and ready for bed. How about it, Stew?"

"Same," Stewart said. "Come on, Dante, let's head upstairs." He deposited his cup in the sink and started to follow Haskell out of the kitchen. He turned back, however, and with a big grin said, "Wouldn't it be a hoot if this Millie Hagendorf turned out to be the woman after the yellow-fever book?"

With that he hurried after his partner, nearly tripping over the dog, while I sat at the table, slack-jawed, thinking about what he had said.

NINETEEN

‖‖

Could Stewart be right? Was the woman who inquired for the yellow-fever book at the main library really Millie Hagendorf?

If she was the woman, this put a darker spin on things. How could she know about that book unless Tara had told her? Was she a friend of Tara's? If she was, why hadn't she simply told me?

She might not want to have anything to do with the police, I reckoned. Acknowledging that she knew Tara would mean she'd have to talk to Kanesha at some point. She must have realized that I wouldn't keep that information a secret, not in a murder investigation.

I had to hope that, when the anonymous woman returned to ask about the book at the main library, one of the officers detailed to watch for her would be able to take her to the sheriff's department for questioning. The whole thing could be a strange coincidence, and if it was, the woman surely wouldn't object to answering a few questions.

Or it could be Millie Hagendorf.

Either way I hoped that there would be an answer to this particular part of the puzzle sometime tomorrow. Or the next day. Soon, I hoped.

My brain didn't need any more reason to shift into overdrive. In previous investigations I had been solidly in the middle of them, but this time I was on the sidelines. I knew it was safer for me there, but my bump of curiosity—bigger than the Great Pyramid of Giza, Sean had once claimed—wasn't satisfied with my position. I had little choice so far.

I felt a paw on my thigh. I looked down at Diesel, and he yawned. He was telling me it was bedtime. "All right, boys, let's go upstairs."

A little while later, settled in bed, I called Helen Louise to bid her good night while the cats dozed off beside me. She answered immediately.

"Calling to say good night," I said. "And to wish you happy dreams."

"Thank you, love," she replied. "The same to you. Are you stewing over the murder investigation?"

I heard the teasing note in her voice. She knew me so well.

"A bit," I said. "I can't quite keep my nose out of it because of Tara's connection with the archive. I'll tell you all about it tomorrow. It's been a long day, and it's time to rest."

"All right," Helen Louise said. "See you tomorrow."

There hadn't been a good moment to share this with Helen Louise. Too many people around I didn't want to find out about my involvement, such as it was, in Tara's case. She had left with Laura and Frank, carrying Rosie to the car for them, while they talked about her house. I didn't have the heart to interrupt that.

I had a restless night. My subconscious was busy, and my dreams were unsettling. I woke up one time from a nightmare in which I was with Tara when she was attacked by the hit-and-run driver. I tried to pull her out of harm's way, but she fought me off, telling me to leave her alone. It wasn't any of my business.

When I managed to dredge myself out of that scene, I went to the bathroom on my nightly errand. I had a drink of water and stared at my reflection in the mirror. My expression told me that I was still unsettled by the dream. I took a few deep breaths to center myself and then went back to bed.

That morning I felt better but not my usual rested self. I knew until I heard about the woman who had asked for the yellow-fever book, I would be antsy. There was nothing I could do about the situation, and that was an irritant. Not the best way to start off a Monday morning.

Diesel and I arrived at the office on time. He made himself comfortable in the window embrasure, and I opened my email to check for new messages. There were a couple of college announcements, including one from the president, who shared the news of a significant bequest to the athletic programs. I sighed. Why couldn't someone give that kind of money to the library? Instead of periodic budget cuts, the library could sorely use additional funding. Unfortunately for the library, athletic programs took precedence with alumni giving.

I pushed those thoughts about budgets and athletics away. They only annoyed me, and I needed to concentrate on my work.

I had good intentions, but a stray thought surfaced about the housewarming party. Tara had seen someone or something there that had set off her alleged panic attack. I had asked Sean for the guest list so I could give it to Melba to go over. She knew so many more people in Athena than I did.

With all that had happened since Tara was run over, I had let it slip my mind completely. Melba hadn't mentioned it to me, and I figured she might also have forgotten it. No time like the present, I thought, to ask her about it.

"Come on, Diesel, we're going downstairs to see Melba."

That woke him up, and he was out the door and down the stairs by the time I locked the office and followed him. When I caught up with him, he had his head on Melba's leg. She was stroking his head and back and cooing to him about how wonderful he was. Oddly enough, he never argued with her.

"To what do I owe the pleasure?" Melba glanced up at me with an inquisitive grin.

"I've been forgetting to ask you about that party list I gave you." I took the chair by her desk. "Remember? With all that's happened I forgot about it."

"Well, I didn't forget," Melba said. "Actually, I did forget to tell you that I'd gone through it, but I do have some information for you. Hang on a minute." She pulled out a drawer and rummaged in it. She extracted a piece of paper and gave it to me.

"I checked off everyone whose name I knew, all people who probably had nothing to do with Tara's murder," Melba said. "There are a couple there I know nothing about, though. A tall, good-looking man, probably in his fifties, and woman, maybe forty, who was with him.

"Did you find out anything about them?" I asked.

"No, I didn't stay long enough," Melba said. "Sean seemed to know the man, though. I did see them chatting once. Never did find out what kind of business he's in, but whatever it is, it must be pretty successful. He was wearing a three-thousand-dollar suit, I'm pretty sure."

"If he can lay out that kind of money on a suit, he must be rolling in it." Spending money on clothes like that didn't impress me, frankly, but I supposed that it impressed the kind of people with whom he did business, whatever that was.

"Why don't you ask Haskell about him?" Melba said. "He'll know something, I'll bet. Or ask Stewart, because maybe Haskell told *him*."

"Possibly," I said. "What about these two other names? Do you think those two could be Alberta Garner and P. J. Jackson? I don't recognize either of those names."

"I didn't, either," she said with some asperity. "That's why they're not marked. I don't know who they are, but I think it's likely they're the two people I mentioned. You'll have to ask Sean or Alex about them to find out for sure."

"I'll check with Sean and Alex," I said. "Thanks. Come on, Diesel, back to work."

He meowed in protest. "All right, you can stay with Melba awhile if it's okay with her."

"Of course it is." Melba patted his head. "I'll send him back to you if I have to leave the office for any reason."

"Thanks. See you later." I left and headed back up to the second floor. I intended to give Alex a call straightaway. I didn't want to interrupt her work, but it was close to lunchtime, and she might be ready to take a break for a few minutes.

Back in the office, I pulled out my cell phone and called Alex. She answered after several rings, and I bade her good morning. "I hope I'm not interrupting your work."

"Not at all, I'm just starting my lunch break with your beautiful granddaughter." I could hear Rosie chattering in the background. "What can I do for you, Dad?"

"Give Rosie a big kiss for me," I said. "And besides that, I wanted to ask you about a couple of the people on the guest list for the housewarming party."

"What are their names?" Alex asked. "You know, don't you, that Sean has already gone over this list with Kanesha Berry?"

"No, I didn't know that," I said, chagrined. "But I should have known Kanesha was on top of things. Anyway, the two people I'm curious about are Alberta Garner and P. J. Jackson. Melba went through the list, and those are the only two names she didn't recognize."

"Honestly, Dad," Alex said, "I can't remember them, off the top of my head. They must be people Sean put on the list. Probably some business connection, but I can't recall meeting them myself. Things were so hectic that night, so many people. I knew most of them, but there were a dozen or so that I didn't. Since Rosie came, I haven't been as active in the office as Sean. Besides, you know how easily he makes friends with people." She chuckled. "He's got the gift of gab, as they used to say, and I don't."

"Sean got it from his mother, because I don't have the ease of manner he has with new people." I sighed. "Thanks, Alex, I guess I'll have to ask Sean about them."

"Be prepared for him to warn you not to get involved in this investigation," Alex said in a kindly tone. "We both know you mean well, but Sean does worry about you because he loves you so much and doesn't want to see you harmed in any way."

"I know, and I don't intend to get involved any more closely," I said. "This is simply to satisfy my curiosity, and Melba's, too, about who these people are."

"All right, then. Good luck with Sean."

"Thanks, and don't forget that kiss for Rosie." I ended the call.

Darn. I didn't really want to call Sean and ask these questions, for precisely the reason Alex had articulated. Sean could get so stern and fussy with me, as if I were a recalcitrant child. He wasn't patronizing, but I squirmed a bit nevertheless during these conversations.

Best get it over with. I called Sean's cell phone, and he answered right away.

"Hi, Dad, what's up? Are you doing okay?"

"I'm fine," I replied. "I have a question for you about two of the guests at the housewarming party. Alberta Garner and P. J. Jackson. How do you know them?"

"Why this curiosity about party guests?" Sean asked. "Does this have anything to do with the current murder investigation?"

"Tangentially, I suppose it does," I said, hoping I sounded convincing enough. "I didn't recognize their names, and I simply wondered who they are."

"And whether one of them frightened Tara Martin so badly she had a panic attack." Sean's dry tone alerted me to the fact that he wasn't buying my attempt at passing this off as simple curiosity that didn't involve the murder case.

"Well, that, too," I admitted.

"Dad." Sean invested that one syllable with enough exasperation that I knew what was coming next. "You need to stop getting involved in these things."

"Don't lecture me again, Sean," I said. "I'm not trying to insert myself into the investigation. I simply want to know some things to satisfy my own nosiness. I know that Kanesha is thoroughly capable of solving this crime without any help from me. The fact that Tara worked with me in the archive, and that she left some clues to her activities there, has caused me to be involved to a certain degree, however."

"Okay, Dad." Sean's tone was grudging. "I'll satisfy your curiosity. P. J. Jackson is a lawyer from Memphis. I worked with him last year on a case with Tennessee connections. He has an outstanding reputation, as far as I know. Alberta Garner is client of his, apparently. I told P. J. he could bring her to the party."

"Thanks for the information," I said. "There isn't anything about either of these two people that has struck you as strange or out of the ordinary?"

"Certainly not with P. J. Jackson." Sean paused for a moment. "Alberta Garner seems to be a pretty reserved person. A widow, I think. I really didn't talk to her for more than a minute or two. I did have a longer conversation with P. J. about the case he assisted me with, though."

"Thanks, that helps," I said.

"I know it's useless to tell you to leave this mess alone, but at least be careful, okay?"

"I promise. I'm really just on the fringes this time," I said. "Thanks, son."

"Bye, Dad, love you."

"Love you, too."

I put my phone down and shook my head. Sean was never going to stop worrying about me, and I appreciated that he was so concerned for my welfare. He had learned, however, that I wasn't going to limit my life in order to stay wrapped up in cotton wool so I couldn't get hurt. I wished we didn't have to go through this dialogue every time, though.

Diesel meowed loudly as he came through the door to alert me to his presence. He padded toward me and paused by my chair so that I would be sure to acknowledge him. I told him what a good boy he was and rubbed his head a few times. Satisfied with the attention, he jumped into the window behind me and settled down for a nap. We would be heading home for lunch before long.

I was able to focus on cataloging for a while, until I heard a knock on the open door. I glanced up to see Ryan Jones in the doorway. He didn't appear happy.

TWENTY

"Hello, Mr. Jones," I said. "Anything I can help you with?" I stood as he approached my desk. I could hear Diesel grumbling behind me on the window embrasure.

"You sure as hell can." Jones stopped about a foot in front of my desk and glared at me. "Why didn't you tell me about Tara? I'd'a gone to see her in the hospital if I'd known she was there."

"I'm sorry about that," I said. "I was under strict orders not to share the news with anyone. The police didn't want word getting out to the hit-and-run driver that she was in the hospital." That wasn't true, of course, but I'm sure I was right about what the authorities would have wanted in this situation.

Jones appeared deflated at my response. He moved slowly to the chair in front of the desk and sank into it. "I never thought of that." He wiped a hand wearily across his face.

"I'm so sorry," I said, and I meant it. His emotion seemed genuine to me. Had he been a friend of Tara's? I decided to ask him. "Was Tara your friend?"

He looked at me, his eyes narrowed. "Sorta. I mean, I mostly knew her when she first came to town. Then I didn't see her for a while, until she needed a phone. I found one for her."

"I see." I really didn't, but I figured I had better be careful about pressing him for details. "Have the police talked to you about Tara?"

He shook his head. "Hell no, man, I don't want to be talking to no police. I don't need the hassle."

"Maybe you can talk to me instead," I said, backing off from the idea of dealing with the authorities. "We really need to know where Tara lived. You see, we don't think Tara Martin was actually her name. They need to find out if she has any family or friends who should be informed about her death. And they need to know who she really was."

Jones regarded me for perhaps fifteen seconds with an expression that seemed to me highly suspicious. I was afraid that he was going to get up and walk out of the office without talking anymore. To my surprise, he didn't move from the chair, and suddenly spoke.

"I don't know nothing about any other name. That's the only name I knew her by," he said with seeming conviction. "She told me she came from Memphis. Where she lived?" He shrugged. "She was homeless when she first got here, but at some point she scored some cash somehow and left the homeless group she was with. Never could get her to say where she was living."

"How long ago did you first meet her?" I'd had no idea that Tara had been homeless, though in some ways it didn't surprise me.

Jones cocked his head to one side as he thought about it. "Maybe six months ago."

"And when was it she left the homeless group?"

He thought again, then said, "Maybe around Thanksgiving. Before, I think."

"How did she get in touch with you to get her a phone?"

He shrugged again. "She knew how to find me."

"Any idea why she would have destroyed her phone?"

"She was kinda crazy sometimes. If she got mad, no telling what she'd do."

"Then she found you again and asked you to get her another phone," I said.

He nodded. "Yeah, and now that she's dead, I want it back. I got somebody else who needs one."

"The cops have it for now," I said, "but once the investigation is done, they might be willing to release it to you. They know you brought it here and I accepted it on Tara's behalf."

"That would be good, although I don't like dealing with the police," Jones replied, exhibiting more animation than he had shown thus far. "How long do you think it'll be before they nail the bastard?"

"I don't know," I said. "They don't have much to go on. Do you have any idea why someone would want to kill Tara?"

He stared at me for perhaps ten seconds this time. Then he shook his head. "Nah, no idea."

I didn't believe he was telling me the complete truth, but I didn't know how I could get him to trust me enough to tell me absolutely everything he knew. If only Haskell or Kanesha would suddenly appear. Maybe they could get out of him some of what they needed to know.

The next moment, my jaw dropped when I saw Haskell in the doorway. How on earth? Melba appeared right behind him. Then I knew she must have seen Jones come into the building. She called or texted Haskell to hurry over. She later confirmed this with me.

Jones saw my expression of surprise and turned quickly to look behind him. I heard him utter an imprecation under his breath before he turned back to glare at me.

"I didn't call anybody," I said, but he didn't appear to believe me.

Haskell and Melba came into the room. Before Haskell could speak, Melba said, "I called the deputy. I saw you sneaking into the building. You must be Mr. Jones."

Now it was Melba's turn to receive the glare.

Haskell closed the office door and stood in front of it. "Mr. Jones, glad we finally found you. I need to talk to you about the late Tara Martin. How's about you come with me to the sheriff's department so we can have a chat?"

Jones muttered more imprecations under his breath. He got slowly to his feet and reached for a pocket. Haskell's gun was out and trained on Jones so quickly that it seemed it was there already.

"Raise your hands," he said, and Jones complied instantly.

"You're not under arrest," Haskell said in a milder tone. "You're going with me to talk to the chief deputy who's in charge of the murder investigation. If you try to get away from me, things will be a lot harder for you. Do you understand me, Mr. Jones?"

Jones's shoulders slumped. "Yeah, I do. Let's go." Haskell put away his gun and came forward to pat Jones down. He extracted a small knife from Jones's pocket and stuck it in his own pants pocket. Then he grasped Jones's arm. Melba opened the door for them, and we watched them go. Melba came over and sank into the chair vacated by Jones. We regarded each other solemnly.

Diesel now came to see Melba, and we sat there in silence while she gave my cat the attention he wanted. When we both had regained our composure over the shock of the encounter, we began to talk at once. I held up my hand for silence.

"Thanks for calling Haskell," I said. "I wanted to do it, but there was no way I could with Jones sitting right there."

"I figured that was the case. Lucky I saw him sneaking into the building," Melba said. "Didn't know for sure who he was, but he looked like the guy you told me about. Did he tell you anything useful?"

"Not really. The only thing I found out was that Tara told him she was from Memphis. He also said she was homeless when she first got to Athena about six months ago. Then, around Thanksgiving she found a place to live, but she never told him where that was."

"She must have either had money with her when she arrived or she got hold of it later," Melba said.

"Jones said she got money from somewhere around Thanksgiving. Said he didn't know the source of the money, but I have a feeling he actually knows more about Tara than he's willing to let on, though."

"Maybe Kanesha can get it all out of him," Melba said.

"If anyone can, she can," I said.

"Thinking about that money," Melba said slowly, "I'm wondering if Tara was involved in a bank robbery. That would explain why she was so private about her life. And why she changed her name."

"That's a good guess, although it's really far-fetched," I said. "I hadn't really thought about it, but it would explain a number of things if that's what happened."

"She must have seen someone involved in the robbery at the housewarming party." Melba warmed to her theme. "Maybe Tara made off with more of the money than she was supposed to, and the other person involved managed to track her down somehow."

"I talked to Alex about those people on the guest list that you didn't know," I said. "She didn't know them, either, but Sean told me about them."

"It must be one of them," Melba said. "Everyone else was local."

Melba rose and blew a kiss to Diesel. "Enough of this. We're not really getting anywhere. I'd better get back downstairs to my desk." She turned and walked out of the office.

A thought struck. "Hey, come back," I called out.

Melba reappeared in the doorway. She frowned. "What is it?"

"I forgot to tell you what Sean told me about those two strangers at the housewarming party."

She exchanged the frown for an expression of eager anticipation as she came back to the chair and made herself comfortable. "Okay, give."

"Sean said the man is a lawyer in Memphis named P. J. Jackson. He helped Sean with a case last year with Tennessee connections. Alberta Garner is a wealthy widow who is a friend of Jackson's."

"Maybe he's her boyfriend." Melba grinned. "Or maybe he isn't."

"That's as may be," I replied. "Sean didn't comment on that. He said he spoke only briefly to the woman."

Melba shrugged. "You need to find out more about them if you can."

"I'll do some searches and see what I can turn up," I said. "It would help if I knew what they look like."

"Why don't you call that guy at the paper here, Ray Appleby? He was there taking photographs, and I think the paper is probably going to run a piece on the party sometime this week. He might have caught them on camera."

"Excellent idea," I said. "I'll do that. Ray owes me a favor or two for some of the scoops I've given him on past murder investigations."

"Right." Melba stood and gave Diesel a couple of head rubs. "Now I really have to get back downstairs before Andrea sends the Mounties out to find me."

I chuckled as she left. Our mutual boss was one of the most laidback people I'd ever known. She knew Melba wouldn't stray far or for too long.

I checked my cell phone for Ray Appleby's number and clicked on the call icon. A few rings later, a gruff voice said, "Appleby."

"Hi, Ray," I said. "This is Charlie Harris. How are you doing?"

His tone lighter, Ray said, "Doing pretty good. Listen, I want to talk to you about that dead woman, Tara Martin. I saw that she was working part-time with you in the archive."

"We could do that," I said slowly. "I'm not sure how much I can tell you. That's my only connection to this." Kanesha had warned me not to talk to the press, but I didn't have to share what little I knew with Ray.

"You could give me some human-interest stuff, you know, tell me what she was like to work with, that sort of thing."

"Sure," I said. "That wasn't exactly why I was calling, though."

"Really?" Ray's tone had sharpened again. "Why did you call?"

"You were at my son's housewarming party, I believe," I said. "Taking pictures. Are you going to write some kind of feature for the newspaper about it?"

"Yeah, working on it now," he said. "So? You want me to mention you and Helen Louise in it? Or something else?"

"What I really want is to see the pictures you took," I replied.

"You want to make sure I got your good side?" He guffawed.

"No. I want to see if you got pictures of a couple of people there who aren't locals. A woman and a man."

"Why are you interested in them?" he asked. "Is this something to do with the murder investigation?"

"I honestly don't know," I said. "Melba told me she didn't know them."

"And if Melba doesn't know them, they're definitely strangers in town," Ray said smugly.

"Well, yes," I replied. "Could I get a look at your pictures?"

No reply was immediately forthcoming. I could almost see the wheels turning in Ray's agile brain.

"Tell you what," he said abruptly. "How about I come over to your place around four. I'll bring the pictures and let you look at them. How would that work?"

"Sounds good."

"I'll be there," he said.

"See you then." I put the phone down and checked my watch.

It was a few minutes after three-thirty. Might as well head home now.

I hadn't long to wait before I heard the front doorbell. I hurried to the door to admit Ray Appleby. "Come on in." I stood aside and waved him in. "Let's go to the den." Diesel and Ramses walked ahead of us after giving Ray a good sniff-over.

In the den Ray pulled a thumb drive out of his pocket. "All the pictures are on here."

I gestured to my computer. He went over to the desk and inserted the drive into my computer and called up the appropriate file. He then stood back so I could sit at the computer and go through the pictures. He appeared to have taken at least a hundred, if not more.

I glanced at a few of them, noting that Sean and Alex looked particularly fine that night. My handsome son and his beautiful wife. I couldn't help smiling.

Ray leaned over my shoulder and took control of the mouse. "I think I know the couple you're looking for. I didn't recognize them, either, and I knew almost everyone else. I'll find them for you." He scrolled down a couple of screens and then suddenly clicked on a photo to enlarge it. "There." He stood back. "Is that them?"

I took a good look at the man and woman. My eyes widened. I started to tell Ray he was wrong. The woman I saw was none other than Millie Hagendorf.

TWENTY-ONE

‖‖

So Millie Hagendorf was really Alberta Garner. What a weird twist.

Ray had evidently been watching me closely. "Do you recognize one of them?"

I had to think quickly. If I told Ray, I knew he would run with it. I needed to tell Kanesha and Sean about this woman and her two identities. Now I was more curious than ever to know why she wanted access to the archive. Had she been working with Tara or against her? Was she Tara's killer?

I decided to tell Ray what I knew. He had access to sources that I didn't, and he might be able to settle the question of the woman's real identity. "She came to the archive to talk about volunteering with me. She gave her name as Millie Hagendorf, though. But Sean knew her as Alberta Garner. She claimed to be a writer, and the name she gave me is her pseudonym."

Ray drew in an audible breath. "Is that so? I've never heard that name before. Are you sure it's the same woman?"

"Absolutely sure. Sean told me that Alberta Garner introduced herself as a widow. She was with P. J. Jackson, whom Sean does know. He's a lawyer from Memphis."

"Interesting. I wonder what her game is," Ray said.

"I do, too," I replied. "I didn't take to her. She came across as cold and hard to me. I've already decided not to accept her as a volunteer. She told me she's a romance writer and is working on a book about an archivist. She said she wanted to do research to make the background believable. I looked the name up on the internet but couldn't find anything about her."

"Sounds to me like she's after something in your archive," Ray said. "Do you have any idea what?"

I was pretty sure I knew what she was after, but I didn't think I could tell Ray exactly what it was. "I don't really know."

Ray frowned at me. I knew he was feeling frustrated. He sensed a big story, and I wasn't coming across with any information he could use. "You can't give me any more than that?"

"I really can't," I said with real regret. "Kanesha would have my hide if she knew I was talking to you now. Let alone if I let slip something that's part of the ongoing investigation."

"I hear ya," Ray said with deep feeling. "I don't want to be on her bad side, either. That woman scares the life out of me sometimes."

"She's as formidable as they come." I looked back at the screen. "Would you mind if I kept a copy of this photo? I'd like to show it to Melba before it hits the paper."

Ray shrugged. "Sure, go ahead."

I saved the photo we were looking at. Ray waited until I had finished; then he ejected the thumb drive from the computer and put it back in his pocket. "I'll see what I can find out about these two. Mr. Jackson and Ms. Hagendorf-Garner."

"I really appreciate it, Ray," I said. "I'll be happy to talk to you later, after the investigation is complete, if you like."

"Sounds good," Ray said. "Knowing you, based on your history of these things, there's bound to be something juicy I can write up." He grinned.

I escorted him to the front door, with the help of Diesel and Ramses. The latter started to follow Ray out the door, and I made a dive to scoop him up before he got outside. "Bad kitty," I told him. He ignored me and stared after the departing Ray.

I held on to him until the door was shut and locked. Then I put him down. "You can't go off with just anyone," I said. "We'd miss you if you did that."

Now he stared up at me, obviously not worried at all. I told him to scoot, and he ran into the kitchen.

"Come on, Diesel, let's go back to the den for a minute."

Back at the computer, I emailed a copy of the photograph to my work address and to Melba's, with a note explaining what it was.

I decided to send Sean the photo also, because I wanted him to identify these two people as Garner and Jackson so I could be absolutely certain who they were. If he did, then I would know for sure that Millie Hagendorf was up to no good. I asked him in the message to let me know as soon as possible. I did tell him how I had got a copy of the photo, but I didn't tell him about my conversation with

Ray Appleby. If he knew what I'd told Ray, he would probably lecture me again about getting involved.

I decided to do a little searching via the computer for Alberta Garner and P. J. Jackson. I found little of use to me. The persons I turned up didn't seem to connect with the two persons in the photograph. There was an Alberta Garner from Memphis, but she was an octogenarian. Obviously not Millie Hagendorf. Had Millie assumed Alberta's identity for some reason? It was entirely possible. Was she in any way tied to the elderly Alberta Garner? I couldn't find a connection.

P. J. Jackson turned up so many hits that I could have gone blind trying to sort through them all. Adding Memphis to the search strategy didn't help. What came up after that was pretty unhelpful. Not knowing what the initials stood for was a big hindrance to the search. The initials brought up too many useless hits. Even using searching techniques that we librarians used to narrow results didn't really help. Perhaps I gave up too soon, but it had already been a long day, and I was tired. I left the computer and went back to my recliner.

I hoped Ray Appleby would have better luck than I did. He no doubt had sources in Memphis he could call on, if these persons did have connections in that city. They could be from anywhere and simply have used Memphis because it was a large enough city and not far from Athena. Memphis had more than double the population of Jackson, our capital city.

I itched to call Kanesha to ask her about these two people, but I knew that was a nonstarter. Haskell, on the other hand, might tell me a little something.

I texted him the two names and asked him whether he knew who they were? I suggested that one or both of them might have been the source of Tara Martin's panic attack.

A few minutes later I received a text in return from Haskell. All it said was *Under investigation.*

I had to be satisfied with that. At least Kanesha was aware of these people and the possibility that they could somehow be involved in Tara's death. It didn't soothe that burning itch of mine, but it helped.

Melba called me. Without preamble, she said, "That woman is Millie Hagendorf."

"Yes, she is," I said.

"I don't think I really got that good a look at her at the party," Melba said. "I'd swear that her hair that night was brunette and not red."

"That's how it looked to me," I said. "But either that or the red hair had to be a wig. The face was distinctive enough, though."

"Yes, she looked stuck-up both in the photo and in person," Melba said.

I smiled. "If she's going about in disguise, she's going to have to learn to watch her expressions. That stuck-up face gives the game away."

"I wonder if either of those is her real name," Melba said. "What is she after?"

"Something Tara had, I reckon," I replied. "Otherwise she wouldn't be so keen on *volunteering* with me in the archive. I don't know what she expects to find. I've already found what Tara hid."

"She doesn't know that," Melba said.

"No, she doesn't," I said, "and I intend to make sure it stays that way. I'm not going to allow her access to the archive if I can help it."

"It's your call, and there's nothing she can do about it," Melba said. "Do you think Ray Appleby might turn up anything?"

"He has ways of getting information that neither of us has," I said. "I didn't find anything on the internet, except that there's an elderly Alberta Garner in Memphis who appears to be a wealthy woman."

"Interesting," Melba said. "Maybe our Millie is impersonating her."

"Possibly," I said. "I wish I knew what story she was telling people, besides what little she told Sean."

"All she has to do is swan around and pretend to be rich," Melba said. "You know how that intrigues most people, and they'll swallow anything if they think a person's rich."

"I'm going to see if Sean will tell me if he knows anything more about her," I said. "Did she know Tara would be there?"

"How could she know that, unless Tara told her?" Melba asked.

"That's a very good question." I had a sudden idea. "I'm going to send that photo to Helen Louise to see if she remembers seeing either of those two in the bistro." I had remembered what Helen Louise told me about a man who had asked about Tara. I shared that with Melba.

"Jackson could be that man," Melba said. "That's what you're thinking, right?"

"Yes, I think it's highly possible, and if Helen Louise identifies him, that proves that there is some sort of link to Tara. What it is, we'll have to find out."

"Send it to her now," Melba urged.

I went back to my computer and forwarded the message with the attached picture to Helen Louise's personal email. Once I had done that, I texted her and asked her to check her email for the photo as soon as she had time. I didn't tell her why I wanted her to look at the photo, but I knew she would be curious enough to do it.

Returning to the call with Melba, I said, "Done. I'm betting that Jackson is the same man."

"I bet he is, too," Melba said. "If only we could find out why they were after Tara."

"And whether one or both of them wanted her dead," I said.

I had an alert that a new call was coming in. Helen Louise. I said a hasty goodbye to Melba and answered Helen Louise. "Hello, sweetheart, did you look at the message?"

"I did, and that's the man," Helen Louise said. "You know the one I mean."

"I do, the man who was asking about Tara at the bistro," I said.

"Exactly. And seeing that picture reminds me that where I saw him originally was at the housewarming party. Do you think he is the reason Tara had the panic attack?"

"I think it's entirely possible," I said. "But get this. The woman in the photo is Millie Hagendorf. She's the one who came to talk to me about volunteering in the archive. Sean said she told him she was Alberta Garner."

"This stinks like week-old fish," Helen Louise said. "I'd better let Haskell know right away about this."

"Definitely," I said. "I texted him about the woman, and all he replied was *Under investigation*. So they're looking into them now, and so is Ray Appleby." I shared with her my conversation with Ray.

Helen Louise laughed. "Ray is like a terrier. He'll dig up something, I'm sure."

"Rats in a hole, no doubt," I said, and she laughed again.

"I need to get back to work. Talk to you later, love," she said.

I called Melba back and shared the gist of Helen Louise's side of the conversation with her. "Looks like things are developing fast," she said.

"I hope so. I want this investigation to be over with. I don't think we're safe with Tara's killer still out there. They haven't found what they're looking for, and I don't think they'll quit until they do."

"Or Kanesha stops them," Melba said with satisfaction.

"I'm praying she does, and soon," I said.

"In the meantime, you be on the alert," Melba said. "I'll be keeping my eye on that front door, and I'm going down right now to make sure the back door is locked. We don't want anyone sneaking in that way."

During the evening I did my best to keep my thoughts away from the mysteries surrounding Tara. Instead, I read until supper was ready. Neither Stewart nor Haskell was present, so I was left to enjoy Azalea's meatloaf, green beans, mashed potatoes, and cornbread on my own. I gave Diesel and Ramses bites of green beans, plus some chicken from the fridge that Azalea had left for them.

After that I read for a while until it was time to turn in. The house remained quiet except for the noise of the paws that ran up the stairs to my bedroom. I changed my clothes for my bedtime wear and climbed in alongside Diesel and Ramses. Helen Louise called, and we chatted for a few minutes. She wanted to run over the menu for our reception again. She had decided to change one of the desserts and wanted my opinion. I gave her my thoughts on profiter-oles, macarons, and religieuse as options, and we settled on having all three of them. I would have eaten any of Helen Louise's pastries happily, but I thought she wanted me to feel that I was really a part of the decision-making.

Diesel, Ramses, and I had a quiet night, and when the alarm went off, I felt rested and ready to face the day. I immediately thought of Tara, however, and I worried that something could have happened during the night.

Neither Stewart nor Haskell appeared for breakfast, and Azalea bustled out of the kitchen right after serving me, so I didn't have a chance to talk to her before it was time for Diesel and me to head to work.

We arrived about fifteen minutes early, and Melba was not yet in. We went on upstairs, and I settled in to work. I glanced occasionally at Tara's desk. I turned back to my cataloging and was able to focus on it until I heard a knock at the door and turned to see a tall, distinguished-looking man about my age standing there.

TWENTY-TWO

IIIIIIIIIIIIIIIIIIIIIIIIIIIIIIIIIIIIIIIIIIIIIIIIIIIIIIIIIIIIIII

After that moment of surprise, my memory kicked in. I had seen a picture of this man. He was P. J. Jackson, the lawyer from Memphis.

"Good morning." I rose from my chair. "Can I help you?"

My visitor strode forward, hand extended. I stepped around my desk to meet him.

"I'm P. J. Jackson, Mr. Harris." We shook hands. "I'm glad to meet you."

Diesel jumped down from the window to come meet the visitor. Jackson appeared slightly startled, but he held out his fingers for Diesel to sniff. "What a beautiful animal. This is Diesel, I assume?" He scratched Diesel's head.

"Yes, he is," I replied. "How do you know his name?" I gestured for him to take a seat, and I returned to mine behind the desk. Diesel allowed another scratch of the head before he returned to his window seat.

Jackson seated himself and crossed one leg over the other. I noted the expensive shoes and the silk socks. The latter matched his tie. His suit appeared tailor-made for his tall, slender, but muscular frame. I had no doubt this was an expensive suit. The man seemed to ooze success, confidence, and affability.

I gazed past Mr. Jackson to see Melba appear in the doorway. Her curiosity, and her appreciation of a good-looking man, had brought her to my door. I signaled her to come in.

"Mr. Jackson, this is my friend Melba Gilley. She's the administrative assistant to the head of the library."

Jackson rose to shake Melba's hand, and I noted his appreciative gaze as he looked down at her. Melba didn't quite simper, but her smile was definitely friendly.

"How do you do?" Melba said.

"Very well, and you?" Jackson replied.

"Just fine." Melba tore her gaze away and pulled the chair from Tara's desk. She situated the chair by my desk so that she could continue to gaze at Mr. Jackson. He resumed his seat and smiled at Melba.

"What can I do for you, Mr. Jackson?"

He switched his attention to me. "I rather think that I might be able to do something for you, Mr. Harris."

"Please, go ahead," I said, intrigued by his words.

"You perhaps are aware of the fact that I worked with your son on a case last year."

I nodded to indicate that I did know.

"I went by his office last week when I came to town simply to say hello, and we ended up having lunch together," Jackson said. "That's when he told me about the housewarming party, and he invited me to attend, as I planned to be in Athena for several days. I accepted, and I attended, along with one of my clients from Memphis, who also was in town."

"That was Alberta Garner," I said.

Jackson inclined his head. "Yes, it was. Ms. Garner is actually the reason for my visit to you today." He paused. "Ms. Garner is what you might call quirky, also unpredictable. She has a vivid imagination, and sometimes she pretends to be someone else."

"Like a romance writer named Millie Hagendorf?" Melba said.

With a pained expression Jackson said, "Yes. She has always been an avid reader, particularly of detective stories. She sometimes fancies herself as a feminine version of Sherlock Holmes and assumes disguises."

Jackson appeared serious, so I didn't laugh as I would have liked to. "Do you have any idea why she came to my office and pretended to be a romance writer?"

"I'm afraid that might be my fault," Jackson said. "I learned of your sleuthing adventures from your son. He's rather proud of you, you know."

"That's nice to hear," I said, secretly delighted.

"I mentioned you to Ms. Garner, and she became determined to meet you," Jackson said. "I suggested that Sean might be able to arrange an introduction, if you were willing, but she declined. Her enthusiasms come and go quickly, and I assumed she had forgotten about it." He shook his head. "I found out last night that she had approached you in the guise of Millie Hagendorf."

"She did," I said. "She told me she was thinking about including an archivist and an archive in a book, and she wanted to volunteer here in order to get to know more about what I do and so on. I told her she would have to go through our HR office and be vetted."

"Did she do that?" Jackson asked.

"She did," Melba said. "I got notice of it from HR."

Jackson appeared surprised. "I didn't realize she'd gone that far. She didn't tell me that part."

"I'll tell you frankly, Mr. Jackson," I said. "I had no intention of accepting her as a volunteer. She rubbed me the wrong way, and I was suspicious of her motives."

Jackson shrugged. "I doubt she would ever have actually worked as a volunteer. She will have to return to Memphis soon to take care of a number of things there."

"That's good," I said. "I wish her well, but I hope she won't waste any more of my time with this masquerade."

"I can assure you she won't," Jackson said. "Her business here will soon be accomplished." He started to rise.

"I have a question for you," I said.

Jackson settled back in the chair. "Certainly. What is it?"

"What is Ms. Garner's connection to a woman named Tara Martin?"

Jackson regarded me quizzically. "Why do you think there's a connection?"

"Instinct," I said. "Having Ms. Garner appear here right after Tara was run over was a big coincidence."

"Very well," Jackson said. "Yes, there is a connection between the two of them. Ms. Martin is suspected of stealing something really valuable from Ms. Garner, and we came to Athena to find Ms. Martin. Sadly, we never were able to find her, let alone talk to her."

"That's too bad," I said. "I'm sorry to hear that Tara was a thief. She was a hard worker, but she didn't let anyone get close to her."

"That was her way," Jackson said as he rose again.

I debated whether to ask Jackson if his client was a suspect in Tara's murder. Melba forestalled me.

"Did Ms. Garner run Tara down?"

Jackson appeared taken aback by Melba's blunt question. After a moment he said, "I don't believe so. She and I have spoken with your chief deputy, Ms. Berry, and accounted for our entire time here in Athena."

"How did Ms. Garner know to come to Athena to look for Tara?" Melba asked.

"She heard that Ms. Martin was here from someone who knows them both," Jackson said. "I believe his name is Jones."

Melba and I shared a startled gaze. Ryan Jones was the link between the women. He told me how he knew Tara, but how on earth did he know Alberta Garner as well?

I voiced this question to Jackson. He shook his head. "I don't know. Ms. Garner hasn't told me. Now, if you'll pardon me, I really must be going." He nodded first to Melba and then to me. "Good morning." He turned and exited my office.

Melba and I sat and stared at each other for a moment. Jackson's unintentional bombshell had hit us pretty hard.

"Jones," I said. "Knowing that makes me suspicious of that whole homeless story he told me about Tara. I bet he made it all up. He must have known Tara in Memphis before she came here."

"Why did she come to Athena, of all places?" Melba asked.

"I have no idea, unless there's a connection we know nothing about," I replied.

"Possibly," Melba said. "Maybe we'll find out at some point. Now, I wonder what Tara stole. Obviously something really valuable. A painting? Jewelry? Money?"

"Could be any of those things," I replied.

"What about a rare book?" Melba asked.

"Possible," I said. "I'd think it'd have to be worth millions, though, for someone to be killed over it."

"Especially when they haven't recovered it," Melba said.

"We don't know for sure that it hasn't been recovered, whatever it is," I said. "Someone may actually have it and be long gone with it. Otherwise, why kill Tara? The killer must have gotten it from her, wouldn't you think?"

"I suppose so," Melba said. "But why was it necessary to run her down like that?"

"The killer could have done it out of anger," I said. "Even after recovering whatever Tara stole."

"What if Tara had a partner in the theft of whatever it was," Melba said slowly, "and the partner knew where it was but didn't want to share?"

"That's possible," I said. "That would make more sense of Tara's death. You may have hit it on the nose."

Melba looked pleased. "I have my moments."

I laughed. "You have plenty of them."

She rose from her chair and pushed it back into place at Tara's old desk. I realized I would be thinking of it as *Tara's desk* for a while. "I need to get back downstairs. I've got a ton of things to do."

Diesel and I bade her goodbye. I checked my watch and found to my surprise that it was almost two-thirty. I had an hour to go if I stuck to my usual schedule. Considering how much time I had spent on Tara's case, however, I should probably put in several hours' worth of overtime to make up for it. I decided to come to work tomorrow, normally one of my days at home. I really owed it to the college to put in the time.

I worked an extra half hour before calling it quits for the day. Diesel and I headed home.

"You're late today," Azalea said when we walked into the kitchen. Ramses immediately came to rub heads with Diesel. I bent to give him some scritches, and he purred in response.

"I worked a little overtime," I said. "I needed to make up some time spent on nonwork business."

"Like investigating this murder?" Azalea's bland expression didn't fool me. I always knew when she was teasing. "Does Kanesha know about this?"

"I'm not investigating the murder," I said. "Kanesha is aware of what involvement I have. I'm really on the sidelines on this one, for all practical purposes."

Azalea smiled. "Don't let her intimidate you, you hear? You help her, even though she don't like to admit it."

"Easier said than done," I replied. "There are some new leads in the case." I told her about the Memphis lawyer's visit to my office.

Azalea frowned. "That Ms. Garner sounds like a snake to me. You better watch out for her."

"I agree. I don't trust her at all," I said. "Dinner at the usual time?"

"Yes. Leftover meatloaf but some fresh vegetables," Azalea said.

"Do me a favor and take that little rascal with you." She pointed to Ramses. "He's been dogging my steps wanting food all day long."

I laughed. "I'll make sure he gives you some peace." I reached down and scooped him up in my arms. "Come on, you little pest. Give Azalea a break." He meowed happily and butted my chin with his head. Diesel meowed to let me know he didn't approve of the attention Ramses was getting. "Don't be selfish, Diesel. Let's go upstairs and change out of these work clothes."

Still carrying Ramses, and with Diesel leading the way, I made it to my bedroom. The cats made themselves comfortable while I changed. I decided to take a short nap. I closed the door so that Ramses would stay in the bedroom, and I set the timer on my phone for an hour. I did my best to quell my thoughts to keep my brain from occupying itself with the investigation into Tara's murder. Instead I concentrated on the forthcoming wedding and honeymoon.

On those pleasant thoughts I drifted off with the cats beside me. I awoke to the sound of the timer on my phone letting me know that my hour was up. I turned off the timer and sat up on the side of the bed. I yawned a couple of times before heading into the bathroom to splash water on my face and comb my hair.

The time was five-thirty when we made our way downstairs to the kitchen. Dinner would be served at six, and then Azalea would be off home.

I found Stewart in the kitchen, chatting with Azalea. He turned to greet us with a smile. We exchanged pleasantries about how our days had gone, and then I asked Stewart whether he expected Haskell home for dinner. To my pleasure, Stewart said he did. I hoped to get some information from Haskell.

Stewart insisted that he would serve the meal and urged Azalea to head on home. She put up only a small protest and allowed herself to be persuaded. Stewart had a way with her, and the two adored each other.

"I'm glad you talked her into going home," I said after she was safely out of the house. "I worry sometimes that she's working too much here."

"Don't let her hear you say that," Stewart said. "You know as well as I do that she's going to do as she pleases, and nothing we can say will slow her down."

"I know," I said. "I keep thinking Kanesha will step in and talk her into retiring."

Stewart laughed. "Yeah, I can see that working. Not."

I grinned. "You're right."

Haskell arrived home a few minutes after six. He washed up and, still in uniform, sat down to eat. Stewart served us meatloaf, roasted potatoes, and English peas, along with Azalea's homemade rolls. I purposely didn't bring up anything to do with the investigation. I waited instead until we were having coffee and pecan pie to test the waters.

"I had a visit from a lawyer from Memphis today," I said. "His name is P. J. Jackson. Have you met him?" I addressed the question to Haskell.

"I have, as a matter of fact," Haskell said. "He brought his client, Ms. Garner, to talk to Kanesha."

"Ms. Garner admitted that she knew the victim," Haskell continued. "Said the victim had stolen something from her, although she wouldn't say how. That's all the lawyer would allow her to say."

TWENTY-THREE

llllllllllllllllllllllllllllllllllllllllllllllllllllllllllllllllllllllll

"Jackson wouldn't let her say any more than that?" I asked. "That's about all he told me and Melba. They've got to be hiding something."

Haskell shrugged. "I agree. Kanesha appeared to take his word for that. She told them, however, not to leave town without her permission. The lawyer agreed, though Ms. Garner appeared angry about it."

"I'd love to watch Kanesha in action," Stewart said.

"I would, too," I said. "Especially with this woman. I wonder if she realizes that a sheriff's deputy is my good friend and lives in my house."

"I don't know," Haskell said. "She's pretty brazen, so if she knows, I don't think it will slow her down. Myself, I think she was in cahoots with Tara Martin and is after whatever Tara had."

"Do you think she could be the murderer?" Stewart asked.

"Can't rule her out," Haskell said. "But if she was working with Tara to steal the money, I don't think she'd kill Tara until she knew where the money was."

"What do you mean about money?" I asked. "How do you know that's what Tara stole? Jackson said only that it was something valuable."

Haskell looked uncomfortable, and I thought he must have revealed something he shouldn't have. He confirmed that right away.

"You're not supposed to know that, either of you," he said sternly. "I know you're not going to forget it, so I'll tell you one more thing. Those numbers you found in that book, Charlie? They represent a Swiss bank account number."

Stewart and I exchanged glances. That must mean there was a significant amount of money involved.

"Are you going to be able to find out who the account belongs to?" I asked.

"The sheriff's department can't, but perhaps the FBI can. They're working on it already. We have to prove that the account is connected to the murder. Since all we have is the account number, we're kind of stuck. If we knew who owned the account, it would help."

I frowned. "If Tara wrote down the account number and hid it so that someone else could find it, surely she must have kept a record of the other information necessary, like the name of the account holder, passwords, and so on."

"We think she did," Haskell said. "We still haven't found out where she was living. If we can find that out, we may be able to turn up the account information."

"I don't think she hid it in any of the books she handled," I said.

"I checked only the one box, though, the one that I found the account number in. Tomorrow I'll go through all the other boxes she handled and see if anything turns up. I'll let you know the minute I find anything."

"That's a good idea," Haskell said. "Since she hid the account number that way, she might have done the same thing with the other pieces we need."

"What about P. J. Jackson?" I asked. "I'm sure Helen Louise let you know he was the man who was asking about Tara at the bistro."

"She did," Haskell said. "We asked him about that, but all he said was that he was acquainted with her. I think he's stonewalling. He knows a lot more than he's telling."

"Athena PD is keeping close watch on her and Mr. Jackson," Haskell continued with a wry smile.

"Good," I said. "I've been meaning to ask, what happened with Ryan Jones?"

"We checked him out," Haskell said. "His real name is Ryan John Marsh, and he's done time for some minor stuff. Not known to be dangerous, just unlucky at getting caught."

"Is he involved in the cell-phone thefts that have been going on?" Stewart asked.

"We think he might be," Haskell said, "but we don't have any concrete evidence to connect him to the thefts."

"When did he show up in Athena?" I asked.

"Far as I know, several weeks ago," Haskell said with a shrug. "Why do you ask?"

"Did Jackson mention Marsh's connection to Ms. Garner and Tara?" I asked.

"Yes, but he didn't elaborate much beyond that," Haskell said, "but we're digging further into all their backgrounds."

"I'd say this is all a pretty strange coincidence, wouldn't you?" I asked.

Stewart nodded. "Sounds like more than a coincidence to me."

Haskell said, "I've learned that when you have these notions, there's often something to them."

I felt gratified at hearing that.

"Let's get the kitchen cleaned up." Stewart pushed back his chair and stood. "I'm ready to go upstairs and relax." He and Haskell exchanged smiles.

I pretended not to notice as I also rose to help. Stewart sent Haskell upstairs to change, and the two of us tidied the kitchen. I bade Stewart good night, gave Diesel and Ramses a few cold English peas apiece, and then we, too, headed up the stairs.

I didn't usually go to bed this early, but I didn't feel like watching television. Instead I decided I would read in bed until Helen Louise and I had our nightly phone call. Before long, those calls wouldn't be necessary, because we would finally be sharing a bed. For the rest of our lives. That made me so happy.

Sorting through the pile of books on my nightstand, I finally settled on Margery Allingham's *More Work for the Undertaker*. I had read it at least twice already, but the last time had been about a decade ago. It was one of my favorites of her books, and I looked forward to immersing myself in it again.

I was well into the middle of the book when Helen Louise called. After the usual remarks that a couple soon to be wed exchanged, I asked Helen Louise about P. J. Jackson, the man who had inquired about Tara. "What was he like?"

"He was pleasant and appeared to be genuinely concerned about Tara," Helen Louise said. "Well-dressed, attractive, good manners."

"Very smooth," I said. Then I told her about his visit to my office today, especially what he told us about Ms. Garner's penchant for disguises.

"Good grief," Helen Louise said after I had finished my story. "How does she keep track of who she is? That's nuts."

"I wonder why she thinks these multiple identities are necessary," I said. "Seems to me she has complicated things more than is necessary."

"I agree," Helen Louise said. "Maybe she gets her jollies from masquerading as other people."

"Could be," I replied. "But I don't see the logic in it."

"From what you've told me about her, she sounds pretty arrogant. She probably does think that we Athena hicks are stupid." Helen Louise laughed derisively.

"Kanesha's going to show her that was a mistake before long." I only wished I could be on hand when it happened.

"Do you think she could be the killer?" Helen Louise asked, her tone now serious.

"I really don't know," I said. "She's as good a possibility as anyone else. She knows Tara's real identity."

"What a rat's nest this all is," Helen Louise replied.

"True, but unfortunately we don't know how many rats are involved." That thought depressed me, but then I figured Kanesha probably knew more about potential rats in the case than we did. I was sure if Haskell were free to tell us what was going on with the investigation, we would both feel better. Time seemed to be slipping away, and as time went on, the murderer seemed more and more elusive.

"Kanesha will get there," Helen Louise said with conviction.

"She always has before," I said. "With or without my interference."

"The good thing this time is that you're working closely with Haskell and Kanesha and not putting yourself in the direct line of fire."

"I know, sweetheart," I said. "I'm trying to keep myself out of things whenever possible."

"Time to bid you good night, love," Helen Louise said. "It has been a long, tiring day."

"Rest well," I said, and she responded with, "You, too."

I smiled as I laid my phone on the nightstand. I was so incredibly lucky when it came to the women in my life. First, my beloved Jackie, my wife of many years and mother of our children. And now Helen Louise, another amazing woman. I wasn't sure I deserved this kind of luck, but I wasn't going to question fate.

I wasn't ready to turn out the light, so I went back to Albert Campion and his adventures with the undertakers. Allingham's rich imagination and her way with words never failed to engage me, and soon I was deep into the book again.

When I turned the last page, I checked the time, and it was a few minutes past midnight. I yawned and put the book aside. I didn't regret staying up to finish the book, although I knew I would pay for it tomorrow. Diesel and Ramses lay sound asleep beside me on the bed. I turned out the light and soon fell asleep.

The alarm went off all too early the next morning, and I thought briefly about not going in to work. Then I remembered I had told Haskell I would examine the rest of the books Tara had worked on to see if I could find anything else she might have hidden. In the bathroom I dashed cold water on my face before putting on my robe and making my way cautiously down the stairs.

I found Diesel and Ramses in the kitchen, begging Azalea for bacon as usual. She rarely cooked sausage anymore because of the spices they contained that weren't good for cats. Since I loved bacon—a bit too well for my cholesterol—I didn't mind having it for breakfast so often.

Forty-five minutes later Diesel and I were in our usual places in the archive office. I had gone into the rare-book room to start retrieving the boxes of books that Tara had processed and to bring them back to my office. I kept them organized by box number, Tara's system, and started on the first box.

The search for any clues Tara might have left in the books was tedious, and I soon developed a headache from the eye and shoulder strain. I stopped to take some aspirin and rest my eyes for a few minutes. I was midway through the second box when my cell phone rang. Ray Appleby was calling.

"Hi, Ray, what's up?" I asked.

"Hey, Charlie, got some news for you," Ray said. "I heard from a source at the sheriff's office that they've found out where the murdered woman was living, and they're investigating the place now."

TWENTY-FOUR

"Does your source leak information like this on a regular basis?" I asked, both intrigued and appalled. I wondered if Kanesha knew she had someone in her department with loose lips.

"Often enough," Ray said. "Now, do you want to hear about this or not?"

"I want to hear," I replied promptly.

"Okay, then," Ray said. "Now, the reason it took this long to find out anything is that the landlady has been on an Alaskan cruise, and she didn't get home until yesterday. She didn't see the newspaper accounts of the murder until this morning, but she got in touch with the sheriff's department right away."

"I'm glad she did. The sheriff's department needs every bit of information it can get," I said. "What's the landlady's name? And where does she live?"

"Her name is Caroline Burnes, and she lives not far from where the Martin woman was run down," Ray said. "On Eleanor Drive, if you know where that is."

"Vaguely," I said, trying to place it on my mental map of Athena.

"It's not hard to find. Anyway, Martin was renting a room over Ms. Burnes's garage."

"Know anything else?" I asked.

"Not at the moment," Ray replied. "The SD is going through the apartment, looking for information on the dead woman. Maybe you can get your boarder to talk when he gets home tonight." He laughed. "If you do, let me know. Otherwise I'll have to wait till my source coughs up some more information."

"My boarder doesn't tell me anything that's not approved by the chief deputy," I said. "I doubt I'll get anything out of him tonight to interest you."

"Keep me in mind anyway," Ray said. "Later."

I put my phone down to resume going through books, looking for hidden clues Tara might have left in them. I had to stop periodically to rub my shoulders and rest my eyes. Going page by page through the books and checking their bindings was tedious work. Several books had in excess of five hundred pages, and I thought my eyes would bug out before I finished them.

I managed to get through three boxes before I decided to take a longer break from the task. "Come on, Diesel, let's go downstairs. I need coffee."

Diesel slid out of the window embrasure and followed me out of the office. I paused long enough to lock the door. I didn't want any surprises.

The coffeepot sat empty in the staff lounge. I made a fresh pot, enough for four cups of coffee. The way I felt at the moment, I figured it would take at least two to revive me. Melba liked coffee in the afternoon, and she could probably finish off the remaining two cups. Our boss, Andrea, was bubbly enough without resorting to caffeine in any form.

I texted Melba and invited her to join me in the lounge for coffee. I added two words that I knew would be irresistible. *New information.*

Sure enough, Melba appeared in the lounge in under a minute without taking the time to reply to my text. The coffee wasn't quite ready, so she took a seat on the sofa with me, leaving room for Diesel in the middle. He moved to put his head in her lap, and she stroked him while we talked. What a sponge my cat was.

"What's the new information?" she asked.

"Ray Appleby called me. He has a source inside the sheriff's office, and he told me they found out where Tara was living. She was renting a garage apartment on Eleanor Drive from a woman named Caroline Burnes. Do you know her?"

"*Of* her, I do. Not personally," Melba said. "She's apparently crazy as a Betsey bug with scads of money. Everyone wonders why she doesn't move out of that neighborhood since she could afford a nice house in a safer area."

"The location at least explains why Tara had me drop her off at that apartment complex," I said.

Melba nodded. "Yes, it's just a couple of streets over from Eleanor Drive."

"The cops are there now going through the apartment, trying to find more information on Tara," I said. "I'm sure Ray will hear about what they find, if anything, before I do. He seems to think Haskell will tell me things like that."

"He and Stewart dated a few times years ago," Melba said with a sniff. "He's probably jealous of Haskell."

I laughed. "That might be." I glanced at the coffeemaker and saw that it had finished. I got up to pour coffee for both of us, but I handed Melba her mug. What she put in her coffee at any time varied, depending on how she felt about her weight. She always looked trim to me, but there were times when she claimed she had gained weight and needed to lose five or ten pounds.

"I sure hope they find out something that can bring this whole mess to a conclusion," Melba said as she added cream and three spoons of sugar to her coffee. Evidently this wasn't one of the times she was concerned about her weight. I hid a smile as I watched.

I added my usual two spoons of sugar and a large dollop of cream to my own cup. We settled ourselves on the sofa again, and Diesel resumed his position with his head in Melba's lap.

"I hope so, too," I said. "Surely they'll find something there to tell them who she really was. I wonder if she had any family at all."

"These days, you can never tell," Melba said. "She might have been an only child like you and me, with no cousins, parents, and so on still living."

"True." I had a sip of my coffee.

"Do you think she embezzled money from someone?" Melba asked.

"If there's a Swiss bank account involved, there's probably chicanery in there somewhere. Some person is bound to be missing that money, I should think, and may have been willing to kill to get it back." I shared with Melba what Haskell had revealed about the numbers I had found inside the yellow-fever book.

"Or maybe Tara had a partner in the embezzlement who was willing to kill to take it for themselves," Melba said.

"Either way is possible," I said. "I've been going through more of the books that Tara processed for me, looking for any more hidden bits of information. So far, nothing, except a headache and a sore neck. Oh, and tired eyes, too."

"Are you planning to put in a full day today?" Melba glanced at her watch. "It's nearly lunchtime now. Why don't you go on home and call it a day."

"I want to get through at least one more box," I said. "This coffee is perking me up a bit. Then I'll probably go home for lunch. I'll decide after that whether to come back for work this afternoon."

"Sounds like a good plan." Melba rose, gently dislodging Diesel. She went over to the coffeemaker and topped up her mug, adding more sugar and cream. "Thanks for making this. I'd better get back to my desk."

Diesel padded after her, obviously in need of more attention. He was so sadly neglected after all.

I remained in the lounge a few minutes longer, enjoying my coffee and feeling comfortable on the sofa. I was tempted to stretch out on it for a short nap, but I knew better than to doze off at work. Andrea was pretty lenient about things, but even she might draw the line at staff napping on work time.

I refilled my cup with the last of the coffee, dumped the grounds, and rinsed out the pot before heading back to the office. All was quiet on the second floor as I unlocked my door and stepped inside.

I spared a baleful glance for the boxes of books I had yet to go through. I decided I would look over one more box before I headed home for lunch, and possibly for the day.

About fifteen minutes later Diesel sauntered in, looking rather pleased with himself. He was really shameless when it came to begging attention from his favorites, particularly Melba. I patted his head before he climbed into the window. "We'll be going home for lunch soon," I said, and he meowed in response.

I turned back to the book I was examining. Oddly enough, it was a book on the 1878 yellow-fever epidemic in Mississippi. I finished leafing through the pages without finding anything unusual. I held the covers open wide in order to examine the interior of the spine, expecting to find nothing. To my surprise, however, I spotted a slender piece of paper inside. I found my tweezers and pulled the paper out. Laying the book aside, I carefully unfolded the paper I had found.

Another string of numbers. I counted them, and again there were twenty-one. This string looked different from the one I had found before, but given the number of digits, it had to be another Swiss bank account number, I thought.

I texted Haskell to tell him what I found, and he responded within a couple of minutes to say that he was on the way to retrieve it. I told him I would wait in the office until he could get here.

I put my phone aside, grabbed a piece of scrap paper, and copied the numbers onto it. I folded my copy and stuck it in my pocket. There was probably no point in my having copies of these bank account numbers, but I figured there was no harm in having a backup, just in case.

Out of curiosity I went into the back end of our library system and called up the bibliographic record of the book. I had scanned it a couple of days ago when I checked all the books on Tara's spreadsheet, or at least I thought I had. When I looked at the tag for local notes, I found a notation similar to the one I had found in the other yellow-fever book. This time it was #11 TM.

I frowned. Why hadn't I noticed this when I had looked at it before? I opened Tara's spreadsheet and searched for this title on it, and there it was. I had to put it down to human error on my part. I had overlooked it somehow.

When Haskell turned up a few minutes later, I pointed to the paper on the desk. He put it carefully in an envelope using my tweezers. "Thanks, Charlie," he said. "Looks like potentially another account number."

"That's what I thought," I said. "I should have found it sooner. I somehow overlooked it before when I was going through the records of the books Tara had handled. I feel stupid for not having found it earlier."

Haskell smiled. "You're only human, Charlie. The important thing is that you found it. I'm going to take it back to Kanesha right away. She'll appreciate it." He hesitated a moment. "Kanesha might want to impound all the boxes that Tara worked with, but I'm not sure we have the manpower at the moment to go through them. It's probably better that you keep doing it for now until I talk to her about it."

"Good," I said. "I hope she appreciates that I'm trying to keep my nose out of this case as much as possible and not out trying to investigate on my own."

"She does, I'm sure." Haskell laughed. "You know, she really does like you, Charlie."

"I'm glad to hear it," I said truthfully. "Are you involved in the search of Tara's apartment?"

Haskell's eyes narrowed. "How do you know about that?"

Oops. I probably shouldn't have asked that question.

"I might as well come clean," I said with a grimace. "Ray Appleby called me and told me that y'all had heard from Tara's landlady."

"How did he find out?" Haskell asked, his tone grim.

"He says he has a source in your department, or maybe it's in the police department," I said. "I'm not sure which."

"I think we'd better find out and put a stop to any leaks," Haskell said. "Kanesha will want to talk to Appleby, and I'm sure the chief of police will, too. Now, why did he call *you*?"

"I called him first," I said. "I wanted to see the pictures he took from Sean and Alex's party the other night. I was looking for pictures of Alberta Garner and P. J. Jackson. He said he would share them with me, and I invited him to my house."

"He knew you were interested in the case," Haskell said, "so he shared his scoop with you. Probably because he thought you might know something to trade for it."

I shrugged. "I didn't tell him anything about the numbers that I found, so unless his source knew I found them, I doubt he knows about them. Now, back to my original question. Have you found anything in that apartment that tells you who Tara really was?"

"We did find an old driver's license," Haskell said. "I can't reveal the name, however. If Kanesha knew I told you this much, she'd probably scalp me. We're working on tracking down information on her under that name. We haven't found anything so far that sheds light on those Swiss bank account numbers."

"I guess you'll have to dig further into her past to find out anything to connect her with them."

"We will. I'd better get going," Haskell said. "Hope to see you tonight at dinner."

"See you then," I called after his retreating figure.

They had found an old driver's license. That was something. I wondered whether Ray Appleby's source knew that, and whether the source knew the name on that license.

I was surprised they hadn't found anything else. Surely Tara would have had something more with information about those accounts within easy reach.

If they hadn't found it in her apartment, where else might it be?

TWENTY-FIVE

IIIIIIIIIIIIIIIIIIIIIIIIIIIIIIIIIIIIIIIIIIIIIIIIIIIIIIIIIIIIIII

I reasoned that, since Tara had hidden the two account numbers in books and that mysterious key in her desk, it was likely that she might have hidden more here.

That left the archive office and the rare-book room. Tara had had only restricted access to the rare-book room. She'd had to go into it a few times to switch out processed boxes with ones awaiting processing, but I couldn't recall that she'd spent any extra time doing that. She could have espied a good hiding place, however, while she was in there. I might as well look.

Not until after lunch, though. I needed a break from going through books, and I was ready for food. I would come back here for the afternoon and go through the rare-book room. The rest of the boxes of books Tara had processed could wait a bit. Right now I was focused on finding a notebook or papers that Tara might have hidden. They weren't in the boxes of processed books, so the rare-book room was the logical place to look.

"Come on, Diesel," I said. "Let's go home."

We were back in the office scarcely an hour later. I checked my email in case anyone had sent anything, but there was nothing new.

I took Diesel into the rare-book room with me. I usually didn't, but with the strange people who had been in and out of the office, I didn't want to leave him alone. I even locked the archive office door. I was probably being overly cautious, but I didn't want to take any chances.

I also locked us in the rare-book room. I texted Melba to let her know where we were, however, in case she needed me for any reason.

Standing only a couple of steps inside the room, I looked around, trying to think as Tara might have if searching for a good place to hide something. Perhaps a small notebook? If she had hidden scraps of paper, it might take months to find them. I knew the shelves and the contents of this room pretty well, but I hadn't memorized the position of every book on every shelf. I was certain, anyhow, that Tara would have been careful to put things back the way she found them in order to make sure no one noticed what she had hidden.

The easiest thing for Tara to have done, I considered, would have been to hide something behind the books on a shelf. That would be the easiest search to perform, although it required a lot of removing books and then putting them back in place. I would get my aerobic exercise during the search.

I started with the nearest range of shelves and began methodically taking out books from the center of the shelf and stacking them on the floor. That way I could reach with my arm to either side to feel for anything hidden there. The shelves closer to the floor were harder to search, because I had to get down on my hands and knees. I would be stiff tomorrow from all the exertion, but this had to be done.

By the time I had worked my way around the room and through every set of shelves, I was tired, dusty, and frustrated. My major discovery was the dust that had accumulated since the room had last been cleaned. I would see to that in a day or two.

I found absolutely nothing hidden behind the books on the shelves. Diesel had followed along with my search for about fifteen minutes before he got bored and found a spot for a nap. I felt like curling up beside him now. The remaining option was to search through the books themselves, but I didn't have the energy to start that this afternoon. I'd have to think more about this idea that Tara could have hidden anything else here.

Time to head home and have a nice, relaxing hot shower to soothe stiff muscles that would be even more sore tomorrow. I woke Diesel, and we left the rare-book room. I made sure the door was locked. I unlocked the archive office to retrieve my jacket and other effects. Then we headed down to the parking lot.

Once we reached home, after greeting Azalea and Ramses in the kitchen, I went immediately to my bedroom, stripped off my clothes, and turned the shower on full blast. Diesel had remained downstairs, letting me stand under the blessed hot water without scratching on the shower door, wanting to get me out.

I felt like warm rubber when I eventually got out of the shower.

The water still ran hot, so I hadn't exhausted the supply. I toweled off thoroughly and sat on the edge of the bed to cool down. Drowsiness threatened to pull me down on the bed for a nap, but I resisted. If I napped this late in the afternoon, I would have trouble going to sleep tonight.

I went into the bathroom and splashed cold water on my face to wake me up, then held my wrists under the water to help bring my body temperature down. Once I felt cooler, I dressed in casual clothes and went downstairs to the kitchen, feeling relaxed and limber.

After a brief conversation with Azalea about dinner, I collected Ramses and went to the den, with Diesel leading the way. I made myself comfortable in my recliner, with Ramses in my lap and Diesel stretched out on the floor beside us. I pulled out my phone and texted Helen Louise, asking her to call me when she had a moment.

She called me within a minute. I realized that she was not working at the bistro today, and I could have called her instead.

"Hello, sweetheart," I said. "Enjoying your day off?"

"Mostly," she said. "I've been going over wedding arrangements to make sure everything is moving ahead properly."

"Have I forgotten to do anything I should have by now?" I felt a bit anxious because I had so little to do, compared with what Helen Louise was overseeing.

She laughed. "No, not that I know about. Take a look at the schedule and see."

"I will, I promise."

"Good. What have you been up to today?"

I told her about my fruitless searches in the rare-book room, and she commiserated.

"Have you heard any more about Jackson, the man who was asking about Tara?" Helen Louise said.

"No. I found another slip of paper hidden in one of the books Tara processed. It had numbers on it, too. Different from those on the first slip I found."

"So a second Swiss bank account, most likely."

"I believe so," I said. "I wonder if and when they'll be able to find out who's the owner of the accounts."

"Unless someone comes forward with proof of ownership, it could take a long time. The Swiss banks guard those accounts closely."

"They're notorious for it," I said. "Can you imagine what it would be like to have that kind of money secreted in a tax haven?"

"No, I can't," Helen Louise said. "It makes me furious that the rich get away with it and don't pay their fair share of taxes."

"I agree with you on that." I was comfortably off, thanks to my inheritance from my aunt, along with my pension from Houston for my years in the public-library system. I was scrupulous, however, in paying my taxes and resented those who managed to avoid paying their due.

"Good thing that we agree on such matters," Helen Louise said. I knew she was smiling.

"Exactly, or I would never have asked you to marry me," I said in a mock-indignant tone.

"You cad." Helen Louise laughed.

We exchanged a few more remarks before we ended the call. I put away the phone, grinning like an idiot. She was truly a wonderful woman, and I felt so incredibly lucky that she loved me.

I put the phone aside and debated what to do until dinner was ready. I couldn't quite make up my mind and ended up turning on the TV to watch old sitcoms from the fifties and sixties on my favorite nostalgia channel. I had seen the episodes multiple times over the years, but this was comfort viewing for me. I didn't have to think much about what was happening, and I could relax with the familiar.

After almost half an hour of this, I was beginning to doze off, but my phone alerted me to a new text message. To my surprise, I discovered it was from Kanesha Berry.

Can you come to my office now? Need to discuss something with you.

What on earth did she have to discuss with me? I wondered. Did she think I was sticking my nose into the case? All I had done was share information with her office. I couldn't think of any way in which I had overstepped boundaries.

I texted back that I would be at her office within twenty minutes. I needed to go upstairs to change. The cats accompanied me. A few minutes later I was back in the kitchen with Azalea. I explained where I was going and asked her to keep an eye on Diesel and Ramses while I was gone.

"What do you think she wants?" Azalea asked.

I shrugged. "I have no idea. I can't figure out why she wants to see me. I've been keeping my nose out of the case as much as possible."

"With that daughter of mine, you never know." Azalea shook her head. "Don't let her bully you."

Easier said than done, I thought, but aloud I said, "I won't. I'm hoping I'll be back in an hour or so." I headed out to the garage.

Nearly fifteen minutes later I reached the sheriff's department headquarters. I found a parking spot straight away. I headed inside. The deputy on duty at the desk recognized me and waved me on to Kanesha's office. I thanked her and headed down the hall. As I neared Kanesha's room I saw that the door was slightly ajar. I could hear her talking, whether to a person actually in the room with her or on the phone, I couldn't tell, because hers was the only voice I could hear.

I stopped a couple of feet away from her door to listen. I heard the faint murmur of a low-pitched voice that sounded vaguely masculine. I stepped forward and knocked on her door. Kanesha looked up and acknowledged me.

"Come on in, Charlie," she said.

I stepped into the office. To my surprise I saw that the person with Kanesha was a woman. Perhaps in her seventies, the woman had short blond hair liberally streaked with gray, an alert gaze, and intensely focused green eyes.

"Good afternoon," the stranger said, extending a hand. "Glad to meet you, Mr. Harris."

I took her hand and almost winced at the strong grip with which she shook my hand.

"Glad to meet you, too." I looked to Kanesha to make the introduction.

"Charlie, this is Caroline Burnes," she said. "She was Tara

Martin's landlady, and she has some interesting things to share with you."

I looked back at Ms. Burnes. "I'm certainly intrigued."

Kanesha motioned to a chair near the one in which her other visitor sat. "Have a seat." She got up to close her office door.

Ms. Burnes reached toward Kanesha's desk to retrieve a folder that she handed to me. "Go ahead and take a look," she said.

My eyes widened in shock when I glanced at the first piece of paper in the folder.

TWENTY-SIX

I was staring at a newspaper clipping with a startling headline.

MEMPHIS WOMAN DISAPPEARS AFTER EMBEZZLING FROM SISTER

There was a picture of the subject of the headline. I had to stare hard at it for nearly a minute before it finally penetrated my brain that I was looking at a picture of Tara Martin.

She was barely recognizable, because the woman in the picture had styled hair, makeup, and jewelry. Tara had, most of the time, kept her face averted or her head downcast, so I rarely ever had a look at her full-on. But this was Tara.

Except that wasn't her name. According to the article, her name was Georgia Canterbury. There was no picture of her sister, but I had a sudden inkling who her sister was based on what Georgia looked like in the picture.

Millie Hagendorf and Alberta Garner resembled the woman in the picture. I scanned the article quickly while Kanesha and Ms. Burnes waited.

"This is amazing," I said. "I thought she was hiding from someone or something. She must have spotted her sister at my son's housewarming party. That's why she bolted."

"What are you talking about, if you don't mind my asking?" Ms. Burnes tilted her head at me in an inquisitive posture.

"Tara was working at the bistro on the square. They catered a party for my son and daughter-in-law about two weeks ago, and Georgia"—I stumbled slightly over the name—"suddenly ran out of the back of the house. When I finally found her, she said she'd had a panic attack because of all the strangers in the house."

Ms. Burnes sniffed. "I'd have a panic attack myself if I spotted the sister that I'd stolen millions of dollars from."

I looked at Kanesha, who nodded. "The FBI has been searching for Ms. Canterbury for nearly six months."

"She didn't make it far from Memphis," I said. "You'd think she would have headed out of the country as fast as she could." *To Switzerland,* I thought.

"Her embezzlement was discovered almost immediately," Kanesha said. "The FBI was on her trail pretty quickly, and all major airports with international flights were alerted to be on the lookout. She went to ground here instead, though I'm not sure why she chose Athena, of all places."

"I wish I could answer that for you," Ms. Burnes said. "She didn't confide in me at all." She gestured to the folder I still held. "I found that on the desk in her apartment when I went up to check on her right after I returned home from my cruise to Alaska. It was open. She owed me a month's rent."

"Did you realize then that she had been murdered?" I asked.

Ms. Burnes shook her head. "I'm not normally nosy about my tenants' private affairs, but this girl always struck me as odd. I hoped she had left the money for me in the folder. She usually left it on the desk for me to collect. When I saw that, I didn't recognize her in the picture. I thought it was just some story she was interested in. I knew she liked to watch true-crime shows on television."

"When did you realize that Georgia and Tara were the same person?" I asked, wondering why Kanesha was not taking part in the conversation. I glanced at her, but as usual her expression gave nothing away. Surely she had heard all this already and had asked the same questions.

"Not until I saw the paper the next morning with the stories about the murder. I looked at the picture in the paper, and it hit me suddenly that she and the embezzler were probably the same woman." Ms. Burnes shrugged. "That's when I called the sheriff's department as requested in that article."

"We really appreciate that you got in touch with us so quickly, Ms. Burnes," Kanesha said. "We were at a standstill trying to figure out who the victim really was and where she had been living."

"That's what it said in the paper," Ms. Burnes said.

"How long had she been renting from you?" I asked.

"Nearly three months," Ms. Burnes replied. "She answered an ad in the paper in mid-November, I think it was."

That jibed with what Ryan Jones had told me. I presumed he had told Kanesha the same thing.

I went back to the article to check something. "Says here she was a skilled computer person in the financial sector."

"Her sister confirmed that," Kanesha said.

"So Georgia obviously knew how to steal the money and put it somewhere else," I said.

"Yes," Kanesha replied with a warning glance.

I figured she didn't want me to say anything about Swiss bank accounts. I blinked to let her know I understood.

"Was this folder the only thing you took from Ms. Canterbury's apartment?" Kanesha asked.

"Yes, it is," Ms. Burnes said. "I didn't touch anything else, I can assure you."

"Thank you, Ms. Burnes." Kanesha rose. "We'll ask you to make a statement before you leave, if you have time."

"I do," Ms. Burnes said.

Kanesha picked up the phone, punched in a number, and spoke into the receiver. "Ms. Burnes is ready to make a statement." She replaced the receiver.

Now Kanesha rose and indicated that Ms. Burnes should come with her. I started to rise, but Kanesha shook her head. I waited for Kanesha to return.

"Why did you ask me to come here?" I asked as soon as Kanesha appeared. "I mean, I appreciate finding out who Tara really was, and I confess I had eventually figured out she must have stolen money."

"Partly because you've been helpful without interfering and going off on your own, the way you usually do," Kanesha remarked as she resumed her seat at the desk. "Partly because I need to pick your brain."

"Okay, go ahead and pick," I said, trying not to sound smug.

"You finding those numbers the victim hid in the rare books was an important clue to what we were dealing with. We knew almost right away that they were Swiss bank account numbers, but that was all. We were looking for a major theft, but we didn't zero in on Georgia Canterbury until Ms. Burnes brought us that folder."

"Why did her sister show up and go through those imperson-ations?"

Kanesha shrugged. "I think she hoped to retrieve the stolen funds without any help from the FBI. She's an odd woman."

"So was her sister," I said. "Any idea about the source of the money?"

"Inheritance," Kanesha said. "They had a very wealthy father who left the bulk of his estate to his older daughter, Ms. Garner. Ms. Canterbury had married a man he didn't like or trust, so he wouldn't leave her money."

"What about the man?" I asked. "Is he in the picture anywhere?"

"We're not sure," Kanesha said. "The problem is that we don't have a picture of him. Ms. Garner gave us only a vague description of him. Says she only met him once, and that was about seven years ago. There was no picture in the victim's effects, so we're working blind."

"What about Ryan John Marsh?" I asked, struck by a sudden inspiration. "The lawyer, P. J. Jackson, said that Marsh knew both the sisters."

"We're digging further into his background. We're looking for connections to both the sisters," Kanesha said.

"Surely the most likely suspect in the murder is the sister or the husband," I said.

"Normally, I would agree with you," Kanesha said. "Ms. Garner pointed out, however, that it made no sense for her to kill her sister without knowing how to get back the money that was stolen."

"Good point," I said. "Are you sure she doesn't know how to retrieve the money?"

"Not completely, which is why I'm keeping Ms. Garner high on the list of suspects. It's a very short list," Kanesha said.

"How did they track her to Athena? She seemed to have covered her tracks pretty well."

"Apparently Ms. Garner thought Athena was the most likely place for her sister to hide, because their maternal grandmother lived here when they were children," Kanesha said.

"Looks like she was right," I said. "Do they have any other family in Athena?"

Kanesha shook her head. "The grandmother was the only one, and she died around twenty years ago. She was a widow at the time. Her daughter was Ms. Garner and Ms. Canterbury's mother."

"What was the grandmother's name?" I asked. Melba would be fascinated to hear about this connection. I wondered if the grandmother's name would stir up any memories.

"Her last name was Hart, Lizzie Hart, I think Ms. Garner said."

The name didn't ring any bells for me, but I was willing to bet that Melba probably knew it. "It wasn't smart of Tara, I mean, Georgia, to try to hide here from her sister."

"It wasn't, but perhaps she hadn't planned far enough ahead before she embezzled the money," Kanesha said. "Or she thought that her disguise was enough to keep her sister from tracking her down."

I remembered the incident with the phone that Tara had destroyed. I mentioned it to Kanesha.

She shrugged. "I suppose it could have been Ms. Garner, but we don't know. Mr. Jones wasn't able to give us the number for that phone. Or he lied about it."

"Whoever it was, Tara feared that person. She sounded angry, and Melba, who overheard the exchange, also thought she sounded frightened." I paused for a moment. "Speaking of Jones, was he able to provide any help at all? Who is he, exactly?"

"To answer your second question first, Jones is a man of many trades apparently. He hasn't been in Athena long. What we've discovered is that he does all kinds of things for money. Nothing illegal so far. He doesn't stick to one job."

"Like selling refurbished cell phones," I said.

Kanesha nodded. "To answer your first question, Jones gave us some of the victim's background for when she first arrived in Athena. I have a couple of deputies working with the homeless group she lived with to see if any of them knows any more about her."

"I hope you can find out more."

"I'm hopeful we can," Kanesha said. "Now, I have a question for you, but an explanation first. One thing we expected to find when we finally tracked down the victim's real home but didn't was some kind of documentation related to those Swiss bank account numbers. You haven't found anything like that at the archive office, have you?"

"No, I haven't," I said. "I'm going through the boxes in the rare-book room, though. She could have hidden something there. Haskell said you might not have the manpower to go through them, so I'm happy to do it."

"Haskell is right. We're stretched thin at the moment," Kanesha said. "I have a court order to remove the computer she was using in order to examine it thoroughly. It's possible she might have put something on it."

"Why didn't you do that sooner?" I asked.

"We have to do these things by the book," Kanesha said. "It takes time to arrange. A couple of my officers are there right now to retrieve the computer."

"I'm sure I'll hear about it before long from Melba," I said.

"No doubt," Kanesha said in a wry tone. "I think that what we're looking for is most likely on that computer. Now that we know more from the victim's sister about what we're dealing with, it shouldn't be that hard to find."

"No further leads to the killer?" I asked.

"Not that I'm prepared to discuss with you," Kanesha said.

I had expected a statement to that effect, more or less, so I wasn't surprised. I had no official standing, after all, and Kanesha did things officially almost always.

I rose. "This has certainly been an informative meeting. Thanks for sharing what you did with me. I really do hope that you'll soon be able to identify Tara's killer and bring her, or him, to justice. She deserves it, despite the fact that she was an embezzler."

"Allegedly." Kanesha surprised me with that word.

"What do you mean?"

"We have only Ms. Garner's word for it that her sister embezzled the money," Kanesha said. "What if Ms. Garner or an associate embezzled the money and framed the victim?"

Dumbfounded, I stared at Kanesha.

She flashed a brief smile. "In my job, you have to think of every possible angle."

I shook my head as if to clear it. "That's one angle I never would have considered. I have to hand it to you. That's a clever twist."

"Remember that if I ever decide to run for sheriff." Kanesha rose. "Thanks for coming in. If you happen to run across anything else that might be pertinent to the case, let Haskell or me know right away."

"I sure will," I said, and at the time, I meant it.

TWENTY-SEVEN

On the way back home I continued to think about Kanesha's statement that Tara might not have been the embezzler. It was an interesting idea and a plausible reason for her disappearance and taking on a different name and a disguise. If Tara was truly innocent of embezzlement, why had she hidden those account numbers? If they were the original account numbers, then surely the sister had them. The only reason I could think of for hiding them was that the money had been moved into new accounts and Tara wanted to keep them secret from anyone who might find her.

If that was the case, then Tara must have been the embezzler. Kanesha had to consider every angle, but this one didn't seem plausible to me. I decided I wouldn't waste any more mental energy on it. It was all out of my hands anyway.

I found Stewart and Haskell in the kitchen when I returned home.

Ramses and Diesel greeted me with meows and leg rubs, and I patted their heads in thanks.

"Dinner's ready to put on the table," Stewart informed me. "Azalea left about ten minutes ago and charged me with serving. Have a seat."

"Thanks." I did as I was bidden. "What's on the menu tonight?"

"Corn on the cob, green beans, hamburger steak with mushrooms, onions, and gravy. And of course homemade rolls." Stewart set a glass of tea at my place, and I took a sip. Nice and chilled, the way I liked it.

"I heard that Kanesha called and asked you to come to her office," Haskell said. "Did you meet Ms. Burnes?"

"I did, and I was fascinated by what she brought. We finally know Tara's real name, though I can't get used to calling her Georgia," I said.

Stewart set a plate in front of me, then did the same for Haskell. Resuming his seat with his own plate on the table, he said, "Haskell's been telling me the story. He says the photograph in the newspaper clipping shows a very different-looking woman than the one you knew."

"She was actually an attractive woman, well-dressed, coiffed, and wearing jewelry. Nothing like the Tara I knew," I said.

"An effective disguise," Stewart said.

"Somebody saw through it, though," Haskell said. "Otherwise she wouldn't have been murdered."

"I was interested to find out there was an Athena connection," I said. "Tara's maternal grandmother lived here, and Tara and her sister visited her. So Tara was somewhat familiar with our town."

"What was the grandmother's name?" Stewart asked.

"Lizzie Hart," I replied. "I'm going to ask Melba if she knew her, or if she knew the family. I'll be surprised if she doesn't."

Haskell smiled. "I don't know how she does it, but she's like an encyclopedia when it comes to people in this town."

"I vaguely remember a Hart family," Stewart said. "I think that Mrs. Hart might have worked in the mayor's office when I was a kid. I went with my father to see the mayor when I was six or seven, and a nice woman gave me some bubble gum. I think she was a Mrs. Hart."

"That's a nice memory," I said.

Conversation lapsed for a few minutes while we all concentrated on our dinner. I had to dissuade Ramses from climbing onto my lap to sample my food. I also had to tell Diesel firmly there was nothing for him on my plate. I finally relented, however, and gave them each a few bites of hot buttered roll. That seemed to satisfy them.

Near the end of the meal, Haskell turned to Stewart. "What day is it that we're supposed to have dinner with Mike and Pete? I can't remember."

Stewart pulled a small notebook out of his shirt pocket. "I'll check my calendar." He began flipping pages.

"Why don't you keep things like that on your phone?" I asked. This notebook seemed to be a new thing with Stewart.

"Because it's tedious to use the calendar on my phone. It's simpler to write it in my notebook calendar." He paused his flipping and told Haskell, "It's a week from tomorrow," he said.

"Thanks. I'll put it on my calendar. Seven o'clock as usual?"

"Yes." Stewart put the notebook back in his pocket and tapped it with his right hand. "I never go anywhere without this now. I'd hate to lose it."

"I'm always anxious that I'll leave my phone somewhere and I'll be lost without it. It's ridiculous, really, how dependent I am on the thing," I said.

"That's why I keep the notebook," Stewart said. "I might lose it, of course, but it's more easily replaced than a lost phone."

"Good point," I said. "Now, what's for dessert?"

After we finished the remains of the lemon icebox pie, I helped Stewart clean up in the kitchen. Haskell had to head back to the sheriff's department for work.

"I know you'll be glad when this case is solved," I said. "I imagine Haskell will be, too, so he doesn't have to put in extra time."

"Kanesha relies on him a lot," Stewart said. "He likes working with her, because she's no-nonsense. She gets things done, unlike her predecessor as chief deputy. Haskell didn't like working with him."

"I'm glad they've got a good working relationship," I said.

"I am, too, though sometimes it feels like there are three people in our relationship," Stewart said wryly.

"I think Helen Louise probably feels that way about Diesel."

Stewart laughed at that. "At least Diesel doesn't have you working long hours some of the time."

"No, he's really good about that," I said lightly.

We had finished in the kitchen. Stewart went upstairs to retrieve Dante to let him outside in the backyard for a while. I headed to the den, along with the cats. I wanted to call Helen Louise and Melba to tell them both what I had learned about Tara's real identity.

I called Helen Louise first, but the call went to voice mail. I left a brief message. Next I called Melba, and she answered right away.

"I've got some news to share," I said.

"Helen Louise called off the wedding," she replied.

Her tone was so serious I felt jarred for a moment. Then I recovered. "Haha, very funny."

Melba laughed. "Had you going for a second, didn't I?"

"Only a second. Now, do you want to hear my news?"

"Of course. Go ahead."

I told her about Kanesha's calling me to come to her office. Then I related the story of Ms. Burnes, the folder with the clipping about Tara, a.k.a. Georgia, and the embezzlement.

"We were right, then, about money being involved somehow," Melba said.

"Alberta Garner, who also used the name Hagendorf, is her sister," I said. "They came here as children to visit their maternal grandmother. Her name was Lizzie Hart. Did you know her?"

"Miss Lizzie? Of course I knew her. Everybody did," Melba said.

"I don't remember her," I said.

"You never remember anybody," Melba said tartly. "Miss Lizzie was the mayor's secretary when we were kids. He stayed in office for what seemed like forever, and Miss Lizzie worked for him the whole time. She retired when he finally lost an election. Died a few years later, as I recall."

"How did you get to know her?" I asked. "Were you in the mayor's office a lot for some reason?"

"No, of course not. My daddy didn't like the mayor. Miss Lizzie was a member of my church growing up. She taught Sunday school, and I was in her class when I was ten years old or so. She was a sweet lady, and everybody loved her."

Melba and I had attended different churches in our youth, so that was one explanation for my lack of acquaintance with Miss Lizzie Hart. The other was that I had never visited the mayor's office. I couldn't even remember the mayor's name. I thought about asking Melba, but I didn't want to give her the satisfaction of showing off her memory more than she already had.

"Hang on a moment," I said. "I'm getting another call. Oh, it's Helen Louise. I'll talk to you later."

Melba said bye, and I ended the call. I answered Helen Louise. "Hello, sweetheart. I've got interesting news for you."

"Hello, love. What's the scoop?"

I filled her in on what transpired in Kanesha's office. When I finished, I asked her whether she had known Lizzie Hart.

"I remember her a little bit," Helen Louise said. "I went to the mayor's office with my mother a couple of times. I don't know if you remember this, but my mother served on the city council for several years when I was a child."

"No, I don't believe I knew that," I said.

"It's immaterial, but it's how I knew Mrs. Hart. She was always pleasant, and she had a candy stash in one of her desk drawers."

"What a sweet memory," I said.

"It's a shame to know that her granddaughters are mixed up in such a terrible thing. One of them murdered, and the other potentially her killer."

"Kanesha is considering whether Tara was framed for the embezzlement and was killed to keep her from revealing the person who did it," I said.

"That's quite a twist," Helen Louise said. "But what about those account numbers that she had? Why would she have them if she wasn't the embezzler?"

"I don't know. I think it's a bit far-fetched that Tara was not the embezzler. Why would the sister embezzle from herself?"

"It's possible that Kanesha knows quite a bit more than she told you about this," Helen Louise said.

"Good point," I replied. "She always does know more than I do about any murder case I'm sucked into."

Helen Louise laughed. "Nothing sucks you into these things, except that gigantic bump of curiosity of yours."

I decided not to dignify the truth of her statement with a disclaimer.

I changed the subject, and we chatted a few minutes more. Then we said goodbye, and I sat in the recliner for a while, thinking about the people involved in the case who knew Tara.

P. J. Jackson came immediately to mind. According to Sean he was highly regarded as an attorney. But attorneys had been known to steal from their clients. What if he had embezzled the money and blamed Tara. He could even be her killer. What if Tara knew he was the embezzler? He might have killed her to keep her from exposing him to her sister and to the law.

The other person was Ryan Jones, a.k.a. Ryan John Marsh. He was connected with Tara for sure, and, according to Jackson, he knew Alberta Garner. Had he been playing one sister against the other? Was he after the embezzled funds for himself?

TWENTY-EIGHT

||||||||||||||||||||||||||||||||||||||||||||||||||||||||||||||||||||||

The more I thought about Jones, a.k.a. Marsh, the more convinced I became that he might be the key to the whole case.

I pulled out my phone and texted Haskell. I had to settle this for my own peace of mind. *Please call me ASAP.* Short and to the point. Haskell might be annoyed with me, but I had to talk to someone about this.

Fifteen minutes later, my phone rang. Haskell was calling.

"Hi, Charlie, what's wrong? Is it Stewart?"

I felt bad for causing Haskell any anxiety about his partner. "No, nothing to do with Stewart."

"Thank the Lord," Haskell said. "So what is so urgent?"

"Have y'all found out any more about this Ryan Jones?" I asked.

"Not more than you've been told already," Haskell said. "The investigation is still ongoing."

"Do you have any evidence that, as Marsh, he has any connection with Alberta Garner as P. J. Jackson claimed?"

"Only that P. J. Jackson represented him in his most recent tangle with the law."

"Interesting," I said. "So you have three possible suspects for Tara's murder."

"Yes," Haskell said. "We have to sort out both motive and opportunity, though. We're still working on those issues. Now, if that's all, I need to get back to work."

"That's it," I said. "Thanks, Haskell."

I put the phone down.

These people with their assumed identities. It made my head ache to think about all the names involved. Ryan Jones, Ryan Marsh, Tara Martin, Georgia Canterbury, Alberta Garner, Millie Hagendorf. I wondered whether P. J. Jackson also had an alias.

There was something shady about Alberta Garner and her use of pseudonyms. If she was the injured party in the embezzlement, why had she felt the need to assume two separate identities? I couldn't figure her out, despite what Jackson had told Melba and me about her quirks. The authorities had to have been looking for her sister and were far better equipped to find her. Why had she taken it on herself to locate her sister?

To make sure Georgia wouldn't be able to talk to the authorities.

That's what my brain told me. But why would she want her sister dead? What was Alberta Garner trying to cover up?

How was Ryan Marsh involved in this? Was he a partner in the embezzlement? Was he on Alberta's side, or had he been helping Tara hide out in Athena? He had admitted to knowing about her from the time she showed up in Athena, and according to Kanesha, Ryan Jones hadn't been here long.

I had no way of sorting all this out. I simply didn't know enough, and I didn't have the resources available to the sheriff's department. I figured Kanesha was liaising with the FBI on this because of the international aspect and the fact that the embezzlement had occurred while Tara was still in Tennessee and she was killed in Mississippi.

Having met Alberta Garner in two of her guises, I thought she was as likely the murderer as either of the men. She had come across as calculating. She wouldn't be happy to have millions of dollars taken from her by anyone, much less her younger sister.

How many millions were involved? I wondered. Even if it was only one million, that was a lot of money. I supposed that when the case was solved, there would be a lot more details in the press. I could satisfy my curiosity then, but the wait would be annoying unless it was all revealed soon.

Enough of this, I decided. This was one I wasn't going to solve myself. I should put it out of my mind and leave it all to Kanesha and her officers. They had appreciated my assistance so far, but I didn't want to wear out my welcome.

A glance at the time on my phone told me that it wasn't yet eight-thirty. Too early to go to bed. I felt restless, and I knew why. My bump of curiosity wasn't satisfied, but there was nothing I could do about that. I needed a good book to read. I had finished the Margery Allingham book, so I looked at the small stack of books I had pulled from Aunt Dottie's heavily laden shelves in the bedroom upstairs that held most of her collection.

One of the books I had pulled was a favorite by Agatha Christie. Even though I had read it before and knew who the killer was, I would enjoy seeing how Christie slipped in the clues to the killer's identity. *The Moving Finger* was what I needed to occupy my mind. I loved Miss Marple, and this was one of her finest cases.

I was halfway through the book when I decided my eyes were too tired to continue. I had also started yawning. The time was now a few minutes past ten, so I should be heading to bed. I had to be up for work the next morning.

"Come on, boys, time for bed." I set the book aside and pulled myself out of the recliner. I checked the kitchen before we went upstairs. No sign of Stewart. I turned off the lights, making sure the outside lights were on along with the hall light for when Haskell came home.

Since Helen Louise and I had talked earlier, I didn't call her like I usually did. Instead I texted her a brief message, wishing her a good night's rest and telling her I loved her. Within a minute, I had a reply echoing my message.

A few minutes later, now in bed with the boys, I turned out the light and settled in to go to sleep. My mind was a bit restless, but I did my best to clear it from anything to do with murder. Instead I filled it with thoughts of the wedding and the honeymoon. Far more pleasant, and definitely more relaxing. I soon drifted off to sleep.

During the night I dreamed about notebooks, probably prompted by Stewart's notebook. I woke up during one of the dreams to go to the bathroom, but by the time I climbed back in bed, that dream had faded. The rest of the night, if I dreamed, I didn't recall it when the alarm went off.

I remembered Kanesha saying they had expected to find something in Tara's apartment that would yield more information, yet they had found nothing.

With rising excitement, I thought I knew why. I also thought I knew where Tara might have hidden a notebook or papers that she wanted to protect from whoever wanted her caught, or dead.

Spotting her sister at the housewarming party had frightened her so badly she either had a real panic attack or pretended to have one so that she could keep her sister from discovering her in the house. She probably knew about the root cellar because that's where Henry had stored the champagne for the night, along with the white wine.

I reasoned she might have hidden her papers or notebook in the root cellar, figuring she would be able to come back to the house for some reason and retrieve it then. She had most likely been murdered before she was able to go back, however.

I hastily finished my shower, shaved, and got dressed for breakfast. I thought about driving out to the farmhouse before work. I could be late. It wouldn't take me a whole hour to drive out, search the root cellar, and drive back to town.

It was still early, however, and I didn't want to bother Sean, Alex, and Rosie at this time of day on what could be a wild goose chase after all. I wasn't absolutely sure that Tara had hidden anything in the root cellar, and I knew Sean wouldn't be terribly happy with me. I could ask him to look, but frankly I wanted to be the one to discover anything Tara had hidden.

Maybe I could go during my lunch hour, I thought. Sean would be at work, and Alex would be up and about. I didn't think she would mind my coming out there during the middle of the day. I decided that was what I would do. I felt a little guilty about going when Sean wasn't at home, but I suppressed those feelings.

My mind made up, I went down to breakfast feeling cheerful. Diesel and Ramses had already gone downstairs, and I found them in the kitchen with Azalea, Stewart, and Haskell. I thought about how I could astonish them all by finding the missing piece of the puzzle in the investigation, and I felt like shouting it out. Totally childish, I realized, but I also didn't want to look like a complete fool if my idea didn't pan out.

There was no mention of the murder case during breakfast. I tried to eat as usual, not rushing through the meal, but I was anxious to get to work. I still had books to go through, although at this stage I didn't count on finding anything else Tara could have hidden. In fact, I didn't see any point now to digging through all the books in the rare-book room. If I didn't find anything hidden in the root cellar, I would probably go back to looking in those books.

Diesel and I bade the others goodbye and drove to work. The weather was pretty dismal today. Cold, with low, dark clouds in the sky that promised rain soon. On days like this, I liked to curl up with a good book, drink hot tea or hot chocolate, and forget about the weather. I hoped there wouldn't be any violent thunderstorms, because I hated being out in them, especially driving in them.

Diesel and I made it into the building before any rain began. Around nine a storm moved through, and I was anxious lest it persist through my usual lunch hour. Fortunately for my nerves, the storm passed in less than thirty minutes, and the sky began to clear.

I busied myself with cataloging, but I kept an eye on the clock. At ten I phoned Alex to make sure she would be at home. I didn't like the idea of going out there when no one was home, because it wasn't my house. Normally I didn't think either Alex or Sean would mind all that much, but given that I was on the hunt for potential clues, I knew Sean would get annoyed with me if I went out there when the house was empty.

Alex answered right away, and after the usual inquiries about her and Rosie, I asked her if it would be okay for me to drive out there during my lunch hour for a quick visit.

"Of course you can," Alex said. "You know Rosie and I always are happy to see you. Rosie loves you so much."

My precious granddaughter. I felt guilty about what I planned to do. I decided I would confess what I was up to once I was there with Alex and Rosie. I doubted Alex would tell me not to do it and mind my own business. I thought she understood my endless curiosity and didn't really mind it.

"All right," I said. "I'll see you around twelve-twenty."

"You'll bring Diesel, won't you?" Alex asked. "You know he and Rosie adore each other."

"Yes, he'll be with me," I said.

"Great. I have some cold chicken, and I'll whip up some chicken salad for us for lunch. I'll save some chicken for Diesel."

I protested that it was too much trouble, but Alex wouldn't be dissuaded. I gave in. I'd had her chicken salad before, and it was savory, not sweet, the way I liked it best.

"See you soon," I said, and ended the call.

A few minutes later someone knocked on the door. I looked up to see Ryan Jones standing there.

I stood. "Come in, Mr. Marsh. What can I do for you?"

TWENTY-NINE

Judging by the man's expression, I guessed he was not in a good mood. He advanced into the room, scowling as he came.

"How did you get that name?" he demanded.

"From the sheriff's office," I said. "Have a seat."

He cursed under his breath, but not so softly that I couldn't make out the words. He had quite the vulgar vocabulary.

"What is it you want?" I asked.

He took the seat indicated and glared at me. "I want you to tell me what Tara hid here."

"Why should I tell you anything? The sheriff's department is aware of what I've found. You don't really think I'd hold back on them, surely."

"There's a lot of money at stake here," he replied. "You might be after it yourself."

"That's absurd," I said. "I'm not a thief."

Marsh's eyes narrowed. "You think I am."

I shrugged. "I don't see what your connection is with any of this, unless you killed Tara, or Georgia, I should say. Did you know her?"

He considered me for a moment, perhaps deciding what he could tell me that would help his case.

"Yeah, I knew her and about a sister," he said. "Tara hated her." He paused. "And Tara and I were married once."

That was certainly a revelation, and it could explain a number of things. "Were you still married at the time of her death?"

He shrugged. "She was supposed to be getting the divorce. I don't know if it ever became final. I left it up to her."

Kanesha would find out, if she hadn't already. "Why did she hate her sister?"

"Because Alberta was Daddy's favorite and got all his money when he died. Tara didn't get much of anything."

"Did Tara steal from her sister?"

He grinned. "She sure did. She found the information she needed, and she transferred it all into a Swiss bank account." The grin faded. "The problem is, I don't know anything about the account itself or how to access it."

"The sheriff's department has the account numbers," I said. "I'm afraid I can't help you. You still haven't told me why you should get the money if it belonged to Tara's sister."

"Tara promised to share it with me," Marsh said.

"Even if you were divorced?"

"Yes," Marsh said, his tone one of defiance. "Tara and I were cool."

"Did she put any of that in writing?"

257

"No, but she swore she would," he replied.

"Since Tara stole it, I think that would negate any promise she made to you. I don't think you're ever going to get your hands on it."

He cursed again, this time including remarks about my antecedents. I simply sat and looked at him. Behind me, I could sense that Diesel was restless. He didn't like the energy in the room. I wanted to reassure him, but I didn't want to turn my back on Marsh. I didn't trust him an inch.

Abruptly, he got up and stomped out of the room. I heard his heavy footsteps as he hurried downstairs. I relaxed, not realizing how tense I'd been while he was in the room. I turned to Diesel and stroked his back.

"He's gone now, boy, so no need to be worried. I'm sure we've seen the last of him." He calmed down as I continued to pay him attention.

Melba came into the office. "What was that guy doing here again? Should I have called Haskell?"

I told her about the encounter. "It was over pretty quickly, so I don't think Haskell could have got here in time."

"I hope you don't have to deal with him after this," Melba said.

"I hope so, too. I have a feeling Kanesha will wrap this case up pretty soon," I replied.

"Good. Well, I'm going back downstairs. Let me know if you need anything." She blew a kiss to Diesel before she left the room.

By now it was a quarter to eleven. Forty-five minutes before I planned to leave for my drive out to the farmhouse. I did my best to stay focused on cataloging, but I was too jittery. I kept glancing at the time on the computer every two or three minutes.

Somehow I managed to wait until nearly eleven-fifty-five before I locked the office door behind us and headed to the car. I told Diesel we were going to see Rosie, and I thought that *Rosie* was one word he understood. The minute I said it he started chirping and trilling, happy sounds. He knew he was going to see his adored Rosie. Ever since their births, Diesel had loved both grandchildren and watched over them like a nanny whenever he was in their presence.

I kept my speed as I drove only a few miles above the limit after we reached the outskirts of Athena. According to the digital clock in the car, I turned into the farmhouse driveway on the nose of twelve-fifteen.

Alex and Rosie greeted us at the door. Rosie squealed with delight at the sight of Diesel, and he trilled for her. Alex gave me a hug and a kiss on the cheek before she started to shut the door behind me. She stopped suddenly in the act of closing the door.

"Something wrong?" I asked.

"No, probably not," she said with a slight frown as she closed the door and locked it. "There was a car on the road near the driveway. It had stopped, but then it moved off."

"Probably someone trying to find the right house," I said, though inwardly I was a bit alarmed. Had Marsh followed me here? Why would he? I wondered. He couldn't have any idea of the reason I came here today, surely.

I brushed that thought aside and scooped Rosie up into my arms. She giggled and kissed me repeatedly. "How's my best girl?" I asked. She gabbled at me in return. She was so adorable like this, and I was looking forward to the time when she made actual words we could understand.

Diesel chirped anxiously, wanting Rosie back at his level. I put her down but held on to her hand as we followed Alex to the kitchen. Diesel stayed right beside Rosie the whole way.

I put Rosie in her high chair at the kitchen table. Diesel sat beside it, determined to keep his eye on her.

"What can I do to help?" I asked.

Alex gestured to a place at the table. "You can sit right there. I'll get everything on the table, and we can eat. If you prefer to make a sandwich, I've got plenty of wheat bread. I also have potato chips. I love having them with chicken salad."

"I do, too," I said. "No need for a sandwich. The chicken salad and the chips will be fine for me."

Alex had already set the table. I seated myself where she indicated while she retrieved the bowl of chicken salad from the fridge, along with some strips of plain chicken for my cat.

Alex poured iced tea for us and gave Rosie a few chips on a napkin. "She had a bottle before you came, but she gets fretful if we're eating and she doesn't have anything."

"Sean was the same at that age," I said, smiling.

"Help yourself to the food," Alex said as she took her own seat. She passed the plain chicken to me, and I tore it into smaller pieces for Diesel. I gave him a few bites before I helped myself.

The chicken salad was every bit as good as I remembered, and I told Alex so. She smiled with pleasure and thanked me.

"What have you been up to, Dad?" she asked. "Besides the usual work, that is." She shot me a mischievous glance.

"Mostly keeping my nose clean," I said. "I have learned a few more things about the investigation, though, thanks to Kanesha."

"Do tell," Alex said. "Ever since that poor woman hid in the root cellar, I've been curious about what's happening."

I decided to circle back to the root cellar after I brought Alex up to date with all that I had learned. When I mentioned Caroline Burnes, Alex grinned.

"She's interesting, isn't she?" she asked.

"Do you know her?"

Alex nodded. "She was a client of my father's, and I inherited her. She can be a handful."

"I've heard that she has a lot of money," I said.

"She has," Alex said. "Client confidentiality restrains me from telling how much, but I will say she can afford to do whatever she likes."

"Good for her," I said.

Alex was as fascinated as I was by the multiple identities of the persons involved with the case.

"Overkill, don't you think? And pardon the infelicitous pun," she said.

"I agree. I can't figure out why they were necessary except for Tara, because she was hiding from the authorities. The whole thing is so bizarre."

"My hat's off to Kanesha if she and her team figure out who the killer is in this case. It's like trying to unravel Christmas lights that have been in the attic for decades."

I had to laugh at that. Diesel nudged me for more chicken, and I dropped a few bits for him on the floor. They disappeared quickly.

Rosie had been patting her chips until they weren't much more than dust, but she seemed happy with what she was doing.

"You mentioned the root cellar earlier," I said as casually as I could. "I've been wondering why Tara hid in there, when she simply could have chosen the catering van. It would have been warmer, and more logical to me."

Alex regarded me with a shrewd gaze. "You think she might have hidden something in the root cellar, don't you?"

No flies on my smart daughter-in-law.

I nodded, feeling sheepish. "I thought it wouldn't hurt to look."

Alex laughed. "You are devious. Here I thought you wanted to spend time with me and Rosie."

"I love spending time with you," I protested, feeling guilty.

"I'm just kidding you, Dad. I know you do." Alex smiled.

"Thank you," I said. "Lunch was delicious. You make chicken salad the way I love it."

"You're welcome," Alex said. "I'm not a great cook, but I do have a few things I make well. Now, if you're finished, why don't you go have a look in the root cellar."

"I will. Do you have a flashlight I can borrow?"

"I do." She got up from the table and went to a drawer. She pulled out a flashlight and tested it. It gave out a good, strong beam of light. "Here you go."

"Thanks. I won't be long."

"We'll be waiting here for you," Alex said.

I wished I had a heavier coat with me. It was chilly enough outside, but I knew it would be even colder in the root cellar. I hoped I would find anything Tara had hidden pretty quickly.

I pulled open the door and stepped inside. Switching the flashlight on, I played the beam around the walls. I decided to start with the area where I had found Tara hiding.

I had to put the flashlight down in order to shift the remaining supplies of wine to the floor of the cellar. A swift examination of each crate showed me nothing was hidden in them. I restacked the crates and cast the light around the area in this corner.

Hoping not to have to examine every inch of the cellar, I focused on a couple of boxes stacked against the wall. Judging by the state of them, I decided they must have been down here for quite a few years.

I made sure the light was focused on the interior as I began to poke about in them. I didn't want to disturb any creature that might be domiciled within.

The first box yielded nothing except filthy, empty jars and a few spiderwebs. No spiders, luckily. The second box had more of the same. I was about to turn away when I spotted something beneath one of the bottles. I pulled the bottle out and focused the light on the object beneath.

Bingo! A small notebook that looked like it had been there only a short time. Hand trembling, I picked it up and opened it. One glance revealed that this was what I was seeking.

THIRTY

Suddenly aware of the deep chill surrounding me, I stuck the note-book in my jacket pocket and left the root cellar. I made sure the door was shut behind me before I climbed onto the porch and opened the door to the house.

I started to enter, but the sound of voices stopped me. Alex was talking to someone, and it wasn't Rosie. Who was it?

I strained to hear more as I closed the door behind me as quietly as possible.

Suddenly I remembered the car Alex had spotted, paused in front of the driveway. Had someone followed me here after all?

It sounded like Alex and the visitor were near the front of the house. I stepped to one side of the hallway and began sidling along the wall, gradually moving closer to the sound of the voices I heard. I glanced into the kitchen. Rosie and Diesel were still there, but

Rosie was now in a playpen in the corner, and Diesel had climbed in with her. They should be fine for a few minutes there.

As I neared the halfway point of the hall, I recognized the second voice. Alberta Garner.

I couldn't see either her or Alex, and I hoped that meant Garner couldn't see me. I looked about for a hiding place for Tara's notebook in the hallway. There was a large painting a few feet back toward the rear of the hall. The notebook was slender enough I thought I could secrete it behind the painting. I moved cautiously back and slid the notebook behind the painting. I made sure it wouldn't fall out before I headed to the front of the house.

"Good afternoon, Ms. Garner," I said as I came into sight of the women.

"How do you do, Mr. Harris," she said. "I came by to express my thanks to Mrs. Harris for having me and my associate at the housewarming party. It was certainly a pleasant occasion."

"As I said, I'm delighted you enjoyed it," Alex said before darting a puzzled glance my way.

Calling unannounced, and uninvited, on someone to deliver thanks in person was not the proper way of doing things. I didn't believe for a minute that was the woman's real purpose. She had followed me from town. She must have some idea that Tara had left something here.

"Why are you really here, Ms. Garner?" I said in a pleasant tone. "Surely a simple thank-you note would have been the proper thing to do."

Ms. Garner shot me a look of pure dislike. "Why should I have any other reason to come here?"

"Because your sister was here at the housewarming party. She had a panic attack when she saw you and ran out of the house. She either had a panic attack or faked one to get away from you. I think you saw her here."

"So what if I did?" Ms. Garner replied, her tone haughty. "I can't help it if my sister was crazy. Why should she be afraid of me?"

I laughed. "You accused her of stealing millions of dollars from you. I've seen the article from the Memphis paper. She didn't want you to get hold of her."

"I had every right to find her," the woman replied, now openly furious. "She stole my inheritance."

"But what about the authorities?" I asked. "Surely the FBI are on the case. They had a better chance of finding her."

"I knew where she would run to," Ms. Garner said. "The FBI was taking too long."

"Because your maternal grandmother lived in Athena when you were kids," I said.

That surprised her but she recovered quickly. "Yes, I figured this was the best place to look for her."

"Did you?" I asked.

"Not until the party here," she said. "I spotted her then, but she ran off before I could confront her. Where did she go?"

"She hid in the catering van," I said. Alex didn't even blink at the lie. "I found her there after searching for her out back. At first I thought she might have run off into the woods. She might have run into the woods before deciding that the van was a better option."

I hoped to deceive her into going into the woods to search, fruitlessly, of course, for Tara's notebook.

Ms. Garner regarded me uncertainly. She must have decided to believe me, because she suddenly said, "Okay, then. Well, that's all I wanted to know. Now, if you'll excuse me, I'll be on my way."

Before she could turn for the door, it opened, and Ryan Marsh stepped into the house.

"Hi, Alberta," he said breezily. "Mr. Harris, Mrs. Harris. Pardon my uninvited entrance, but I have business with this piece of work." He waved in Alberta Garner's direction.

"What the hell do you think you're doing?" she demanded, an edge of fright in her tone.

"Be nice, Alberta. I'd hate to hurt you in front of these nice people," he said. "I have nothing against them, really, although Mr. Harris has frustrated me a couple of times."

"You've got some gall sticking into this. Even if you were married to my sister," Ms. Garner said. "This has nothing to do with you."

"Still the same lovely personality that Tara hated," Marsh said in a mocking tone. "You're such a pleasant person, Alberta. I hate you as much as Tara did."

"Daddy and I both were horrified when Tara married such a no-account loser like you," Ms. Garner said, fairly spitting out the words. "What she saw in you I'll never understand."

While Garner and Marsh were so focused on each other, Alex and I each took a couple of steps back, away from them. Marsh spotted us, however, and shook his head. "Don't go anywhere. This doesn't involve you."

"What do you want?" Ms. Garner demanded, her voice high and shrill now.

"I want Tara's notebook. You must have it," Marsh said. "I need the information in it in order to get access to the account."

"I don't have it, you fool." Ms. Garner screamed the words at him. Then she threw her purse at him, and that startled him into stepping back and tripping. He landed on the floor.

Alex turned and ran to the kitchen, and I moved forward to tackle Marsh. Before I could do so, however, Haskell and another sheriff's deputy came through the door and grabbed both Marsh and Ms. Garner.

I felt limp with relief. "How on earth did you manage to show up at the right moment?"

Haskell, trying to hold on to a wriggling woman, didn't respond for a moment. He got handcuffs on her, and his fellow officer did the same with Marsh. Then he answered me. "We were following Marsh to see what he was up to. He didn't spot us, apparently."

"Thank the Lord," I said.

"There's another car on the way," he said. "One for each of them. Somehow I don't think they'd care to share a ride back to the jail."

"Jail?" Ms. Garner screeched the word. "Why are you putting me in jail? He's the one who needs to go to prison."

"Don't start that," Marsh said. "You killed your own sister. They're not going to pin that one on me."

"You're both going to be held on suspicion of murder," Haskell said.

"You can't do that." Ms. Garner was still screeching.

"I assure you we can," Haskell said. "Why don't you put yours in the car?" He nodded to his fellow officer.

"Sure thing," he said, and led Marsh out of the house, still cursing every one of us.

"Your ride should be here in a couple of minutes," Haskell said to Ms. Garner. I was surprised she didn't scream at him again, but she probably realized it wouldn't do her any good.

"Before you go," I said to Haskell, "I found something you need to put into evidence. Hang on a minute, and I'll get it for you."

I turned and hurried down the hall to the painting where I'd hidden the notebook. I retrieved it, regretful that I wouldn't have a chance to examine it myself. But at least I was the one who had figured out where it was and found it.

Ms. Garner's eyes bulged at the sight of the notebook. She squirmed in Haskell's grasp as I handed it to him.

"Hang on to it until I get Ms. Garner in the car," Haskell said. "I heard it drive up a moment ago. Come on." He led her out of the house.

Alex returned then. "Are they gone?"

"Just about," I said. "They're putting them in separate cars to take back to the sheriff's department."

"On what charge?" Alex asked.

"Suspicion of murder, according to Haskell."

"Did they caution them properly?" she said.

"Not in my hearing, but I'm sure they will," I replied. "Haskell would never forget that."

"No, he wouldn't," Alex said with a smile.

"I wonder which one actually killed Tara," I said. "I wouldn't put it past either of them."

"My money's on the sister," Alex said.

Haskell returned then. "We're about to head back to town. As soon as you can, can you both come by the sheriff's department and make a statement about what happened here today?"

Alex and I both assured him we would.

Haskell grinned at me. "Good for you, Charlie, finding that notebook." He reached out, and I gave him the notebook. He turned and headed out the door, closing it behind him.

"Well done, Dad," Alex said as we walked back to the kitchen. "I think you found the key piece of evidence they needed to finalize this investigation."

"I hope so," I said. "I still don't know who the killer is, though."

"You'll find out soon," Alex said. "I'm sure Kanesha will be appreciative enough to let you know before it's made public."

"Maybe so. I'm sure they have evidence that I know nothing about," I said. "They usually do."

Alex held up a hand as we stepped into the kitchen. Following her gaze, I saw that Rosie was asleep in the playpen. Diesel lay beside her, awake and watching her.

"So sweet," Alex murmured. "He really is amazing with babies. Do you think you can get him out without waking her up?"

"I think so," I replied softly. I took a couple more steps into the room and called to Diesel. He stirred, stretched, and leaped out of the playpen. Rosie didn't move.

Alex came out of the kitchen with us. "This has been an exciting day," she said with a mischievous smile. "I can't wait to tell Sean about it."

I grimaced. "Don't hurry on my account."

Alex laughed as she followed us to the front door. "Don't worry. I'll make sure he doesn't call and fuss at you."

"I'm really sorry that those two people came into your house because of me. I don't know what I'd have done if they hurt you or Rosie."

"They didn't, and I don't think they would have," Alex said. "They were too focused on each other."

"You're probably right," I said. "Thanks again for that delicious lunch. Diesel and I had better get back to the office."

I heard the lock click into place after Diesel and I stepped onto the porch. "Come on, boy, back to the office."

I didn't break the speed limit on the way back to town, at least not by more than a couple of miles per hour. It was one-twenty-one by the car clock when I pulled into the parking lot behind the building. Melba heard us in the lobby and came out with a frown.

"Where have you been? You're not usually so late back to lunch. Is everything all right?"

"Come on up with us," I said. "I'll tell you everything."

Melba followed us into the office and took her usual chair. "Okay, give. Something's obviously happened."

"It's all over, I think," I said. Diesel stretched out beside Melba so she could reach him more easily. She began stroking him, and he purred.

First I told her about my hunch about Tara's notebook, and then I told her about lunch with Alex and Rosie and all that ensued afterward. She looked appalled when I mentioned that Marsh had shown up.

"Good heavens," she said. "He could have hurt you."

I shook my head. "I don't think we were in all that much danger. He was so focused on Tara's sister, I think he wouldn't have harmed us. She was the one who needed to worry."

"Thank the Lord that Haskell was following him," Melba said.

"Amen to that."

THIRTY-ONE

|||||||||||||||||||||||||||||||||||||||||||||||||||||||||||||||||

Helen Louise joined us at dinner a couple of nights later, so we were four at the table. Azalea had outdone herself with roast chicken, asparagus with hollandaise, new potatoes roasted in the oven, and salad. Helen Louise provided the dessert, my favorite, her chocolate cake.

Haskell was the focus of attention during the meal because I kept asking him questions about the resolution of the murder investigation. Helen Louise admonished me to let Haskell enjoy his meal, and I left off the questions until we reached the dessert.

Haskell kept looking at me with a gleam of humor in his expression. I thought he was enjoying my obvious impatience a little too much, but finally, over the delicious cake and coffee, he told us what we wanted to know. He told Helen Louise and me, that is, because I was sure Stewart already knew it all.

The pets were sated with bites of boiled chicken prepared by

Azalea just for them, and they stretched out and snoozed under the table.

"To go back to your questions, Charlie," Haskell began, "the FBI is handling the embezzlement issue. That's their bailiwick, not ours. They have the resources we don't."

"I figured that," I said.

Helen Louise looked at me and laid a finger across her lips to urge me to be quiet and let Haskell talk. I grinned at her.

"The FBI think Kanesha might be right about Georgia being framed by her sister," Haskell said. "Preliminary evidence is pointing that way. And before you ask, I can't tell you what that evidence is, because the FBI isn't sharing it with us.

"Kanesha thinks that Alberta targeted her sister because they hated each other. She framed her to have her put in prison."

"That's harsh," Helen Louise said, and I flashed her a glance.

"What about those account numbers that Tara, I mean Georgia, hid in the books in the archive?" I asked.

"Evidently Georgia got the information from her sister's computer, then destroyed the hard drive so Alberta couldn't retrieve them. Turns out the notebook was actually Alberta's, and she had recorded the information about the accounts in it.

"Georgia swiped the notebook, and that of course infuriated Alberta. When Georgia disappeared, Alberta had to find her before Georgia could move the money elsewhere. Unfortunately for her, Georgia managed to move it not long before she was killed."

"Who killed Georgia, and why?" I asked, trying not to sound impatient. "It must have been Alberta."

"It was," Haskell said. "The irony of it is that Alberta expected

Georgia to have the notebook with her when she ran her down. That's actually how we found the evidence that's going to convict her."

"What do you mean?" Helen Louise said in surprise. "What evidence?"

Haskell laughed. "Georgia must have been a lot smarter than her sister. She had already hidden the notebook out at the farmhouse. Alberta searched Georgia's body after she ran over her, and she was wearing a coat at the time that shed fibers on Georgia's. We found the coat and enough fibers on Georgia to prove that Alberta killed her. Believe it or not, we also found a couple of fingerprints in the stolen car belonging to Alberta."

"I'm so sorry that Georgia died like that," I said. "But I'm glad she managed to thwart her sister one last time by hiding that notebook in the root cellar."

"Alberta was frantic to find it," Haskell said. "That's why she tried to worm her way into the archive office as a volunteer. She confessed that she was sure Georgia had hidden the notebook somewhere there when she didn't find it on Georgia after she ran her down."

"What was Marsh's part in all this?" I asked. "There certainly wasn't any love lost between him and Alberta."

"No, there wasn't. Marsh knew both sisters, and he helped Georgia get out of Memphis and get established here, originally as a homeless person, under the name Tara Martin. Marsh was claiming to be Georgia's husband, but she had actually finalized the divorce. Georgia accepted his help and played him along, he said, so she could figure out what game he was playing."

"He wanted to get his hands on those accounts himself," Stewart said. "More coffee, anyone?"

We all declined refills. Haskell said, "Yes, Georgia told him that Alberta was trying to frame her, and he knew the sisters well enough to believe Georgia."

"What about that man P. J. Jackson?" Helen Louise asked. "He actually seemed concerned about Tara, um, Georgia."

"I think he probably was," Haskell said. "In an interview he told us that he recognized her pretty quickly. He was the sisters' father's lawyer, and he knew them both. He was highly suspicious of Alberta, and he came to Athena with her to keep an eye on her. He's been pretty helpful with a lot of background on the sisters. That Alberta has been a nasty piece of work for most of her life."

"What will happen to the money?" I asked. "Surely Alberta won't get it because she killed her sister."

"She won't. You can't profit from your crimes, and there's proof of her motive for her sister's murder." Haskell paused long enough to have the final piece of his cake, and he washed it down with the remainder of his coffee.

"The money, once it's recovered," Haskell said, "will, according to the late father's will, go to the children's hospital in Memphis. Something in the neighborhood of five to six million dollars, they reckon."

"That's wonderful," I said. "It's terrible about Georgia's death and what she went through, but at least the money will go to a worthy recipient."

"Is Marsh still being held?" Helen Louise asked.

"No, the charges were dropped, except for his illegal possession of a firearm," Haskell said. "He swore he had a license, but strangely enough, he can't produce it." He rolled his eyes.

"I think that takes care of about everything," Helen Louise said.

"There's one thing Haskell hasn't told you, Charlie." Stewart shot a mischievous glance at his partner. "You really should tell him, sweetie."

Haskell grinned. "Oh, you mean what Kanesha said." He looked at me. "Kanesha said to tell you how much she appreciated your assistance in finding the notebook. We probably would have found it eventually, but you scooped us on it. Well done."

"Thanks, and thank Kanesha for me," I said, really pleased by what Haskell had said.

"That ought to make you feel better after what Sean said to you," Helen Louise said.

"Did Sean rake you over the coals?" Haskell asked.

I squirmed a bit in my chair. "Not exactly, but he wasn't pleased with me. Alex took my side, and that annoyed him, but in the end he just rolled his eyes and gave me a hug. That's probably not the last I'll hear of it, but at least for now, he's stopped fussing."

"Surely he realizes that you couldn't know you'd be followed to the farmhouse," Stewart said.

"Oh, he does, and that's the one thing that's kept my goose uncooked," I said. "Now, who's ready for another piece of cake?"

"I'm ready," Haskell said, and Stewart echoed him. Once we all had a serving of cake, Helen Louise cleared her throat.

"I have a surprise for you, Charlie," she said.

"What is it?"

"It's about our honeymoon," she said.

"In Asheville?" I asked. We had talked about going back there.

"No, but we're still going there." She gave me a mischievous smile.

"Then what's the surprise?" I asked, puzzled.

Stewart and Haskell exchanged grins, and I realized they must know what Helen Louise was going to tell me.

"It's too cold there in February," Helen Louise said, "so we're going in April instead. The weather will be better then, though a bit cool."

"Too cold where in February?" I asked.

"Ireland," Helen Louise said. "I have a cousin who lives there in a big country house, and we're invited to stay with them for two weeks."

A country house in the beautiful Irish countryside? Sounded wonderful to me. A nice, relaxing visit.

"Sounds wonderful," I said. "I can't wait."

ACKNOWLEDGMENTS

As always, I owe a great debt of thanks to my editor, Michelle Vega, and the whole Berkley team: Annie Odders, Elisha Katz, and Yazmine Hassan. They are simply the best. My agent, Nancy Yost, is also simply the best, along with her amazing team.

Most of all, I owe the biggest debt to my readers, whose enthusiasm and support never fail to encourage me. Their love for Charlie and Diesel keeps me going, and I can never thank them enough.